THE DIAMOND SUTRA

THE DIAMOND SUTRA

The Story of the World's Earliest Dated Printed Book

FRANCES WOOD AND MARK BARNARD

THE BRITISH LIBRARY

First published in 2010 by
The British Library
96 Euston Road
London NW1 2DB

British Library Cataloguing in Publication Data
A catalogue record for this publication is available
from The British Library

ISBN 978-0-7123-5090-7

Designed by Bobby & Co, London
Colour reproduction by Dot Gradations Ltd, Essex
Printed in Hong Kong by Great Wall Ltd

CONTENTS

INTRODUCTION

The oldest printed book in the world has been in London for a hundred years, first in the British Museum and now in the British Library. Printed in AD 868, the year King Alfred failed to protect Mercia from the invading Danes, it is well over 500 years older than the first European printing. Although it was on display in the old King's Library in the British Museum for over 30 years, it was only sought out by a few Asian visitors. For everyone else, the Gutenberg Bible, printed in about 1455 and displayed nearby under the (inaccurate) banner heading, 'The Earliest Printed Book', was the pioneer.

The oldest printed book in the world was made in China and is a copy of the Buddhist work usually known as the 'Diamond Sutra' in English, sutras being the discourses or sermons of the Buddha (see Chapter 3). It is just under five metres long and has a beautiful frontispiece depicting the Buddha preaching amongst monks and flying 'angels'. It attracted little attention and is little known. Yet the story of its discovery as part of a race for antiquities in the desert of Central Asia is exciting, and its life in London has been eventful too, including the Blitz of the Second World War which caused considerable damage to the British Museum.[1]

Though the elegant frontispiece is the most striking part, the very end of the scroll contains the most important text since it gives us the date of production. A printed colophon reads, 'Reverently (caused to be) made for universal free distribution by Wang Jie on behalf of (his) two parents on the fifteenth day of the fourth month of the Xiantong reign', a date equivalent to AD 868. Nothing else is known about Wang Jie, though it may be assumed that he was a pious Buddhist, acting in accord with the belief that the repetition of the words of the Buddha or of the Buddha image would bring merit to help the dead escape from the cycle of rebirth. The Diamond Sutra includes passages where the Buddha states that chanting, or repeating aloud, even part of the sutra would confer immeasurable merit. Using the new technology of printing, Wang Jie was able to commission the printing and distribution of hundreds of copies of the sutra, thus accruing considerable merit.[2]

It was not only for their parents that people commissioned copies of the Diamond Sutra. Another (undated) printed edition was made for the spirit of an old ox

ABOVE *The Diamond sutra, the response of the Buddha to questions posed by his elderly disciple, Subhuti, was delivered in a garden. The leaves of the trees can be seen behind the flying apsareses or Buddhist 'angels' at the top of the picture. The Buddha is attended by shaven-headed monks, haloed Bodhisattvas and guardian figures, as well as an emperor and empress to the bottom right.*

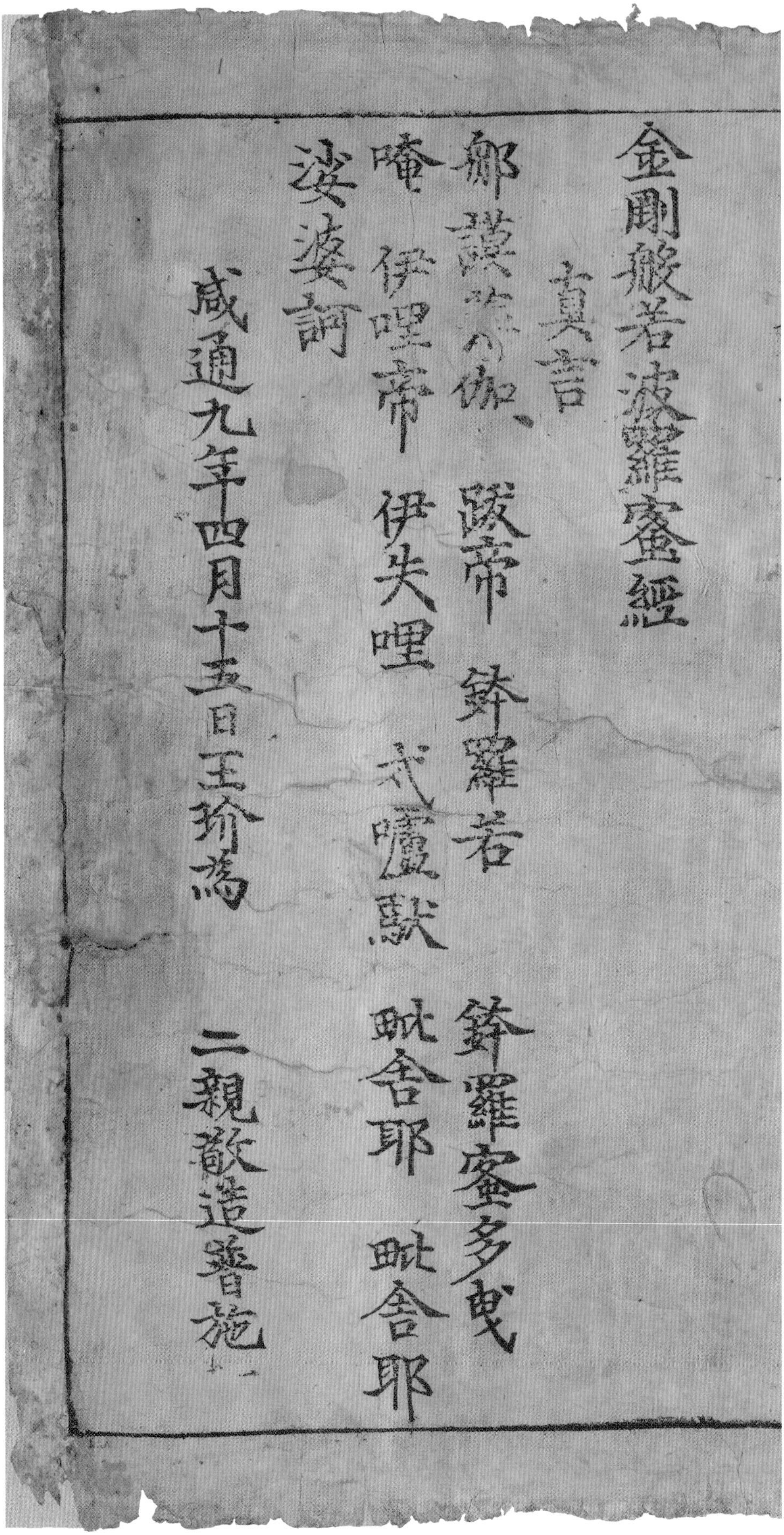
金剛般若波羅蜜經
真言
那謨薄伽跋帝 鉢羅若 鉢羅蜜多曳
唵 伊哩帝 伊失哩 戍嚧馱 毗舍耶 毗舍耶
娑婆訶
咸通九年四月十五日王玠為 二親敬造普施

to be born in Amitabha Buddha's Pure Land (rather than continue to endure the cycle of rebirths as an animal) where the copyist hoped to meet him again.[3] Commissioning or making multiple copies of a Buddhist sutra were means of gaining merit, as was chanting a sutra. Because it is quite easy to memorise, and can be recited in about 30 minutes, the Diamond Sutra has for centuries in China been a favourite sutra for chanting.

This copy of the Diamond Sutra was brought to London by Sir Aurel Stein (1852–1943), a Hungarian Sanskrit scholar, archaeologist, explorer and surveyor who acquired it in 1907 at the Caves of the Thousand Buddhas near Dunhuang in China's western province of Gansu on his second Central Asian expedition. Dunhuang was close to the point where the famous 'Silk Road', a network of trade routes from China to the West, branched into northern and southern routes around the edge of the great deserts at the heart of Central Asia. The Silk Roads were not only used by traders carrying silk and other goods from oasis to oasis but were also the routes by which religions such as Buddhism and, later, Islam entered China.

By the end of the nineteenth century, European archaeologists and explorers had become fascinated by the ancient sites of the Silk Roads that were buried beneath the desert sands. German archaeologists concentrated on excavating in the Turfan oasis, the Russians explored the northern Silk Roads and the rather terrifying Swedish explorer, Sven Hedin (1865–1952), discovered the sources of the Brahmaputra, Indus and Sutlej rivers at considerable cost, losing members of his expeditions and frequently risking death himself.[4] Stein was completely different from Hedin, never losing an expedition member and planning his expeditions with enormous care, having special fur-lined coats made for his fox terrier, ordering Marmite, dried soups (pea and tomato) and Captain Cookesley's desiccated vegetables (excluding onions) and employing Indian assistants to help with surveying, photography and the construction of crates to house his finds.[5]

Though he was considerate towards his expedition staff (and his dogs), Stein was ruthless in his determination to beat all his European archaeological rivals in the

OPPOSITE *At the end of the sutra, the title is listed and then the two characters 'true words' or Buddha-truth, a term used to cover mantra and dharani, chanted incantations, Chinese renderings of Sanskrit. The very last printed line, to the left, contains the date of production (or the date on which production was ordered) followed by Wang Jie's dedication to his parents.*

race for antiquities across the Central Asian deserts. His meticulous planning was also extremely secretive as he sought to mislead his French rival, Paul Pelliot, in particular about his proposed route of exploration. His secrecy paid off and he won one of the most significant antiquarian prizes of all time in the acquisition of this single scroll.

On both his first expedition in 1900–1 and the second in 1906–8, Aurel Stein was supported financially by the Government of India and the British Museum, on the understanding that his finds would be distributed between them. The National Museum in New Delhi houses Stein collections of paintings and stuccos. The documents assigned to India (in Indian languages and scripts and Tibetan) were in fact housed in the India Office Library in London and transferred to the British Library in 1982. Many other artefacts and the Chinese paintings he found at Dunhuang are now in the British Museum, whilst the documents, including the Diamond Sutra, were transferred from the British Museum to the British Library in 1973.

The recent history of the sutra has been complicated. British Museum conservators looked at it with western eyes and thought it fragile. They took advice from Japanese conservators and applied backings to it to support the apparently fragile paper. Applied with the best will in the world, these treatments had something of a reverse effect. Twenty years ago, a decision was made that the Diamond Sutra, a world treasure, should be restored. Seven years ago, that work began and this year it has been completed. Now, stripped of its recent history, the Diamond Sutra is close to the state in which it was when first printed and, at last, paper quality, paper fibres, paper manufacture, even the impression of the printing block, can all be seen clearly.

OPPOSITE *Islam Akhun, 'forger of antiquities'. One of Stein's missions on his first expedition to Central Asia was to track down a prolific source of 'ancient' manuscripts in Khotan. Bought by the British Consul in Kashgar, they were sent to the scholar Rudolf Hoernle in Oxford, who puzzled over apparently unknown scripts. It turned out that Islam Akhun was making the documents himself. In his expedition reports, Stein included this photograph of Islam Akhun with Stein's dog in the background, and Hoernle was forced to abandon his early enthusiasm for these mysterious productions.*

CHAPTER ONE

A RACE

ON 21 MAY 1907, Aurel Stein 'marched off to the sacred caves' near the oasis of Dunhuang, on the western edge of the Lop desert in northwestern China. The oasis, green with cotton plants and shaded by poplars and elms, gave way to 'grey gravel waste' stretching infinitely from a long cliff below rounded sand dunes. Below the cliff was a small stream fringed with tall poplar trees and the cliff behind was 'honeycombed with the gaping mouths of cave temples big and small'. The first of several hundred caves in the cliff had been carved out by a Buddhist monk, Lezun, in AD 366. The cave walls were painted with frescoes and the centre of the caves was usually occupied by a stucco sculpture of the Buddha, all intended as aids to Buddhist meditation which was becoming popular in China at the time. At the height of its popularity as a pilgrimage site in the Tang dynasty (AD 618–907) the caves were probably protected by wooden galleries, but these had tumbled into ruins by 1879 when an expedition from the Hungarian Geological Society passed by. Impressed by the wall paintings, now exposed to the elements, Professor de Loczy told Stein of the existence of these cave temples in 1902 but Stein had since heard rumours in the oasis town of Dunhuang that there were also ancient documents to be found there.[1]

Aurel Stein, born in Budapest in 1862, was on his second Central Asian expedition in search of antiquities and documents for the British Museum and the (British) Government of India. He had studied Sanskrit and written a PhD on Old Persian

and Indology before entering government service in India as Principal of the Oriental College in Lahore and Registrar of Punjab University. In 1900 he set off on his first Central Asian expedition to the Khotan area, and the finds he made in desert sites there had been greeted with great excitement by scholars all over Europe.

His second expedition (1906–9) was more ambitious. Though he told the Government of India and the British Museum (both of whom supported the expedition financially) and British scholars such as the art historian Dr Stephen Bushell about his plans in some detail, he was very cautious about letting them be known further abroad. There was increasing competition to explore the ancient sites of the Silk Road, with the Russian Professor Sergei Oldenburg (1863–1934) planning to excavate at Kucha, a German team led by the two Alberts, Grunwedel (1856–1935) and von Lecoq (1860–1930) digging in Turfan and an announcement in 1905 by Paul Pelliot, a distinguished French Sinologist, that he intended to take a French expedition to various sites in Central Asia, including the Caves of the Thousand Buddhas near Dunhuang.[2]

Towards the end of the nineteenth century, proposals had been circulating at meetings of the International Congress of Orientalists that, archaeologically, Central Asia should be divided into separate areas of work. The Germans could work in Turfan, the Russians along the northern Silk Road and the British in their 'sphere of influence' in Khotan, although as the proposal was mooted, it was noted that the Swedish explorer Sven Hedin was 'meditating a second visit to Khotan'.[3] It was not until he arrived in Central Asia that Paul Pelliot discovered Stein had beaten him to the Caves. He wrote angrily, 'What I reproach him for is that having had a proposal from us that he should not come north of Lake Lop on the understanding that we would not go to the south, by saying nothing, he kept his hands free. Technically he has broken no promises…'[4] It is clear that Stein did feel somewhat guilty for he wrote in February 1906 that he feared that 'my adherence to my original plans [to visit Dunhuang] may alienate me from some of the friendly interest which I have met so far in Paris…' although in his defence, technically, Dunhuang is neither north or south of Lake Lop but due east.[5]

OPPOSITE *One of Aurel Stein's photographs of the exterior of the Caves of the Thousand Buddhas. In front of the long cliff, honeycombed with over 400 caves hollowed out and filled with wall paintings and stucco Buddhist figures, runs a stream bordered with poplar trees. Largely abandoned for a thousand years, when Stein's colleagues on a Hungarian geographical expedition passed by in 1879, many of the lower caves had filled with sand and the protective wooden structures in front of the caves had long since vanished.*

With Paul Pelliot busying himself at sites on the northern Silk Road, Stein proceeded to Dunhuang. He had first visited the caves on 16 March, when he 'passed rapidly from one cella to another' noting 'rows of Bodhisattvas ... figures of Buddhas, singly or in groups surrounded by divine worshippers' and admired 'the dignified severity of the features', 'the rich floral borders' and 'ornate landscapes'.[6] He was unable to stay long since the self-appointed 'guardian' of the caves, a Taoist called Wang Yuanlu, was away collecting alms to restore the caves so, awaiting Wang's return, Stein turned to the excavation and exploration of the long line of Han dynasty beacon towers stretching out from Dunhuang. Whilst staying in the oasis, he had heard from 'Zahid Beg, the intelligent Turki trader of Urumqi who had established himself at the head of a small colony of Mohammedan exiles ... the first rumour ... of a mass of ancient manuscripts which had been discovered by chance several years before hidden away in one of the cave temples.'[7] Since Stein's first interest was the study of ancient manuscripts, he waited impatiently for Wang's return and the end of the annual pilgrimage to the caves, and it was not until 21 May that he was able to return to the caves: 'The thought of the great store of old manuscripts awaiting exploration drew me back to the Caves of the Thousand Buddhas with the strength of a hidden magnet.'[8]

ABOVE *The map shows the silk routes from the ancient Chinese capital of Chang'an (today's Xi'an) to the Mediterranean. The routes skirt the Lop desert beyond Dunhuang and divide again around the Taklamakan Desert to re-join at Kashgar and Yarkand before branching southwards to India or westwards to the Mediterranean and the Black Sea. Aurel Stein preferred to enter China from India via Kashgar.*

ABOVE *In front of a tamarisk cone in the Taklamakan desert, Stein poses for a photograph with his terrier, Dash the Great. On the left are his assistant Ibrahim Beg in a fur coat and his Chinese secretary Jiang in a hat with long ear flaps. Beside Stein are the surveyors Lal Singh and Naik Ram Singh who contributed greatly to Stein's mapping of the area. Behind Stein is Jasvant Singh, Lal Singh's cook, whose caste status meant he could not cook for a European so another cook had to be engaged to cook for Stein. The photograph was probably taken in the autumn of 1907.*

ABOVE *Paul Pelliot examining manuscripts by candlelight in Cave 17, a year after Stein had taken away enough documents to allow him space to work. Painted leaves from the wall painting that decorated the cave before it became a store are just visible on the wall behind him. Paul Pelliot (1878–1945) was a brilliant French Sinologist who also knew many other languages. His linguistic skills, together with the speed at which he worked, enabled him to make a scholarly selection of documents from Cave 17 which are now in the Bibliothèque nationale de France. He was very disappointed that Stein had beaten him in the race to the caves.*

Access was not easy. On meeting Wang Yuanlu, he wrote, 'He looked a very curious figure, extremely shy and nervous, with a face bearing an occasional furtive expression of cunning which was far from encouraging. It was clear from the first that he would be a difficult person to handle.' Stein, however, could match Wang's cunning and instead of making a direct approach,

> started next morning what was to be ostensibly the main object of my stay at the site, a survey of the principal shrines and the photographing of the more notable frescoes. Whilst thus engaged at the northernmost caves near the great shrines restored by Wang ... I cast a glance at the entrance passage, behind the wall of which the manuscript hoard was declared to have been discovered and still kept. To my dismay, I now found the narrow opening of the recess, about 5 feet above the floor of the passage, completely walled up with brickwork. It seemed like a special precaution taken against my inquisitive eyes.[9]

ABOVE *Wang Yuanlu, self-appointed guardian of the Buddhist caves at Dunhuang, gathered funds for their 'restoration'. He is shown to the right of a rather garish modern wall painting depicting the pilgrim monk and eminent translator Xuanzang (c. 596–664). Stein, knowing of Xuanzang's epic trip to India to collect sutras, used his example to ingratiate himself with Wang. He was unimpressed, however, by Wang's restoration efforts, which 'showed how low sculptural art had sunk'.*

Stein and his Chinese assistant, Jiang Xiaowan (?–1922), worked hard to persuade Wang to show them the manuscripts, making special use of the story of the monk Xuanzang (c. 596–664) who had travelled to India to collect Buddhist scriptures which he then translated into Chinese. Stein told Wang 'of my devotion to Xuanzang: how I had followed his footsteps from India across inhospitable mountains and deserts; how I had traced the ruined sites of many sanctuaries he had visited and described…', and within a few days, achieved his first object when Wang

> summoned the courage to open before me the rough door closing the narrow entrance ... The sight disclosed within made my eyes open wide. Heaped up in closely packed layers, but without any order, there appeared in the dim light of the priest's flickering lamp a solid mass of manuscript bundles rising to a height of nearly 10 feet. They filled, as subsequent measurement showed, close on 500 cubic feet, the size of a small room or chapel being about 9 feet square and the area left clear within just sufficient for two people to stand in.[10]

ABOVE *Even after Wang had taken all the documents out of Cave 17 and then replaced all except those he presented as gifts to local officials, many were still gathered together in bundles, often wrapped in a long scroll as a form of wrapper. The fact that they were gathered together in this way suggested to Stein that the deposit was not made in a hurry, and the fact that so many sutras found in the cave were incomplete or damaged suggested that they had been put away as no longer in use. Their extraordinary preservation, in some cases for more than 1500 years, was due to the quality of the paper and the dark, dry conditions of the cave.*

Wang was cautious about handing manuscripts over to Stein for inspection but, in the end, he 'summoned up courage to fall in with my wishes, but … as long as I was on Chinese soil the origin of these "finds" was to be kept entirely secret. He himself was afraid of being seen at night outside his temple quarters. So Jiang took it upon himself to be the sole carrier. For seven nights more he thus came to my tent, with loads which grew steadily heavier and in the end needed carriage by instalments.'[11]

Wang's anxiety was real. Having discovered the hoard by accident in 1900, he had made presents of some of the items he had found to local officials and the most important of these, the Circuit Intendant of Dunhuang, Wang Jiayan, had ordered the sealing of the cave, hence the brickwork that had so dismayed Stein when he first saw it. To allow access, particularly to a foreigner, was potentially dangerous to the self-appointed guardian of the caves, even though Stein took care to maintain good relations with the local officials.[12]

As Stein admitted, his was not a systematic survey. He had no control over what Wang provided and 'there was no time during that hurried search to appreciate properly the antiquarian import of all that passed through my hands'.[13]

> As I worked my way in great haste through the contents of the 'mixed' bundles – we never knew how long we might rely on [Wang's] indulgence – I felt elated and at the same time oppressed by the constant flow of fresh materials pouring down upon us. Even in the case of art relics and manuscripts which were neither in Chinese nor Tibetan, and of which I was able to estimate the full interest, there was no chance of closer examination … But what obsessed me most at the time was my total want of Sinologist training. How gladly would I then have exchanged one-half of my Indian knowledge for a tenth of its value in Chinese! Even with Jiang's zealous help I could never be sure of not leaving behind documents and texts of historical or literary interest amid the smothering mass of Buddhist canonical literature and the like.[14]

In 1908, a year after Stein's visit to Dunhuang, his rival Paul Pelliot arrived. In the words of Arthur Waley, Pelliot 'made a similar haul, not so large as Stein's but more discriminating, since he could read Chinese and Stein could not'.[15] Like Stein, Pelliot was almost overwhelmed by the mass of material.

> At best I had to make a quick examination of the library ... It was not possible to fully unroll the 15–20,000 scrolls there as it would have taken more than six months. But I had to see what each text was and decide whether it offered anything new and make two selections, one of items which had to be acquired at any cost and one of items that I would try to acquire whilst resigning myself to perhaps having to let them go. Despite my efforts it took me three weeks. For the first ten days I tackled about 1000 rolls a day which must be a record, working at 100 miles an hour like a speeding car and afterwards I slowed down a little.[16]

Though Pelliot noted that a few documents were in Tibetan (for the Tibetans had occupied Dunhuang for over 50 years from the late eighth to the mid-ninth centuries), Uighur and Brahmi, he concluded quickly that 'virtually everything here is Chinese'.[17] The speed with which Pelliot said he worked brought ridicule when he returned to France and accusations that his selection was too rapid to be credible.[18]

Stein concentrated his efforts on the non-Chinese materials but he knew a little Chinese and reported in a letter in early 1907 when he was excavating wood-slip records from the ancient beacons near Dunhuang, 'My good [Jiang] could not fix the reign (Chinese chronology is quite exact but a little complex) so it was an exciting hunt in my *Chinese Reader's Manual* which followed in the evening. I felt elated when the first finds proved to be dated to a reign corresponding to 25 to 51 AD.'[19] Stein was using William Frederick Mayer's *Chinese Reader's Manual: A Handbook of Biographical, Historical, Mythological and General Literary Reference*, published in 1874, a useful reference book.[20] Paul Pelliot would no doubt have disapproved of this Anglo-Chinese production by the one-time Chinese Secretary and Translator to the British Legation in Peking, but even he when he arrived at Dunhuang found himself at a considerable disadvantage as he had left his chronological tables behind.

With Stein working with a manual for beginners, how much was his Chinese assistant able to help him? Jiang Xiaowan, a local government clerk, had been hired by Stein in Kashgar on the recommendation of the British Consul George Macartney, and while he was useful as an interpreter with local officials he was unfamiliar with Buddhism and knew nothing of Buddhist terminology. When he first visited the caves, Stein, familiar with Buddhist statuary and iconography from museums in India, reported,

I could readily recognize representations of Devarapalas, the celestial 'Guardians of the Quarters'. In the richly adorned and gaily dressed figures usually flanking the horse-shoe shaped platform which bore the sculptured groups in the large shrines, and here and there also images of the more prominent Bodhisattvas. But for the rest I realized from the first that prolonged study and competent priestly guidance would be needed ... how would my honest secretary, himself a stranger to all the intricate details of Buddhist mythology and iconography, succeed in correctly grasping and reproducing the technical explanations of the hoped for cicerone? [21]

ABOVE *Composite view of bundles of manuscripts in Cave 16, with the door to the side chapel, Cave 17, visible on the right. Stein's photograph shows the characteristic interior of a cave with a seated Buddha figure flanked by attendant Bodhisattvas. The walls of the cave are entirely covered with paintings of Buddhist figures, illustrating the reason they were known locally as 'the Caves of the Thousand Buddhas'. The photograph, which was published in Stein's* Ruins of Desert Cathay *(1912) was a double exposure in which the piles of manuscripts were added to the photo of the cave. It was perhaps made to create the illusion that Stein examined the manuscripts in the caves whilst the truth was that his Chinese secretary Jiang smuggled them out to his tent by night.*

On this first visit to the caves, though Wang was away, a young priest 'borrowed' one of the manuscripts and showed it to Stein and Jiang.

> It was a beautifully preserved roll of paper about 10 inches high and when we unfolded it in front of the original hiding place, proved to be about 15 yards long. The paper, yellowish in tint, looked remarkably strong and fresh. But in a climate so dry and in a carefully sheltered hiding place it was impossible to judge age from mere outward appearance, and with its fine texture and carefully smoothed surface it looked to me decidedly old.

But what was it?

> ... my learned secretary frankly acknowledged that on cursory reading he could not make out any connected sense in the text. This, however, soon found its explanation when, in frequently repeated formulas read out by Jiang, I recognised such words as *pusa* and *bolomi*, the familiar Chinese transcripts of Sanskrit Bodhisattva and *paramita*. I knew how utterly strange the phraseology of Chinese Buddhism is to the average literatus.[22]

Thus only when Jiang read the unfamiliar text aloud to Stein who knew Sanskrit, did it become apparent that this was a Chinese translation of a Sanskrit Buddhist text. Stein was right to suspect that Jiang, not being a Buddhist, though educated and literate, was quite unfamiliar with the religion and, particularly, with its texts. It is in the nature of the Chinese script, with its tens of thousands of different characters, that the vocabulary of Chinese Buddhism, complicated by its phonetic renderings of unfamiliar Sanskrit terms, could be quite unknown and near-incomprehensible to a non-believer.

Overwhelmed by the amount of material and his inability to make judicious selections, Stein decided 'that it was my duty towards research to rescue, if

OPPOSITE *A manuscript of the Ratnakutarapariprccha, the 47th of the Gem Heap sutras, translated into Chinese by Fahu of the Western Jin dynasty (AD 256–316). Some of the fine manuscripts that Stein first saw from the deposit in Cave 17 were visually very striking, like this one, written on fine paper, probably made from hemp and dyed a strong yellow. The calligraphy is even and consistent, written in strong black ink. The wooden roller and the fine blue silk tie are original, dating back to the eighth century.*

According to Stein, Jiang loyally did his best to persuade Wang that

> the removal of the collection to a place of learning in *Da Yingguo* or England, would in truth be an act which Buddha and his Arhats might approve as pious. He also urged that the big sum I was prepared to pay (I hinted at 40 [silver] horse-shoes, about Rs. 5000, and was resolved to give him twice as much, if need be, whatever the excess over my sanctioned grant) would enable Wang to return to a life of peace in his native province ... if Dunhuang should become too hot for him. Or else he could allay any scruples by using the whole sum for the benefit of the temple, which by his restoration he could claim to have annexed as his own with all its contents known or unknown. But all in vain.

Not only did Wang not agree but he moved some bundles of manuscripts back to their 'gloomy prison of centuries'.[24]

Stein persisted and 'the advantage we possessed by already holding loads of valuable manuscripts and antiques, and Wang's unmistakable wish to secure a substantial sum of money, led at last to what I had reason to claim as a substantial success in this diplomatic struggle'. A week later, Stein tried again and Wang 'allowed me to add some twenty more bundles of manuscripts to my previous selections, against an appropriate donation for the temple'. Stein continued to press Wang and, eventually, 24 cases of 'manuscript treasures' and 'five more filled with paintings and other art relics from the same cave' were despatched from Dunhuang. Stein fully realised the clandestine nature of his activities for he noted that when it came to packing, 'there was some little trouble about getting enough boxes without exciting suspicion at Dunhuang. Luckily I had foreseen the chance and provided some "empties" beforehand...'[25]

OPPOSITE *Stein's Chinese secretary at Pakhtakla, 6 July 1915. George Macartney, the British Consul in Kashgar, recommended Jiang Xiaowan, a local clerk, as Chinese secretary to Aurel Stein on his second expedition. Jiang was very useful as an interpreter for Stein when he met local officials, although his literacy did not extend to an ability to read and understand Buddhist texts. Stein remained fond of him and employed him again on his third expedition (1913–16) when they revisited Dunhuang and acquired yet more scrolls from Wang. Jiang's costume of traditional Chinese gown and trilby hat is characteristic of the period after the fall of the last emperor in 1911, when the new Republican Chinese sought ways of modernising their country.*

ABOVE *Camels at Yardang-bulak, 1915. Stein relied on various types of pack animals to transport his equipment and his finds. Crossing into China from India over the Pamirs, he used yaks but in most of the desert areas from Kashgar eastwards, he relied on camels. His preparations for the removal of antiquities and manuscripts were meticulous, with specially prepared boxes in sufficient quantity for speedy removal. The two-humped Bactrian camels were used across Central Asia and into northern China, where only 30 years ago they could still be seen hauling loads of coal on the outskirts of Peking.*

CHAPTER TWO

A CAVE

WHY WAS the Diamond Sutra hidden away at the Caves of the Thousand Buddhas? The existence of a cache of manuscripts and documents there remained a secret from the time that it was deposited, over 1000 years ago, until its rediscovery in 1900. In the last years of the nineteenth century, a wandering Taoist preacher named Wang Yuanlu (1849–1931) came upon the caves and set himself the task of restoring them, collecting money to pay for new wall paintings and sculptures. As he supervised the restoration of Cave 16, he found cracks in the wall that revealed the hidden niche, a tiny side chamber leading off Cave 16, later to be numbered Cave 17.

Cave 17 was of particular significance in the history of Dunhuang for it had been constructed between 851 and 862 in honour of the most important monk in the area, Hong Bian, who died in about 862. Hong Bian was a local monk who had studied Sanskrit and translated Buddhist texts into Chinese. Between 832 and 834 he presided over the carving out of 17 caves. However, it was his support of a local Chinese leader, Zhang Yichao, who drove the occupying Tibetans out of Dunhuang in 848, that led the Emperor of China to issue a decree in 851 allowing Hong Bian to wear purple in commemoration of the return of Dunhuang to Chinese rule. The decree was carved on a stone stele placed in his memorial cave. Apart from the emperor's stele, the cave contained a stone sculpture of Hong Bian set against a wall painting of overhanging pipal trees flanked by attendant figures. At some time in the early eleventh century, Hong Bian's statue was moved to another cave higher up the cliff and his niche, now known as Cave 17, filled with documents, paintings and bronzes.[1]

Though now often referred to as the 'library cave' because of the great mass of more than 50,000 documents that emerged from it, the niche also contained hundreds of religious paintings and many small bronze Buddhist figures. As soon as he had discovered the hoard, Wang Yuanlu removed everything from the niche, presumably to explore the contents but thereby possibly destroying much evidence as to how and why the hoard was deposited in the first place. He made

OPPOSITE *Sutras of the Buddha's name are non-canonical recitations of hundreds, even thousands of different names with different references to or attributes of the Buddha, some mysterious, some beautiful: Buddha of the Mysterious Sound, the Facing the Clouds Buddha, Gold Mountain Buddha, Buddha Without Parallel. Repetition of the names and such sutras were often illustrated. In this case, tiny printed woodblock outlines of the Buddha figure are stamped in two rows between the characters, and the figures were then individually hand-coloured.*

南无福藏佛

南无電明佛

南无師子德佛

南无明讚佛

南无具足讚佛

南无應天佛

南无見有邊佛

南无金山佛

南无勝相佛

南无堅精進佛

南无離畏佛

南无大燈佛

presents of Buddhist bronzes, paintings and scrolls to local officials, probably in order to ingratiate himself and reinforce his unauthorised position at the caves. The local officials, in turn, passed on some of these gifts to higher officials. The local officials seem to have preferred the bronze statuettes which were soon all dispersed.[2]

One distinguished provincial official who expressed interest in the finds was Ye Changchi (1849–1917), who served as Education Commissioner for the province of Gansu from 1902 to 1906 with his office in Lanzhou. He was a scholar, a connoisseur of fine calligraphy who amassed a considerable collection of rubbings of famous stone inscriptions, whose own works include 'On Stone Inscriptions' and 'Poems Recording Incidents of Book-Collecting'. In his diary entry for 30 December 1903, he recorded a gift from the District Magistrate of Dunhuang which included '... an old Buddhist scroll painting depicting a sermon at the festival of water and land ... also four manuscript scrolls all of the *Mahaparinirvanasutra*.' And he continued,

> Dunhuang is hidden in the western wastes, among remote mountains and ancient Buddhist temples, and it is therefore not surprising that it has such progeny. I have heard that these sutras come from a rock cell in the Thousand Buddha Caves and that the door of the cave had been sealed with molten lead and not opened since ancient times. It was only a few years ago that it was discovered and opened. Inside were stone tables and ledges piled high with several hundred scrolls and the sutras I have received are from among these. At the time, the monks and laymen did not realise their value and so divided them amongst themselves.[3]

Ye Changchi did not visit the site itself but mentioned the finds again in his diary on 28 December 1909, with reference to Paul Pelliot's visit to Dunhuang in 1908. 'A Frenchman had taken all the bundles [paying] 200 yuan. This is a pity. The local officials and the people on the borders do not know how to appreciate ancient objects...' The following month Ye wrote,

> Classics, steles and works from the Buddhist canon were all deposited there in the Tang to Song period. The Frenchman Pelliot acquired most of the choice examples to place in the Paris library and an Englishman [Stein]

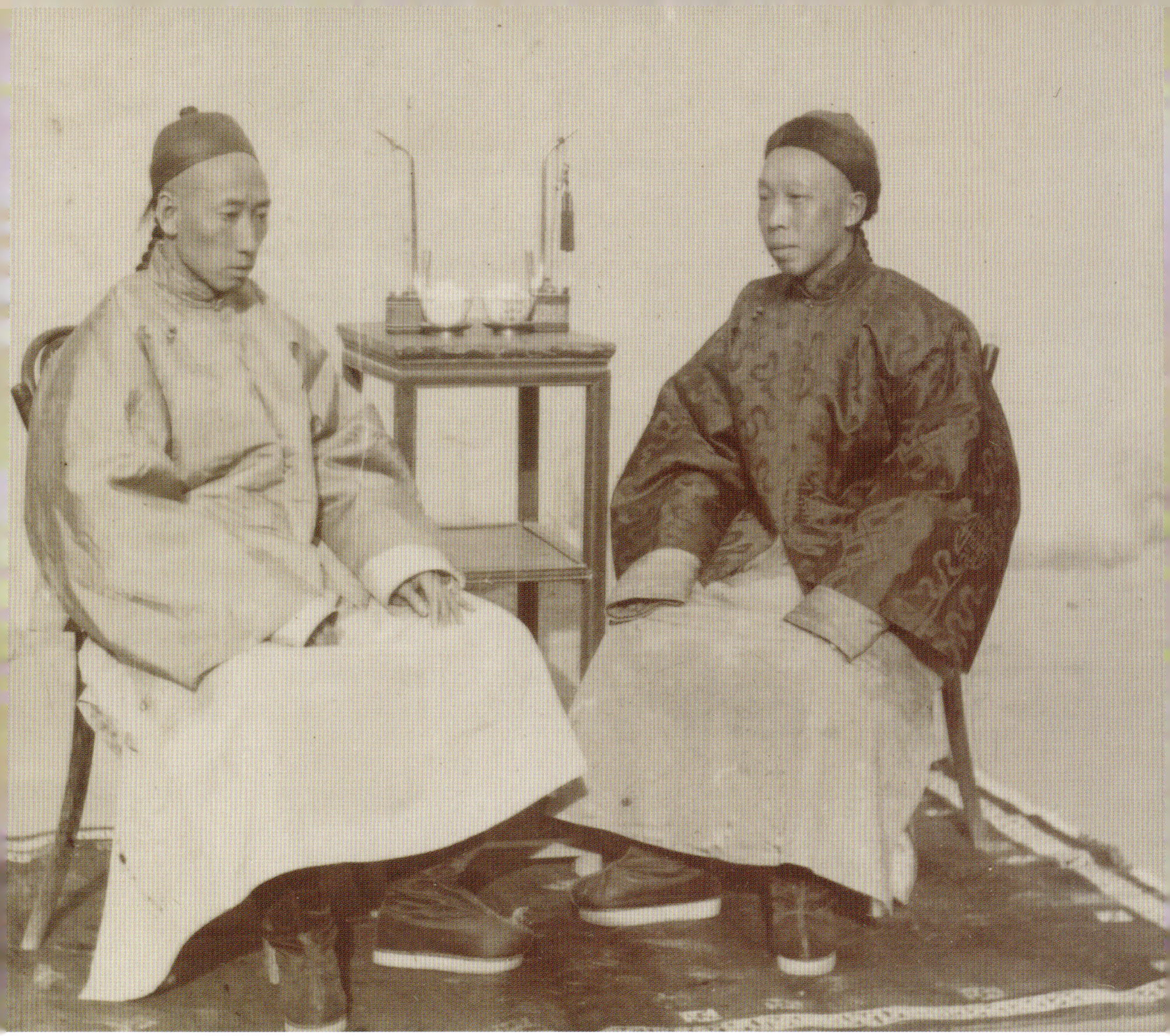

also acquired some odd lots. The Chinese local official turned a blind eye. My circuit took me to Jiuquan but I did not go beyond Jiayuguan which is not more that 1000 li [300 miles] from Dunhuang. By this time I had heard of the discovery of the cave and had also received two Buddhist paintings and five manuscripts. Was it really not possible for its contents to be emptied? What was my role as an imperial envoy? I am ashamed and full of remorse that I dared to blame others.[4]

ABOVE *Chinese secretary Jiang with the Amban (or provincial governor) of Charklik. Through his work in the offices of local officials in the Yarkand and Kashgar area, Stein's Chinese secretary was aware of the significance of Chinese officialdom in the Central Asian desert oases. Stein formally called upon local officials such as the Amban of Charklik (today's Ruoqiang) to the west of Lop Nor and Jiang acted as interpreter (though Jiang knew little English and Stein little Chinese). On his first three expeditions into western China, Stein avoided the capital, Peking, and higher officialdom, preferring to enter China quietly via Kashgar and to deal with lower level officials who provided him with permission to travel in their area.*

Distance and transport difficulties deterred Ye Changchi from investigating the cave. Amongst most other officials there was a general lack of interest, particularly in Buddhist literature. Local officials, trained in the Confucian classics, would have been unaware of Buddhist literature or the history of Buddhism in the area, as was Stein's Chinese secretary. The Chinese government moved very slowly for it was not until 1910, after Paul Pelliot had shown some of his Dunhuang finds to scholars in Peking in September 1909, that the Ministry of Education ordered all the remaining documents to be brought to Peking.[5]

Though few Chinese scholars of the time showed interest in the remarkable find, both Stein and Pelliot advanced theories as to why and when the cache of documents was made. Pelliot was the first to publish his theory that the cave was sealed at a time of imminent invasion, a claim which he made with characteristic certainty.

> The first problem was to determine the rough date of the cache. There is no possibility of doubt. The latest reign dates on the documents are from the early Song: 976–83 and 995–7 and there is not a single Tangut character in the whole library. It is therefore clear that the cave was sealed up during the first half of the eleventh century and probably at the time of the Tangut conquest around 1035.[6] Chinese and Tibetan manuscripts, paintings on silk, hangings and bronze statuettes were piled in higgledy-piggledy with the stone stele [in honour of Hong Bian] engraved in 851. The confused order in which the rolls were sewn into bundles may be attributed to the fear of invasion but I think it more likely a sign of the decadent state into which Chinese civilisation had fallen in the Dunhuang area ... the monks had preserved beautiful manuscripts of the seventh and eighth centuries but did not produce any more and the precious scrolls tore in their clumsy hands. The arrival of the [Tangut] enemy only served to accelerate this decline...[7]

In 1908 Pelliot was probably unaware that the confused state of the contents of the cave owed more to Wang Yuanlu's activities than to the 'decadence' of Chinese civilisation more than 1000 years before. Others have noted that, whatever the effect on the neatness of the hoard of Wang's moving the entire cache out and then putting it back, the fact that, when the original deposit was made, Hong Bian's statue was moved and the entire wall carefully repainted after the cave was bricked up suggests deliberate, planned action rather than panic at the arrival of the Tanguts.

Stein, who knew that Wang had emptied and repacked the entire cave, formed a different opinion as to why the Diamond Sutra and tens of thousands of other paper scrolls had been walled in. He surmised that though they 'had belonged to monastic libraries', they were 'no longer required for use' and 'had been collected from shrines where they had once been deposited and stored away here'.[8]

Chinese scholars today share Stein's view, their conclusions based on long study of local history and the documents themselves. One scholar pointed out that the latest date on a document found in the cave was 1002, over 30 years before the Tangut invasion, which rather contradicts Pelliot's theory that the cave was filled in a panic to protect the manuscripts from the Tanguts. On the other hand, Chinese scholars have suggested that the gradual realisation of the threat posed by the rise of the Turkic Khara-khanids, an Uighur group that ruled Transoxiana from 840 to 1211, might have roused local temples to action. In 1006 the Muslim Khara-khanids invaded the Buddhist kingdom of Khotan which had close links to Dunhuang through the marriage of a Khotanese princess with one of the sons of the local ruler. The arrival of refugees from Khotan may have encouraged local monks to collect and seal up the ancient documents and Buddhist scrolls and paintings that had long been stored in their temples. Their activities were deliberate and not the least hurried. Stein noted that most of the documents had been sewn into 'uniform packets'. From the many and varied colophons and seals on the manuscripts, it is clear that they were gathered from many temples in the Dunhuang area.

Some Japanese scholars advanced the theory that these many manuscripts were discarded because, by about AD 1000, printed Buddhist sutras were arriving in Dunhuang from central China. This theory ignores the fact that the Diamond Sutra, printed in 868, was packed away in Cave 17 along with dozens of other printed items. Fang Guangchang, a Chinese scholar who has been working on Dunhuang manuscripts for some 40 years, concluded that the documents and paintings in Cave 17 were put there because they were no longer usable. He found that sets of scrolls of different sutras were lacking parts, indicating that they had been put aside because they were incomplete and could therefore no longer be used. He also noted that there were no complete sutras written in gold or silver characters in Cave 17, which suggests that these may have been more carefully looked after.[9]

Other indications that the contents of Cave 17 represented a deposit rather than a hoard include the fact that very many of the scrolls were quite worn, or torn and patched. Even the Diamond Sutra had been patched many times before it was placed in the cave. And although the survival of this mass of Buddhist sutras is unique, there are other examples of Buddhist sacred deposits elsewhere in China. In 1996 a great quantity of Buddhist sculptures was found in Qingzhou, in what had once been the grounds of a famous temple. The sculptures all dated from the sixth century but had been 'buried' in the twelfth century and all had been broken before they were buried. The breakages do not seem to have been deliberate or iconoclastic but the result of wear and tear, or fire, and possibly earthquake damage. In the former Mingdao temple nearby, a stone inscription recorded that, in 1004, two travelling monks found 300 broken sculptures in the temple and reverently buried them as an act of piety.[10] When Buddhist images were damaged or ready for replacement, it would have been impious to destroy them, so instead they were carefully buried. The same could have been true for Buddhist sutras. When damaged beyond repair or suffering loss, they were not thrown away but reverently stored, in what was almost a form of burial.

Apart from fine, but worn out or incomplete, Buddhist works, there were a large number of secular documents in Cave 17. Most of these are short items: contracts for the loan of draught animals, sales of slave girls and bolts of cotton, shopping lists and odd items of local government interest such as fragments of official census returns and official gazettes. There were also calendars, club circulars, schoolbooks and fragments of literary works and dictionaries, even copies of

OPPOSITE *Unidentified sutra written in gold on paper dyed with indigo. Paper dyed yellow, the Buddhist colour of solemnity, was commonly used for Buddhist manuscripts although the dye was also protective. Produced from the bark of the Amur cork tree, the dye was insecticidal and prevented worm damage to the paper which was not uncommon. A very small number of coloured papers, pink, pale blue and pale green, have been found amongst the items removed from Cave 17 but, as Chinese scholars noted, though manuscripts written in gold on dark indigo-dyed paper became more popular in the late Tang period, there are extremely few fragments from Cave 17, suggesting that they were treated with especial care to prevent damage within the temples.*

the Yijing, the Confucian classic of divination. These scraps of paper might have survived in the monasteries after being deposited for safe-keeping; but they most probably owe their survival to an old Chinese tradition. This held that any piece of paper with writing on it was regarded as almost sacred and had to be collected 'to save it being put to base uses'. Boxes for the reverent and safe disposal of such papers were often found in Chinese temples.[11]

The smaller pieces of paper thus collected and which ended up in Cave 17 were sometimes used to patch damaged manuscripts or cut out to form cloud collars and crowns and paper flowers to decorate Buddhist figures on festival days and even cut up into tiny squares to be burnt and made into magic medicine.[12] Thus the cave was most importantly a sort of graveyard for texts but also a recycling centre.

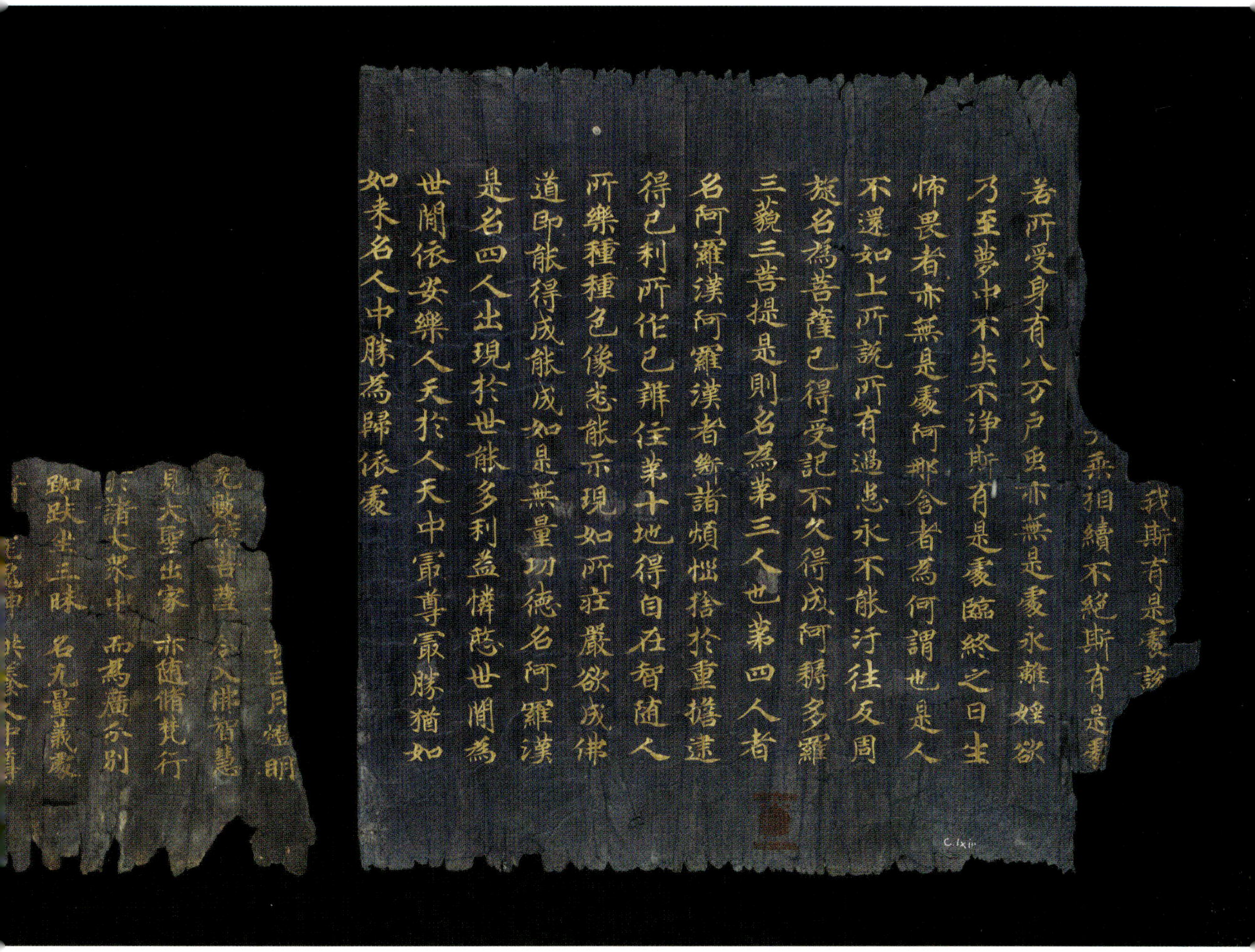
我斯有是處諍
無相續不絕斯有是處
若所受身有八万户虫亦無是處永離婬欲
乃至夢中不失不浄斯有是處臨終之日生
怖畏者亦無是處阿那含者為何謂也是人
不還如上所說所有過患永不能汙往反周
旋名為菩薩已得受記不久得成阿耨多羅
三藐三菩提是則名為第三人也第四人者
名阿羅漢阿羅漢者斷諸煩惱捨於重擔逮
得己利所作已辦住第十地得自在智隨人
所樂種種色像悉能示現如所莊嚴欲成佛
道即能得成能成如是無量功德名阿羅漢
是名四人出現於世能多利益憐愍世間為
世間依安樂人天於人天中最尊最勝猶如
如來名人中勝為歸依處

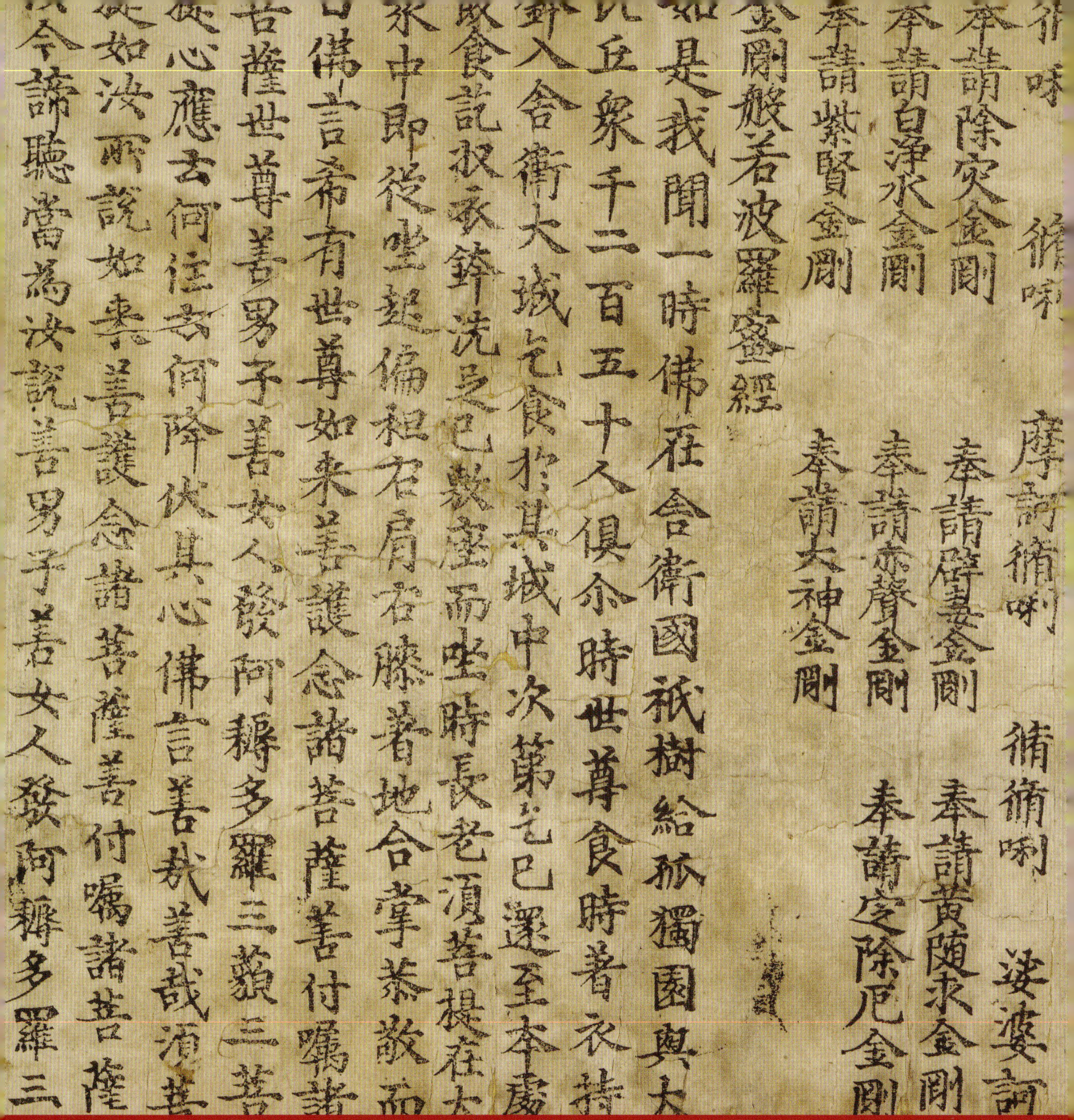

修唎修唎　摩訶修唎　修修唎　娑婆訶

奉請除災金剛　奉請辟毒金剛　奉請黃隨求金剛
奉請白淨水金剛　奉請赤聲金剛　奉請定除厄金剛
奉請紫賢金剛　奉請大神金剛

金剛般若波羅蜜經

如是我聞一時佛在舍衛國祇樹給孤獨園與大
比丘衆千二百五十人俱尒時世尊食時著衣持
鉢入舍衛大城乞食於其城中次第乞已還至本處
飯食訖收衣鉢洗足已敷座而坐時長老須菩提在大
衆中即從座起偏袒右肩右膝著地合掌恭敬而
白佛言希有世尊如來善護念諸菩薩善付囑諸
菩薩世尊善男子善女人發阿耨多羅三藐三菩
提心應云何住云何降伏其心佛言善哉善哉須菩
提如汝所說如來善護念諸菩薩善付囑諸菩薩
汝今諦聽當為汝說善男子善女人發阿耨多羅三

CHAPTER THREE

A SUTRA

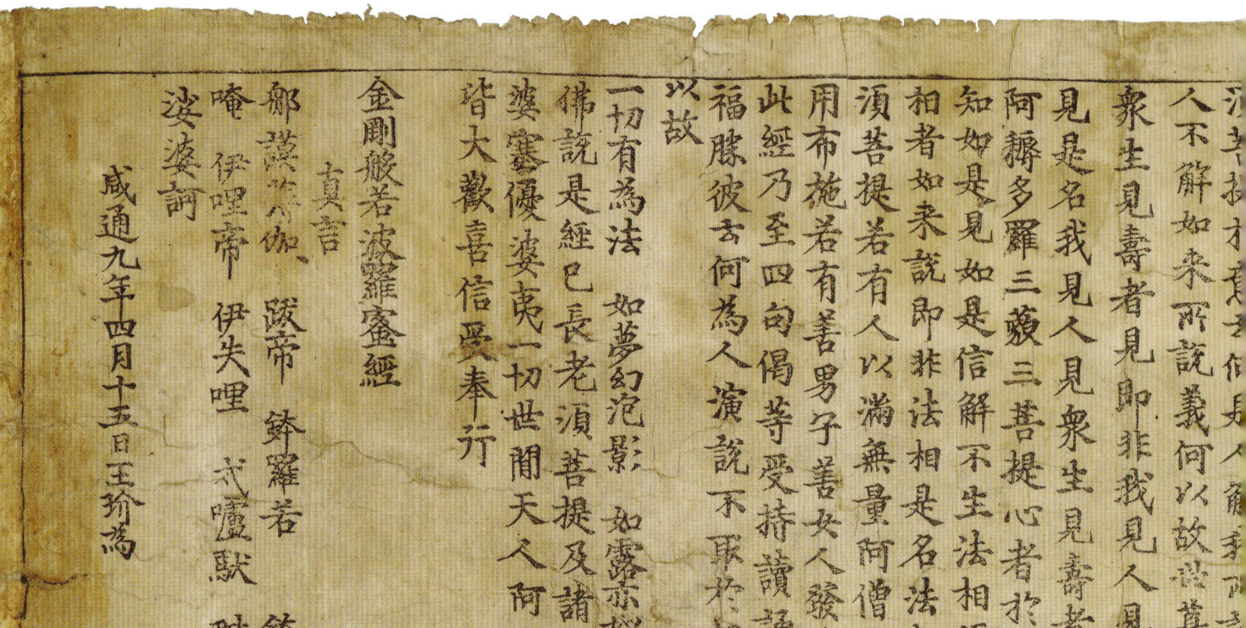
人不解如來所說義何以故世尊說我見人見
衆生見壽者見即非我見人見衆生見壽者
見是名我見人見衆生見壽者見須菩提發
阿耨多羅三藐三菩提心者於一切法應如是
知如是見如是信解不生法相須菩提所言法
相者如來說即非法相是名法相
須菩提若有人以滿無量阿僧祇世界七寶持
用布施若有善男子善女人發菩薩心者持於
此經乃至四句偈等受持讀誦為人演說其
福勝彼云何為人演說不取於相如如不動何
以故
一切有為法 如夢幻泡影 如露亦如電 應作如是觀
佛說是經已長老須菩提及諸比丘比丘尼優
婆塞優婆夷一切世間天人阿修羅聞佛所說
皆大歡喜信受奉行
金剛般若波羅蜜經
真言
那謨婆伽跋帝 鉢羅若 鉢羅蜜多曳
唵 伊唎底 伊失唎 輸嚧馱 毗舍耶 毗舍耶
莎婆訶
咸通九年四月十五日王玠為 二親敬造普施

THE 'DIAMOND SUTRA' and all the other sutras are the discourses or sermons of the Buddha. The Buddha, Siddhartha Gautama of the Sakya tribe in Nepal, probably lived between 563 and 483 BC, and is venerated for having achieved enlightenment and taught a way to salvation. Very little information on his life can be discovered, although there are masses of legends about him, and even his own teachings are difficult to retrieve from the scriptures attributed to him, many of which were clearly composed several centuries after his death. From other pre-existing Indian religions, especially Hinduism, Buddhism incorporated the idea of rebirth, that an individual life was one of a series, whose condition was shaped by deeds performed in previous existences. Buddhists also held the view that animals were part of that cycle of rebirth and some said, for example, that birds had been human thieves in a previous existence. In the early period, Buddhism was also characterised by a rejection of

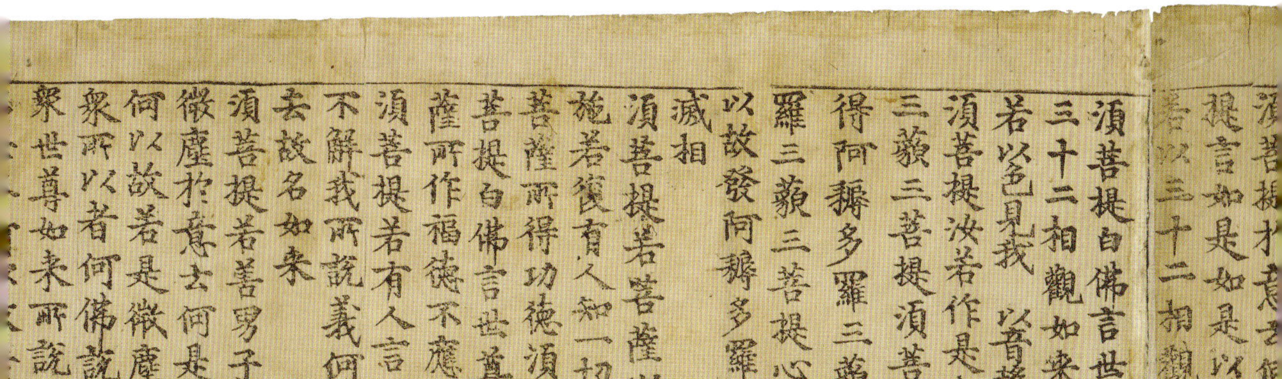

提言如是如是以三十二相觀如來佛言須菩提
若以三十二相觀如來者轉輪聖王即是如來

須菩提白佛言世尊如我解佛所說義不應以
三十二相觀如來爾時世尊而說偈言
若以色見我　以音聲求我　是人行邪道　不能見如來
須菩提汝若作是念如來不以具足相故得阿耨多羅
三藐三菩提　須菩提莫作是念如來不以具足相故
得阿耨多羅三藐三菩提　須菩提汝若作是念發阿耨多
羅三藐三菩提心者說諸法斷滅相　莫作是念何
以故發阿耨多羅三藐三菩提心者於法不說斷
滅相
須菩提若菩薩以滿恒河沙等世界七寶持用布
施若復有人知一切法無我得成於忍此菩薩勝前
菩薩所得功德　須菩提以諸菩薩不受福德故　須
菩提白佛言世尊云何菩薩不受福德　須菩提　菩
薩所作福德不應貪著是故說不受福德
六
須菩提若有人言如來若來若去若坐若臥是人
不解我所說義何以故如來者無所從來亦無所
去故名如來
須菩提若善男子善女人以三千大千世界碎為
微塵於意云何是微塵衆寧為多不　甚多世尊
何以故若是微塵衆實有者佛則不說是微塵
衆所以者何佛說微塵衆則非微塵衆是名微塵
衆世尊如來所說三千大千世界則非世界是

other local beliefs such as the importance of caste, and it denied the efficacy of gods and ritual. However, by the time that the Diamond Sutra was produced in China, Chinese Buddhism had developed very different characteristics, with temples filled with statues of gods of all sorts and special rituals enacted for funerals, the Buddha's birthday, the lantern festival and All Souls' Day.[1]

The historic Buddha, Siddhartha Gautama, was believed to have been conceived immaculately and born, without pain, from his mother's side. Though a prince, living a protected life within the palace, he was said to have gone out into the

ABOVE *Over the subsequent pages, the entire sutra is shown, following its most recent conservation. The end of the sutra (above, left) is at the beginning of this chapter since Chinese books and manuscripts were written from right to left.*

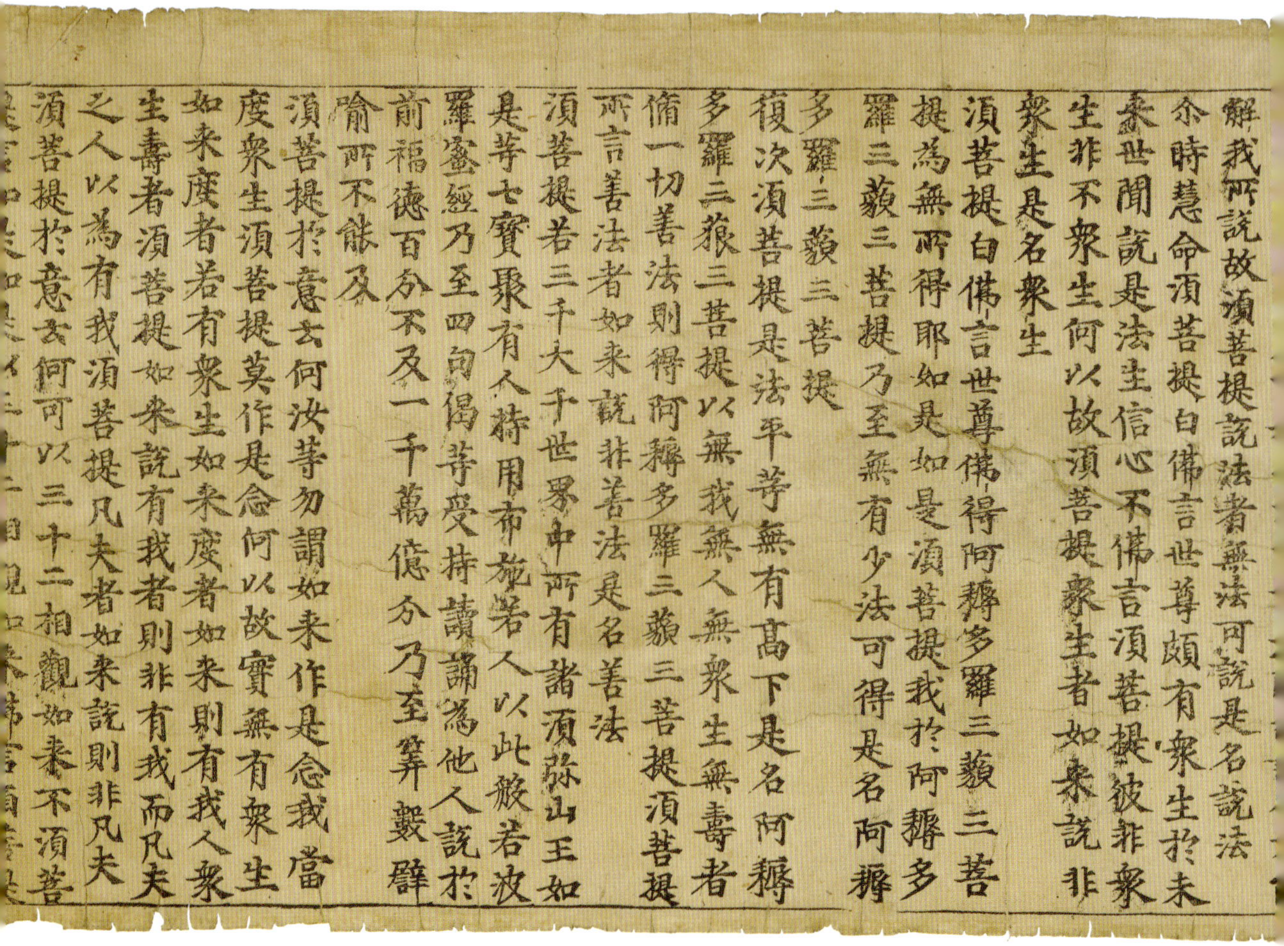
解我所說故須菩提說法者無法可說是名說法
尔時慧命須菩提白佛言世尊頗有衆生於未
來世聞說是法生信心不佛言須菩提彼非衆
生非不衆生何以故須菩提衆生者如来說非
衆生是名衆生
須菩提白佛言世尊佛得阿耨多羅三藐三菩
提為無所得耶如是如是須菩提我於阿耨多
羅三藐三菩提乃至無有少法可得是名阿耨
多羅三藐三菩提
復次須菩提是法平等無有高下是名阿耨
多羅三藐三菩提以無我無人無衆生無壽者
脩一切善法則得阿耨多羅三藐三菩提須菩提
所言善法者如来說非善法是名善法
須菩提若三千大千世界中所有諸須彌山王如
是等七寶聚有人持用布施若人以此般若波
羅蜜經乃至四句偈等受持讀誦為他人說於
前福德百分不及一千萬億分乃至筭數譬
喻所不能及
須菩提於意云何汝等勿謂如来作是念我當
度衆生須菩提莫作是念何以故實無有衆生
如来度者若有衆生如来度者如来則有我人衆
生壽者須菩提如来說有我者則非有我而凡夫
之人以為有我須菩提凡夫者如来說則非凡夫
須菩提於意云何可以三十二相觀如来不須菩

city where he saw an old man, a sick man, a corpse and a religious ascetic. These so-called 'four encounters', the first three shocking and sad, the last inspiring, led him to renounce the world and seek enlightenment. In the legends about his life, he braved many attacks, survived many ordeals and acquired many followers. On his death, enlightened, he achieved nirvana, eliminating the causes of rebirth.

The Buddha's view, transmitted orally by his disciples in the centuries after his death, was that life was essentially painful. This was the first of the 'four noble truths': the suffering of sickness, old age and death, disappointment and frustration. The second noble truth defined the cause of suffering as desire for material things, for illusory pleasure. The third truth was the suppression of

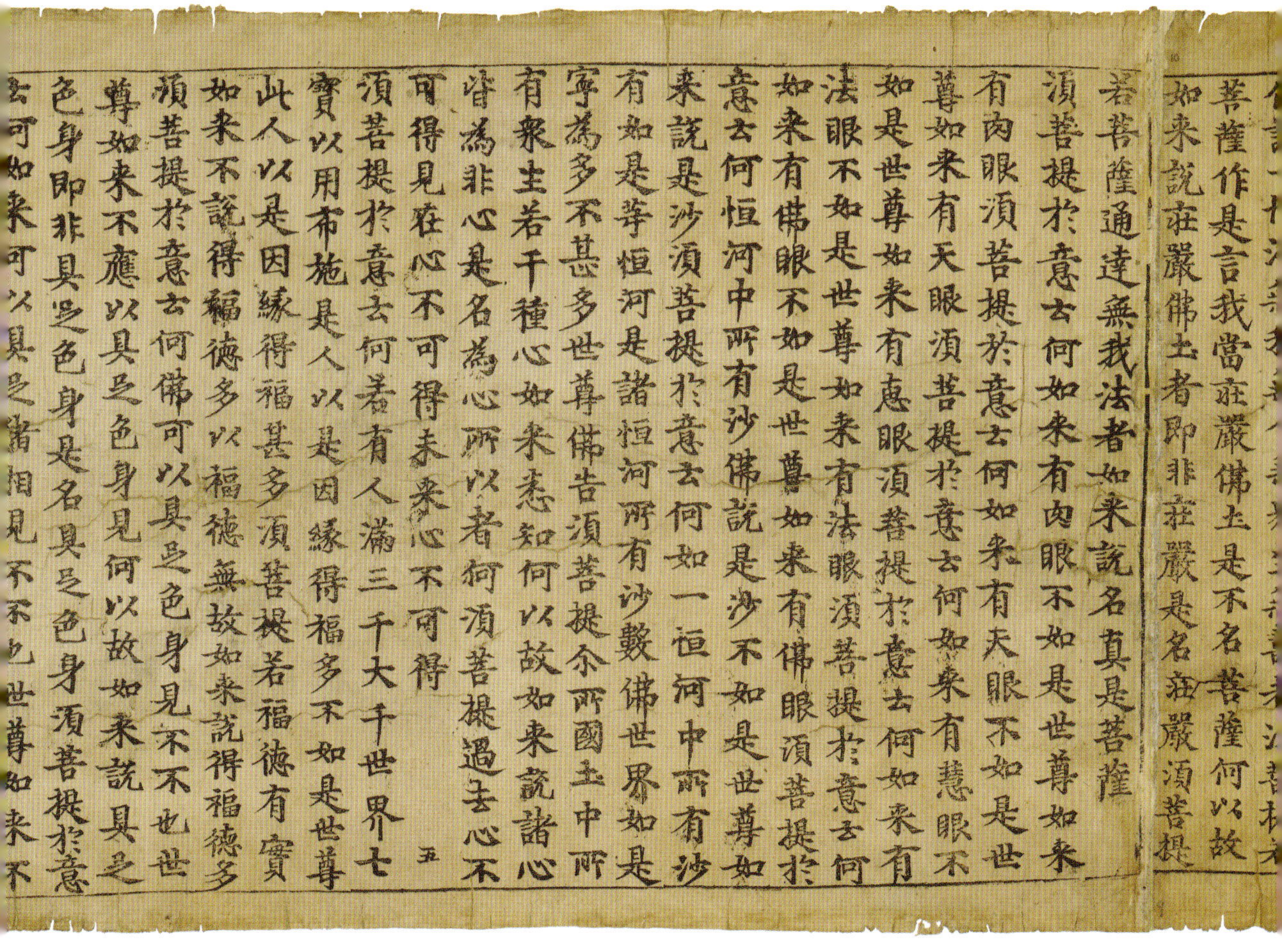
菩薩作是言我當莊嚴佛土是不名菩薩何以故
如来說莊嚴佛土者即非莊嚴是名莊嚴須菩提
若菩薩通達無我法者如来說名真是菩薩
須菩提於意云何如来有肉眼不如是世尊如来
有肉眼須菩提於意云何如来有天眼不如是世
尊如来有天眼須菩提於意云何如来有慧眼不
如是世尊如来有慧眼須菩提於意云何如来有
法眼不如是世尊如来有法眼須菩提於意云何
如来有佛眼不如是世尊如来有佛眼須菩提於
意云何恒河中所有沙佛說是沙不如是世尊如
来說是沙須菩提於意云何如一恒河中所有沙
有如是等恒河是諸恒河所有沙數佛世界如是
寧為多不甚多世尊佛告須菩提尒所國土中所
有衆生若干種心如来悉知何以故如来說諸心
皆為非心是名為心所以者何須菩提過去心不
可得見在心不可得未来心不可得 五
須菩提於意云何若有人滿三千大千世界七
寶以用布施是人以是因緣得福多不如是世尊
此人以是因緣得福甚多須菩提若福德有實
如来不說得福德多以福德無故如来說得福德多
須菩提於意云何佛可以具足色身見不不也世
尊如来不應以具足色身見何以故如来說具足
色身即非具足色身是名具足色身須菩提於意
云何如来可以具足諸相見不不也世尊如来不

desire and the fourth the means to achieve it through the 'noble eightfold path': right view, right intention, right speech, right action, right livelihood, right effort, right mindfulness, right concentration. Fundamental to the four truths was the belief that individuals have no permanent self or soul, for these components are subject to constant change and reassembly into a new life (or rebirth). These changes are not arbitrary but determined by actions, ruled by cause and effect, depending upon meritorious acts to determine reward and retribution in the cycle of rebirth.

The best way to follow the spiritual exercises of the eightfold path was by retreating into a monastery. By clearing the mind of the 'five hindrances' (longing for the world, malice, sloth, distraction and doubt) through 'four stages of trance'

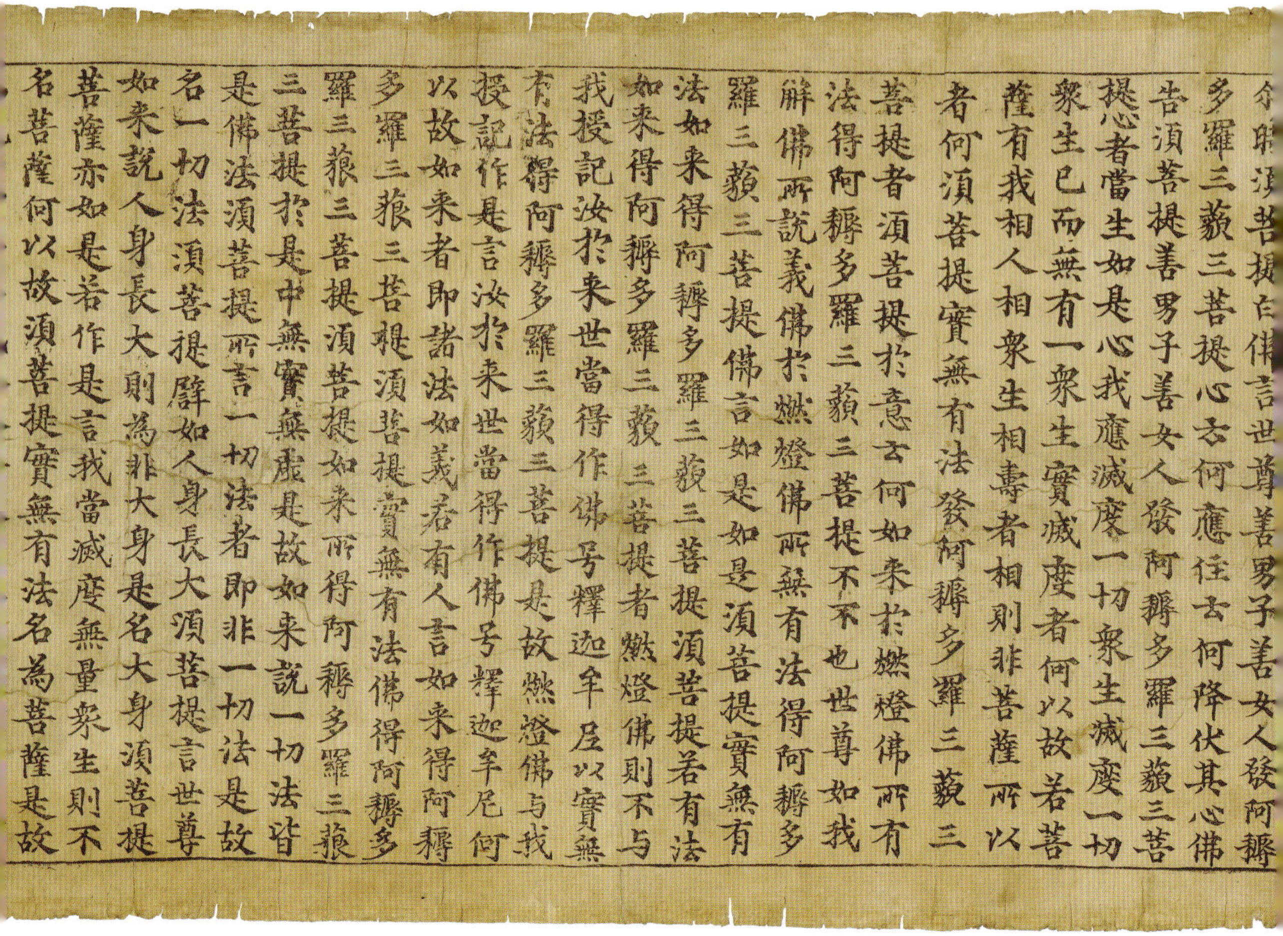
尒時須菩提白佛言世尊善男子善女人發阿耨
多羅三藐三菩提心云何應住云何降伏其心佛
告須菩提善男子善女人發阿耨多羅三藐三菩
提心者當生如是心我應滅度一切衆生滅度一切
衆生已而無有一衆生實滅度者何以故若菩
薩有我相人相衆生相壽者相則非菩薩所以
者何須菩提實無有法發阿耨多羅三藐三
菩提者須菩提於意云何如來於燃燈佛所有
法得阿耨多羅三藐三菩提不不也世尊如我
解佛所說義佛於燃燈佛所無有法得阿耨多
羅三藐三菩提佛言如是如是須菩提實無有
法如來得阿耨多羅三藐三菩提須菩提若有法
如來得阿耨多羅三藐三菩提者燃燈佛則不与
我授記汝於來世當得作佛號釋迦牟尼以實無
有法得阿耨多羅三藐三菩提是故燃燈佛与我
授記作是言汝於來世當得作佛號釋迦牟尼何
以故如來者即諸法如義若有人言如來得阿耨
多羅三藐三菩提須菩提實無有法佛得阿耨多
羅三藐三菩提須菩提如來所得阿耨多羅三藐
三菩提於是中無實無虛是故如來說一切法皆
是佛法須菩提所言一切法者即非一切法是故
名一切法須菩提譬如人身長大須菩提言世尊
如來說人身長大則為非大身是名大身須菩提
菩薩亦如是若作是言我當滅度無量衆生則不
名菩薩何以故須菩提實無有法名為菩薩是故

to the cessation of perception and the elimination of passion, the believer hoped to progress towards nirvana. Lay persons could achieve merit by supporting monks, giving food and clothing and seeking instruction; they could also practise meditation and breathing exercises and follow the monastic discipline in matters of food and clothing. These principles can still be seen in many Buddhist communities throughout the world, although in a number of places Buddhism itself has changed over the centuries to suit local beliefs. Though monasteries did flourish in China, for example, there was a fundamental contradiction between Confucian family duties such as caring for elderly parents and worshipping ancestors in the home on a regular basis and the retreat from family implicit in the lives of monks and nuns. This led to a growth in the patronage of monasteries in China, which became rich through donations of land and treasure. The government felt threatened by this to

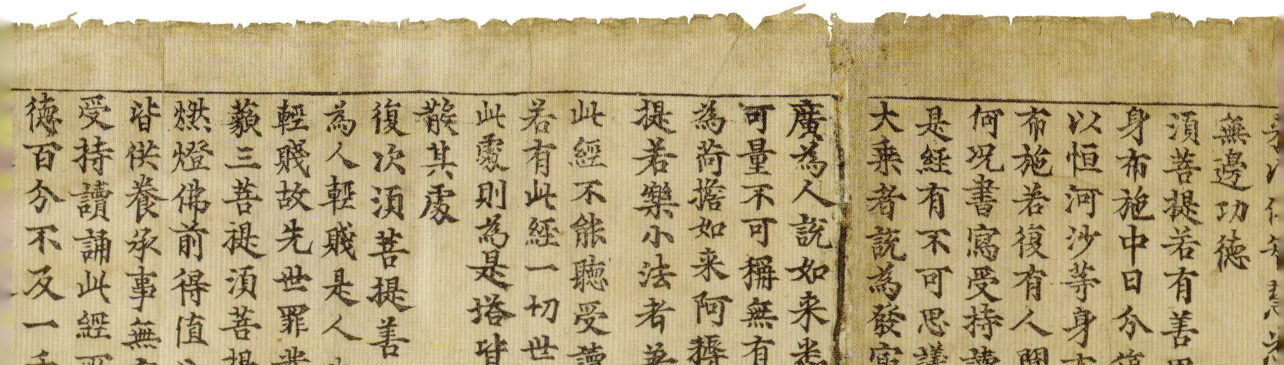

the point that, in 845, Buddhism was officially suppressed with the expulsion of thousands of monks and nuns and the confiscation of Buddhist land and property. Buddhist believers, however, continued to sponsor projects which would accrue merit, as Wang Jie did when he paid for the printing of the Diamond Sutra for universal distribution.[2]

According to tradition, the texts of Buddhism were transmitted orally for several centuries and first written down in Pali in Sri Lanka, with Sanskrit versions written on palm leaves in the second century AD. At a Grand Council held soon after the Buddha's death, a three-fold division of the scriptures had been established. This included the sutras or sermons, the rules for monks (Vinaya) and scholastic commentaries (Abhidharma).[3]

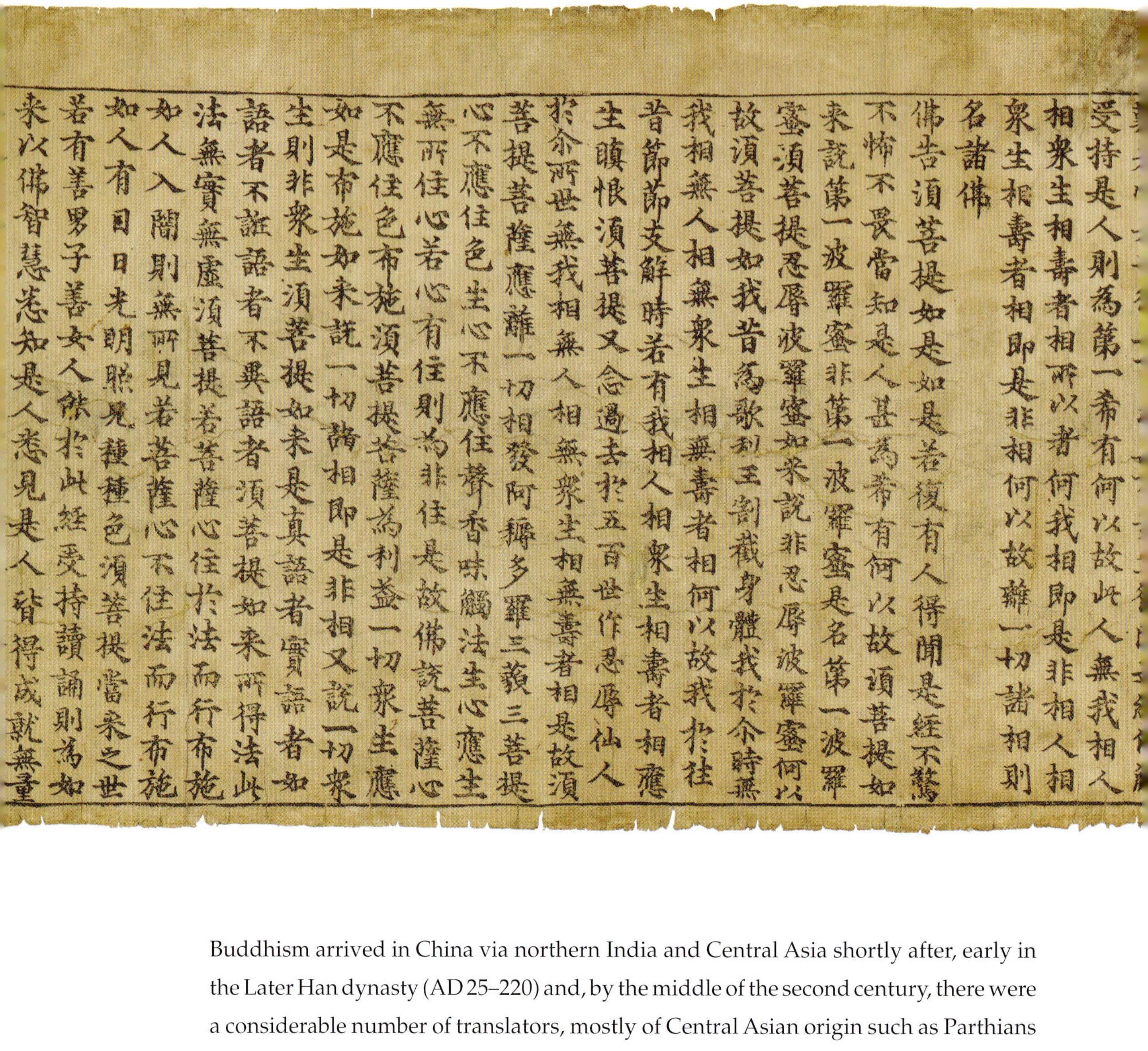

受持是人則為第一希有何以故此人無我相人
相衆生相壽者相所以者何我相即是非相人相
衆生相壽者相即是非相何以故離一切諸相則
名諸佛
佛告須菩提如是如是若復有人得聞是經不驚
不怖不畏當知是人甚為希有何以故須菩提如
來說第一波羅蜜非第一波羅蜜是名第一波羅
蜜須菩提忍辱波羅蜜如來說非忍辱波羅蜜何以
故須菩提如我昔為歌利王割截身體我於尒時無
我相無人相無衆生相無壽者相何以故我於往
昔節節支解時若有我相人相衆生相壽者相應
生瞋恨須菩提又念過去於五百世作忍辱仙人
於尒所世無我相無人相無衆生相無壽者相是故須
菩提菩薩應離一切相發阿耨多羅三藐三菩提
心不應住色生心不應住聲香味觸法生心應生
無所住心若心有住則為非住是故佛說菩薩心
不應住色布施須菩提菩薩為利益一切衆生應
如是布施如來說一切諸相即是非相又說一切衆
生則非衆生須菩提如來是真語者實語者如
語者不誑語者不異語者須菩提如來所得法此
法無實無虛須菩提若菩薩心住於法而行布施
如人入闇則無所見若菩薩心不住法而行布施
如人有目日光明照見種種色須菩提當來之世
若有善男子善女人能於此經受持讀誦則為如
來以佛智慧悉知是人悉見是人皆得成就無量

Buddhism arrived in China via northern India and Central Asia shortly after, early in the Later Han dynasty (AD 25–220) and, by the middle of the second century, there were a considerable number of translators, mostly of Central Asian origin such as Parthians and Sogdians, working, often in teams, to translate Buddhist texts into Chinese. Over the succeeding centuries, thousands of Sanskrit Buddhist texts were translated into Chinese and, in the seventh and eighth centuries, also into Tibetan. In some cases, the Sanskrit originals have disappeared, destroyed in the Muslim invasions of India in the eighth to thirteenth centuries, and only the Chinese or Tibetan versions remain.

There is a surviving Sanskrit version of the Diamond Sutra, and several Tibetan and Mongolian versions, amongst others. There are also eight Chinese translations: the earliest by Kumarajiva (344–413) in about 401, two versions

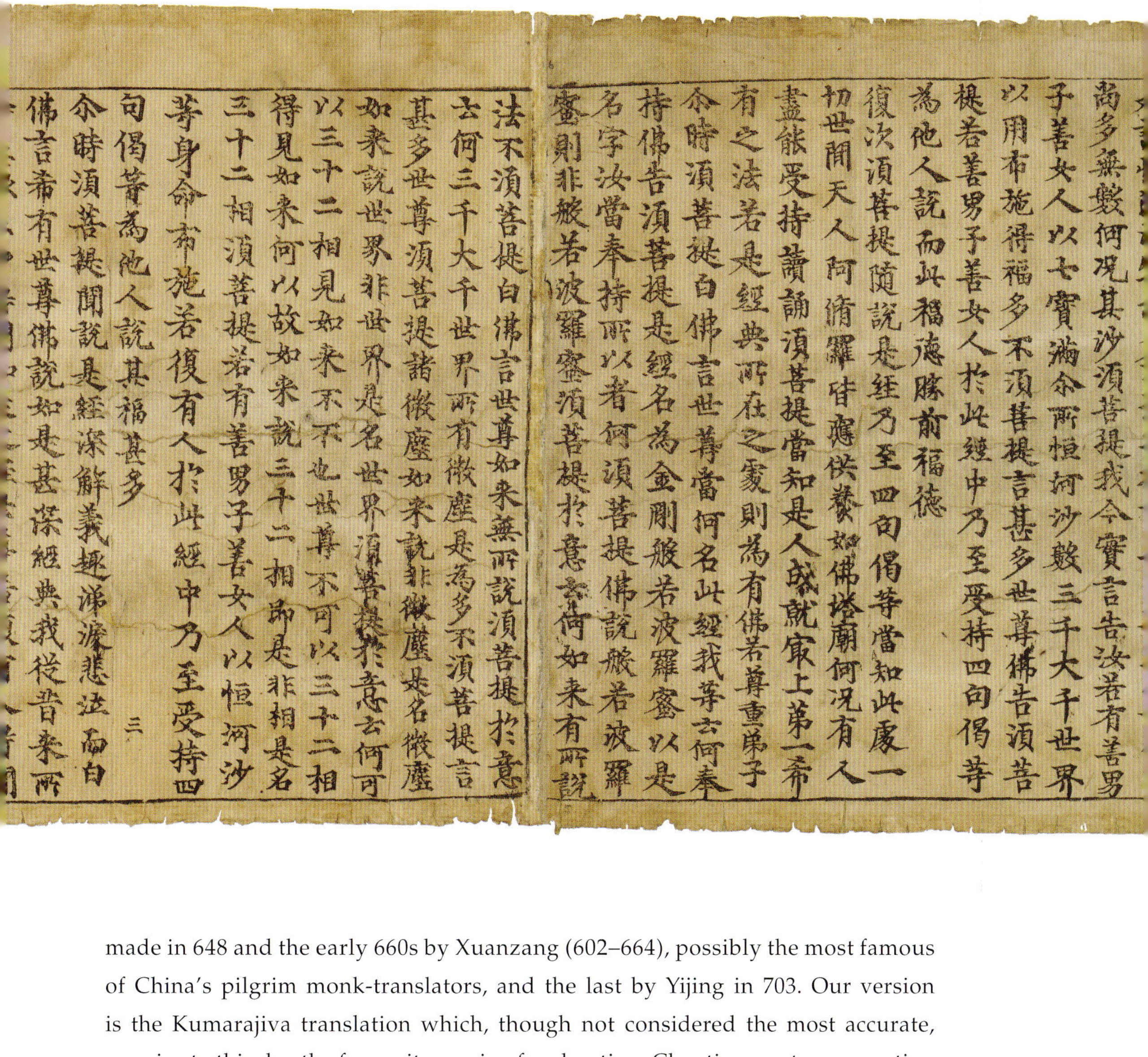
尚多無數何況其沙須菩提我今實言告汝若有善男
子善女人以七寶滿尒所恒河沙數三千大千世界
以用布施得福多不須菩提言甚多世尊佛告須菩
提若善男子善女人於此經中乃至受持四句偈等
為他人說而此福德勝前福德
復次須菩提隨說是經乃至四句偈等當知此處一
切世間天人阿脩羅皆應供養如佛塔廟何況有人
盡能受持讀誦須菩提當知是人成就最上第一希
有之法若是經典所在之處則為有佛若尊重弟子
尒時須菩提白佛言世尊當何名此經我等云何奉
持佛告須菩提是經名為金剛般若波羅蜜以是
名字汝當奉持所以者何須菩提佛說般若波羅
蜜則非般若波羅蜜須菩提於意云何如來有所說
法不須菩提白佛言世尊如來無所說須菩提於意
云何三千大千世界所有微塵是為多不須菩提言
甚多世尊須菩提諸微塵如來說非微塵是名微塵
如來說世界非世界是名世界須菩提於意云何可
以三十二相見如來不不也世尊不可以三十二相
得見如來何以故如來說三十二相即是非相是名
三十二相須菩提若有善男子善女人以恒河沙
等身命布施若復有人於此經中乃至受持四
句偈等為他人說其福甚多　三
尒時須菩提聞說是經深解義趣涕淚悲泣而白
佛言希有世尊佛說如是甚深經典我從昔來所

made in 648 and the early 660s by Xuanzang (602–664), possibly the most famous of China's pilgrim monk-translators, and the last by Yijing in 703. Our version is the Kumarajiva translation which, though not considered the most accurate, remains to this day the favourite version for chanting. Chanting a sutra – repeating the words of the Buddha – is one way of gaining merit. The Diamond Sutra is short and can be chanted in about 40 minutes. It was clearly popular in Dunhuang in Tang times for the 615 manuscripts and two printed versions of the text collected by Stein from Cave 17 came second in number only to copies of the Lotus Sutra.[4]

Like so many of the early translators, Kumarajiva was not Chinese. Born in Kucha, his Indian father was a Brahmin noble and his mother a Kuchan princess. When he was nine years old his devoutly Buddhist mother took him to Kashmir

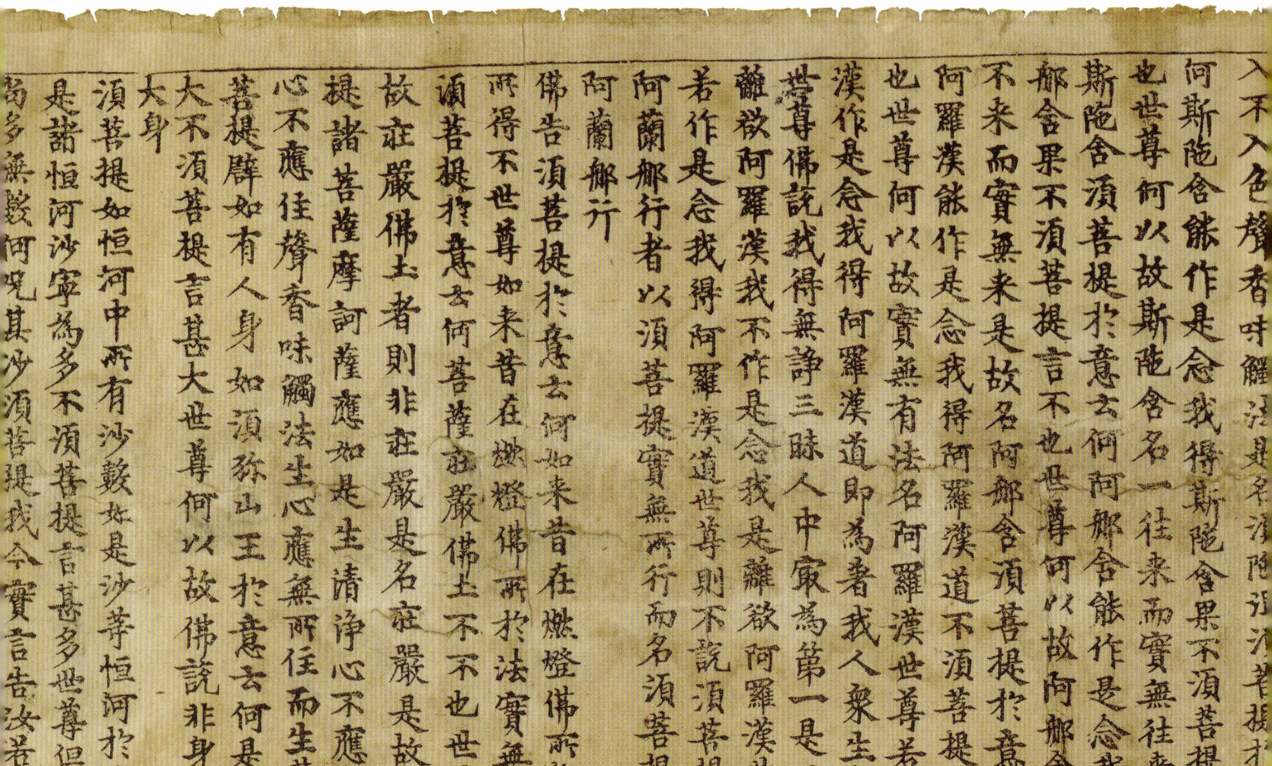

to study. Captured at the age of about 40 by a Chinese force, he learnt Chinese and such was his fame as a Buddhist teacher and scholar that he was fought over by local rulers though he eventually settled in the Chinese capital, Chang'an (today's Xi'an) and made many translations, characterised as smooth and elegant renderings rather than strictly literal versions. Despite his vocation and his skill, he is supposed to have said that reading a sutra in translation, rather than the Sanskrit original, was like eating rice that someone else had chewed.[5]

The Diamond Sutra is one of the Prajnaparamita or Perfection of Wisdom sutras, texts of the Mahayana or Great Vehicle school of Buddhism which developed in southern India in the first century BC or a little earlier, whose aim was Bodhisattvahood: the achievement of enlightenment but postponing personal nirvana to help others on

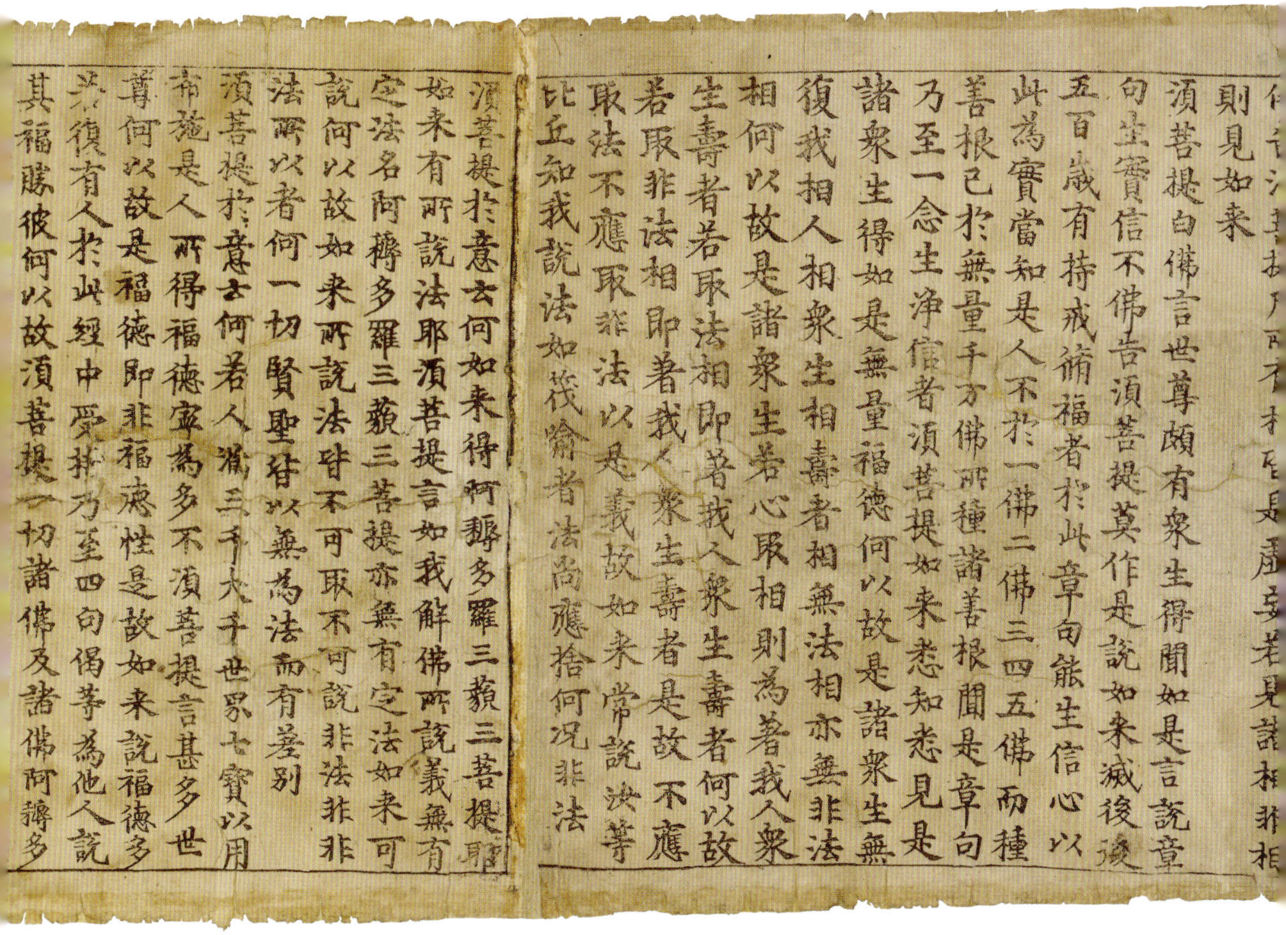
則見如來
須菩提白佛言世尊頗有衆生得聞如是言說章
句生實信不佛告須菩提莫作是說如來滅後後
五百歲有持戒脩福者於此章句能生信心以
此為實當知是人不於一佛二佛三四五佛而種
善根已於無量千万佛所種諸善根聞是章句
乃至一念生淨信者須菩提如來悉知悉見是
諸衆生得如是無量福德何以故是諸衆生無
復我相人相衆生相壽者相無法相亦無非法
相何以故是諸衆生若心取相則為著我人衆
生壽者若取法相即著我人衆生壽者何以故
若取非法相即著我人衆生壽者是故不應
取法不應取非法以是義故如來常說汝等
比丘知我說法如筏喻者法尚應捨何況非法
須菩提於意云何如來得阿耨多羅三藐三菩提耶
如來有所說法耶須菩提言如我解佛所說義無有
定法名阿耨多羅三藐三菩提亦無有定法如來可
說何以故如來所說法皆不可取不可說非法非非
法所以者何一切賢聖皆以無為法而有差別
須菩提於意云何若人滿三千大千世界七寶以用
布施是人所得福德寧為多不須菩提言甚多世
尊何以故是福德即非福德性是故如來說福德多
若復有人於此經中受持乃至四句偈等為他人說
其福勝彼何以故須菩提一切諸佛及諸佛阿耨多

the way. Its title in Sanskrit is *Vajracchedikaprajnaparamita*, and it was first translated into English by the Reverend Samuel Beal in 1864 as the 'Kin-kong-king',[6] but is best known in the English-speaking world as the 'Diamond Sutra', the title of Max Muller's translation (1894). Another possible translation of 'vajra' is 'thunderbolt', in this case 'the perfection of wisdom which cuts like a thunderbolt', and it is clear from the vocabulary and grammar of the Mongolian translations, for example, that this is the more accurate rendering, but the Diamond Sutra remains nonetheless the more popular title.[7]

Our printed edition of the Diamond Sutra begins with an exhortation that is not found in the Sanskrit, nor in any of the standard printed versions of the Kumarajiva translation, such as the great *Taisho Tripitaka* printed in Japan (1924–

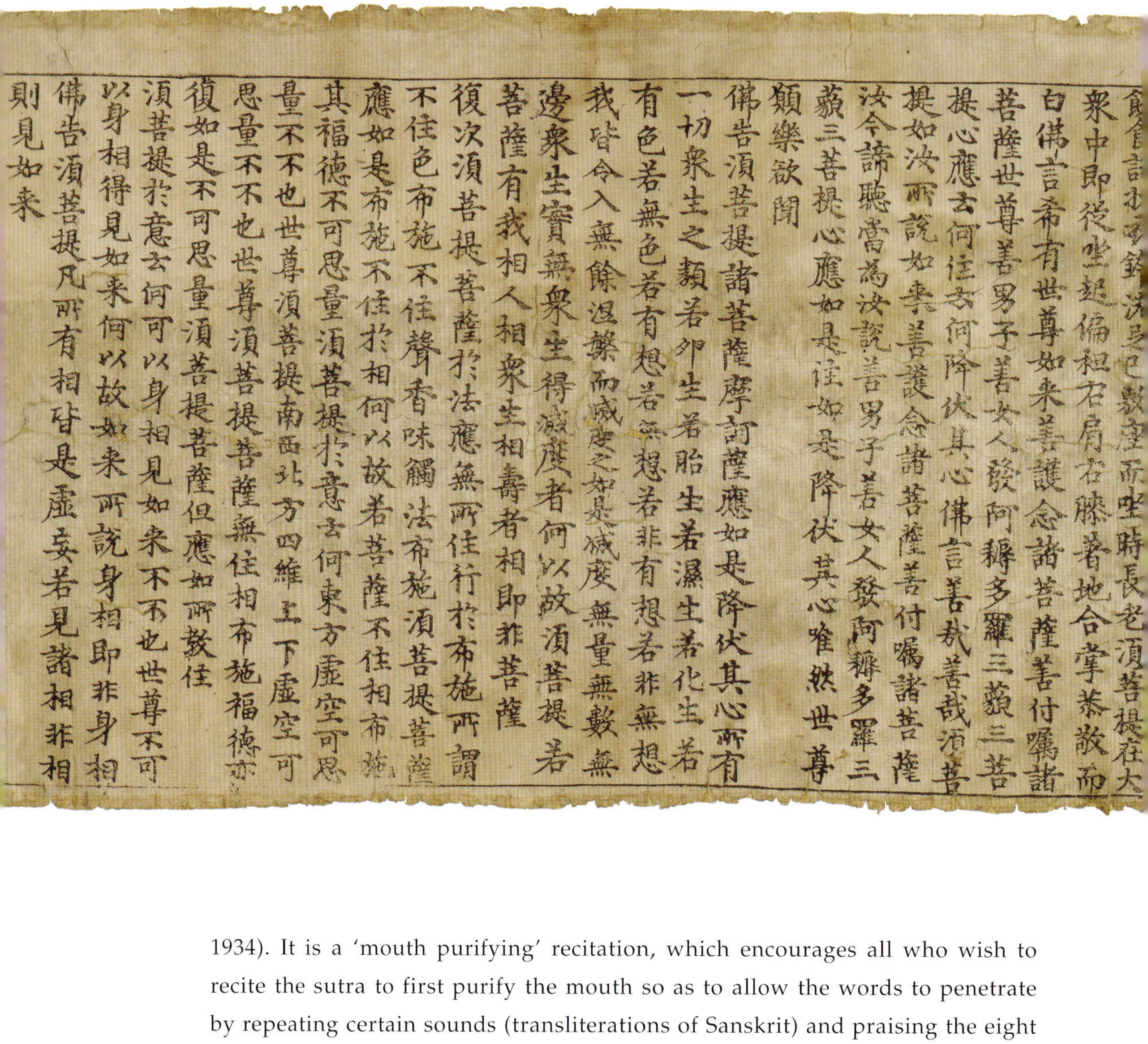
食訖收衣鉢洗足已敷座而坐時長老須菩提在大
衆中即從座起偏袒右肩右膝著地合掌恭敬而
白佛言希有世尊如来善護念諸菩薩善付囑諸
菩薩世尊善男子善女人發阿耨多羅三藐三菩
提心應云何住云何降伏其心佛言善哉善哉須菩
提如汝所說如来善護念諸菩薩善付囑諸菩薩
汝今諦聽當為汝說善男子善女人發阿耨多羅三
藐三菩提心應如是住如是降伏其心唯然世尊
願樂欲聞
佛告須菩提諸菩薩摩訶薩應如是降伏其心所有
一切衆生之類若卵生若胎生若濕生若化生若
有色若無色若有想若無想若非有想若非無想
我皆令入無餘涅槃而滅度之如是滅度無量無數無
邊衆生實無衆生得滅度者何以故須菩提若
菩薩有我相人相衆生相壽者相即非菩薩
復次須菩提菩薩於法應無所住行於布施所謂
不住色布施不住聲香味觸法布施須菩提菩薩
應如是布施不住於相何以故若菩薩不住相布施
其福德不可思量須菩提於意云何東方虛空可思
量不不也世尊須菩提南西北方四維上下虛空可
思量不不也世尊須菩提菩薩無住相布施福德亦
復如是不可思量須菩提菩薩但應如所教住
須菩提於意云何可以身相見如来不不也世尊不可
以身相得見如来何以故如来所說身相即非身相
佛告須菩提凡所有相皆是虛妄若見諸相非相
則見如来

1934). It is a 'mouth purifying' recitation, which encourages all who wish to recite the sutra to first purify the mouth so as to allow the words to penetrate by repeating certain sounds (transliterations of Sanskrit) and praising the eight vajras or thunderbolts, 'the disaster-dispelling, the poison-dispersing, saving, pure, resounding, catastrophe-averting, all-knowing...'[8]

After this unique beginning, which emphasises the power of the sutra as a vehicle of pious recitation (a theme that is repeated in the sutra itself), the text opens in the same way as many other sutras, with a description of the scene. 'Thus I have heard that once the Buddha was staying in Jeta's grove in Sravasti with a large community of 1250 monks.' The next paragraph is shorter in the Chinese version than in the Sanskrit and describes simply how the Buddha put on his

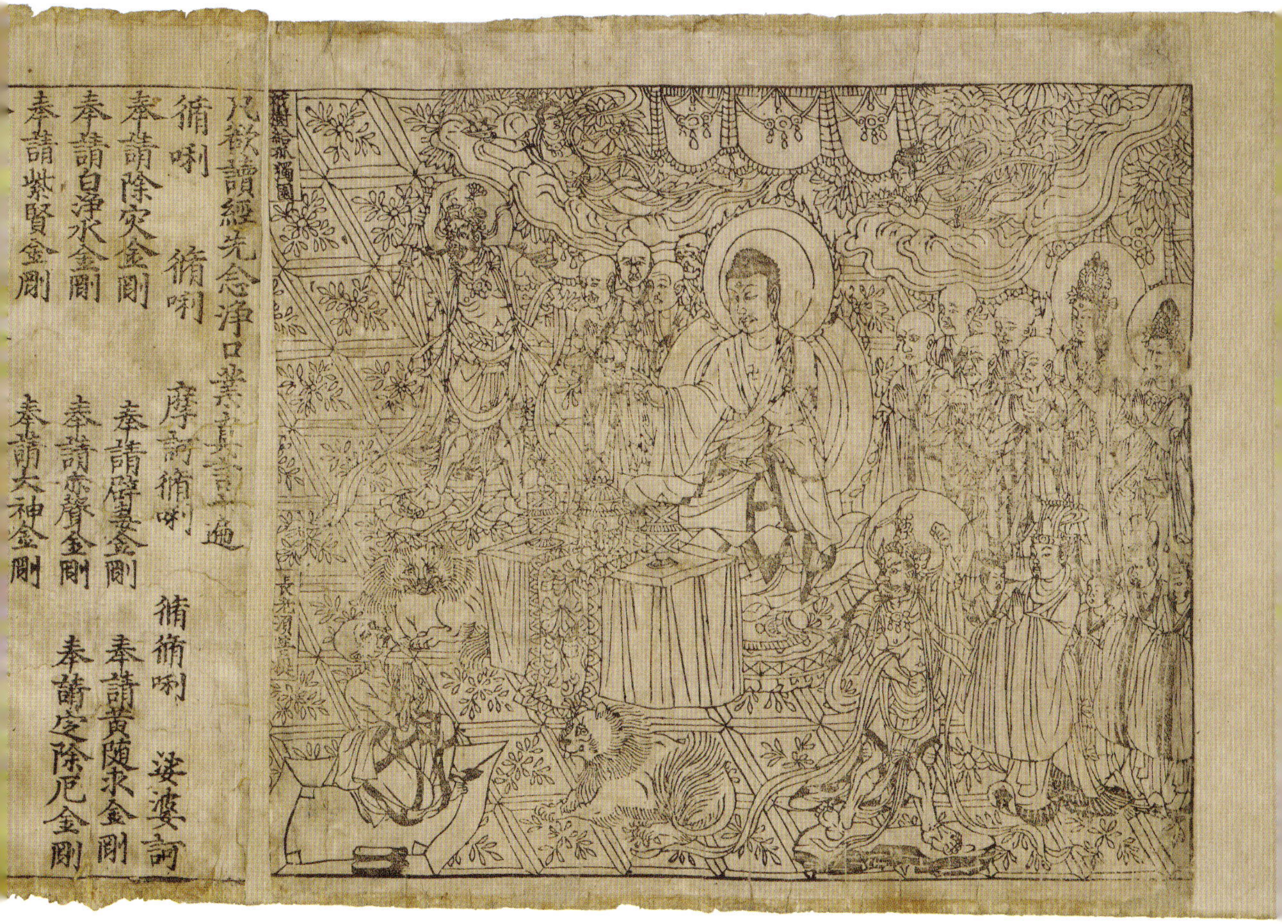

robe, picked up his alms bowl and went into the city to beg for food, going from house to house. When he returned to the grove, he ate his meal and then washed his feet and sat down. In the Sanskrit version, he sat down with his legs crossed as the many monks approached him, prostrated themselves, walked around the Buddha three times and then sat down to one side. In both Sanskrit and Chinese versions, the sutra proceeds in a question and answer format with questions posed to the Buddha by the Venerable Subhuti, shown in the frontispiece as an elderly monk kneeling on a mat in the left foreground.

Subhuti first refers to the high favour which the Buddha grants to the Bodhisattvas and asks how another person seeking to follow the Bodhisattva path should proceed: 'How should he control the mind?'[9] In effect, his question is repeated

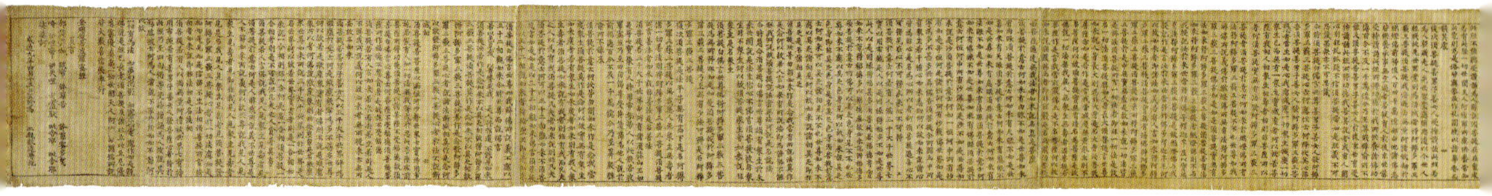

several times throughout the sutra and the Buddha gives similar answers each time. Bodhisattvahood cannot be defined in terms of the physical world, for 'if a Bodhisattva abides in the signs of self, person, sentient being, or life-span, she or he is not a Bodhisattva'. Their acts of charity cannot be measured, as long as they 'practise charity while not abiding in charity'. As if to stress the point, the Buddha then asks Subhuti if it is possible to define the physical characteristics of Buddhahood? Having listened to the Buddha, Subhuti must answer no and the Buddha repeats, 'All things that have characteristics are false and ephemeral.' Another repeated theme is introduced by the Buddha who asks Subhuti if 'someone were to fill this trigalactic megagalactic world-system with the seven treasures [or jewels in the Mongolian translation] as many jewels as the grains of sand on the banks of the Ganges ... would that generate a lot of merit?'

The Buddha continued to say that simply learning one four-line verse from the sutra and teaching it to others would, by comparison, produce an 'incalculable, immeasurable' amount of merit. In the next passage, this is emphasised yet again as the Buddha states that completely memorising the sutra would bring a state of heightened awareness and make even the place of recitation sacred.[10] The teaching of the sutra, and the act of committing it to memory and repeating it, are infinitely more valuable than countless heaps of jewels. This theme is repeated later in the sutra, as a refutation of the misguided idea that the Buddha or Bodhisattvas can be discerned through their physical characteristics. Subhuti seems to need telling twice for he refers to the 32 bodily characteristics of the Buddha whereupon the 'World Honoured One' replies, 'if you try to seek me in form or discern me in sound, these are not Buddhist ways and you will not see me'. In his summary of the non-existence of all things, the Buddha uses verse to state that everything must be seen as 'a dream, an illusion, a bubble, a shadow; like dew, like lightning.'[11]

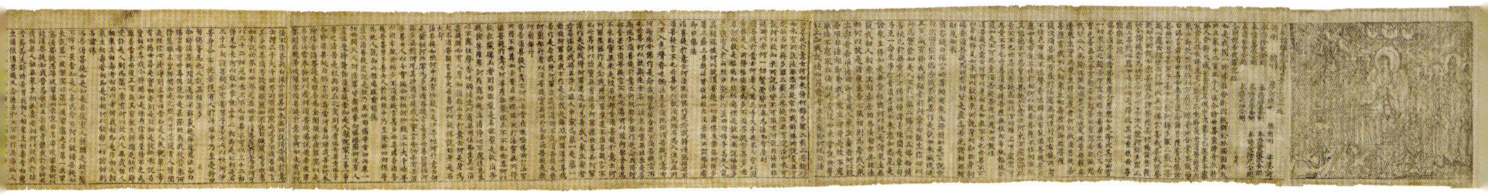

Some aspects of argument in the sutra were in forms familiar to Chinese. The use of high numbers, of 'countless heaps of jewels' as many as 'the grains of sand on the banks of the Ganges' is a familiar style in Chinese where ten thousand stands for myriad and ten thousand times ten thousand for forever. And the negative–positive answers of the Buddha recall the philosophical arguments of Gongsun Long (c. 325–250 BC), most famously the statement 'A white horse is not a horse'. He argued that '"Horse" is that by which we name the shape, "white" is that by which we name the colour. To name the colour is not to name the shape. Therefore ... a white horse is not a horse.'[12]

But the complexity of argument in the sutra stands in contrast to the simplicity of the message that to learn and recite it would bring merit. One Diamond Sutra specialist has said that to read it without chanting is like reading a musical score without hearing the music, and Chinese Buddhists would have been familiar with the chanted form, as part of temple ritual. However, listening to the mumbled hum of ritual chanting (when a cat purrs, the Chinese phrase is 'the cat is reciting the sutras') is a very different activity from intellectual engagement with arguments about form and substance.[13]

ABOVE *The entire sutra is shown above, at a very reduced size. It is printed on six long sheets of paper with the frontispiece on a smaller, separate sheet. The preparation of text and illustration for printing almost certainly involved different people: an artist and a calligrapher.*

CHAPTER FOUR

A PRODUCTION

HOW WAS the Diamond Sutra made? The invention of paper was a significant prerequisite for the production of multiple copies of pictures or text, and Stein knew something of the invention of paper from the two articles published by his mentor Rudolf Hoernle in 1903 and 1904. Hoernle, Secretary of the Asiatic Society of Bengal, had accepted Stein's edition of the Sanskrit epic *Rataranginі* ('Chronicles of the Kings of Kashmir') for publication by the society in 1893 and had become a friend. In 1891, with reference to Hoernle, Stein described 'the pleasure, almost unknown for several years, of being able to talk *con amore* with someone in my own field'.[1] In the first of his articles, 'Who was the Inventor of Rag Paper?', Hoernle stated that 'mixed rag paper ... was known to the Chinese from the very beginning of its invention by Cai Lun, early in the second century AD'.[2] On 26 June, studying a manuscript that Jiang had wrongly dated to AD 86, Stein wrote in his field diary, 'paper was not supposed to have been invented till 40 years later'.[3] Jiang had made a double error in reading a cyclical date (referring to a 60-year cycle commonly used in dates in pre-modern China) on a manuscript, ascribing it to AD 86 rather than the actual date of 416. The manuscript, a unique fragment of a local census, bears the second oldest date in the collection, even if it cannot be pushed back in time to the first century and before the official invention of paper.

In the *Hou Han Shu* ('Official History of the Later Han', AD 25–220, compiled long after, in the fifth century) Cai Lun, a eunuch who served from AD 89 in the imperial manufactory of instruments and weapons, was recorded as reporting to the emperor in AD 105 on his achievement in 'making paper from the bark of trees, remnants of hemp, rags of cloth, and fishing nets ... from this time, paper has been in use everywhere and is universally called "the paper of Marquis Cai"'.[4] As one historian pointed out, the compilation of the official history took place at a time when 'archival materials were no longer available', for, with the fall of the Han and the sacking of the capital at Luoyang, the bamboo slip archives were destroyed and 'the silk scrolls were used as curtains', but the story of Cai Lun's paper production was recorded in another historical account from which the official history was probably derived.[5] 'He initiated the idea of making paper from tree bark, old rags and fishing nets. He submitted the process to the emperor in AD 105 and received praise...'[6]

OPPOSITE AND OVERLEAF *A seventeenth-century work on Chinese technology shows the stages of the manufacture of bamboo paper. Paper can be made of all sorts of materials, from mulberry bark and hemp fibres to bamboo.*

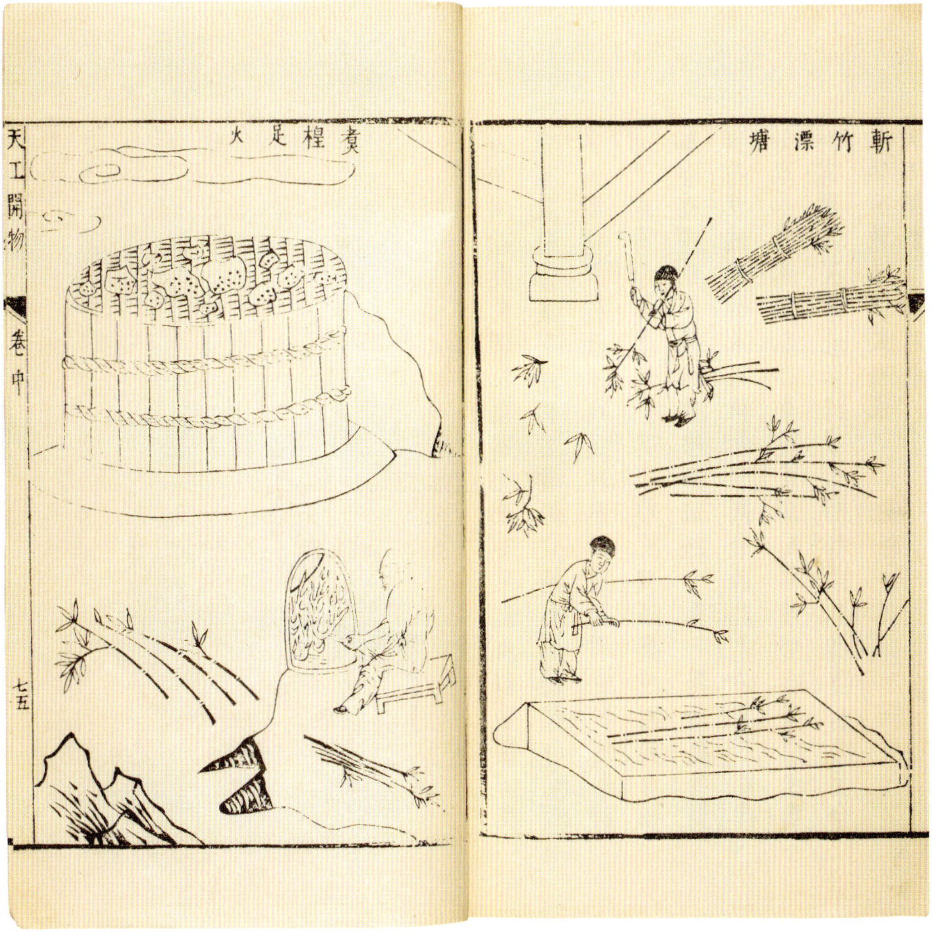

The date in the literary record has been contradicted by archaeological finds of paper dating back to the Former Han dynasty, to the second and first centuries BC.[7] Some of the earliest finds of Han dynasty paper were made by Stein in the first decades of the twentieth century but, since then, significant finds of paper dating back to the second and first centuries BC have been made, most in the same Central Asian desert regions, and they include the world's earliest

ABOVE (right) *In the first stage of production, bamboo is cut, many of the leaves are removed and the stems soaked in a pool of water for 100 days.* ABOVE (left) *The well-soaked bamboo stems are then pounded and mixed with lime and boiled over a fire for eight days. The wooden vat, encircled by ropes of twisted bamboo, conceals an iron pot containing the bamboo and lime mixture. The vat is covered by a bamboo lid weighted down with stones and the fire, below, appears to be fuelled by bamboo. The fibrous mixture is alternately washed and soaked, boiled and strained and mixed with wood ash and rice straw for ten days before a final pounding.*

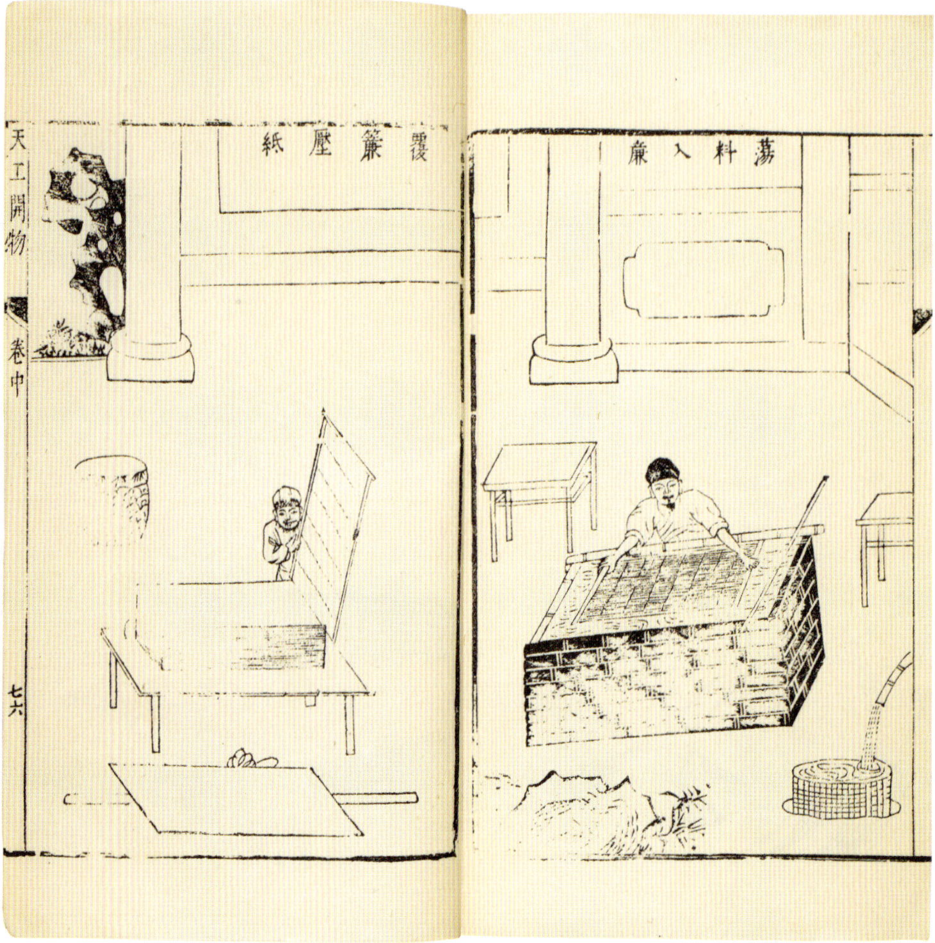

paper map and fragments with the names of medicines written on them.[8] Some Chinese historians, intent upon following the official histories, contend that such early fragments are not true paper but felt, and Denis Twitchett suggested that 'these early papers, made mostly of hemp fibres, were very coarse and could hardly have served as writing materials and were probably intended for wrapping', although the medical wrapping paper served both to carry written text and to wrap.[9] It is probably safest to conclude that Cai Lun's report to the emperor concerned the perfection of paper manufacture, rather than its invention.

ABOVE (right) *The resulting suspension is poured into a square tank and a mould screen, consisting of a removable mat of very fine split bamboo in a frame, is dipped in and raised slowly so that a thin layer of fibres rests on the mat.* ABOVE (left) *The sheets of wet paper are pressed down to remove much of the moisture.*

Paper and felt are very close in manufacture and composition, although we now think of felt as a rather thick cloth made from wool. Paper has been defined as 'a matted or felted sheet of fibres formed on a fine screen from a water suspension' whilst our felt is usually pressed, rather than formed on a screen.[10] The manufacture of paper in China, in the earliest phase using hemp fibres, later, fibres from the bark of the paper mulberry and, even later, bamboo, remained consistent for thousands of years and is illustrated in the early seventeenth-century Ming work on technology, Song Yingxing's *Tiangong kaiwu* ('Exploitation of the Works of Nature').

ABOVE *The last process is depicted in a single illustration running right to left (as all traditional Chinese books were read right to left). The sheets of paper were finally dried on a heated wall, a hollow construction heated by a fire on the right. On the left, the dry sheets of paper are peeled off the wall.*

The raw material, whether hemp, mulberry bark or bamboo, is first pounded, saturated in lime, heated and then steeped in water. A frame, holding a mould, essentially a base made of fine bamboo strips stitched together, is placed in the mixture and carefully raised, so that a layer of fibres rests on the mould. When the water is drained off, the resulting sheet of matted fibres is dried, often against a heated wall and a sheet of paper can then be peeled away.

The great significance of paper in the history of printing is that it provides a very cheap medium for the printed text. In China in the fourth century BC, texts were inscribed on silk, an expensive product. In the Han dynasty, 206 BC–AD 220, everyday documents were written on narrow slips of wood or bamboo, a cheap form of writing material of which many examples were discovered by Aurel Stein near the Caves of the Thousand Buddhas, in the refuse heaps left by the garrisons of Han dynasty soldiers at the western end of the Great Wall. The use of this format led to the Chinese tradition of writing from top to bottom (as if still on a narrow slip of bamboo) rather than horizontally left to right, a style which persisted until the early twentieth century and is still used today for traditional calligraphy.

The perfection of the manufacture of paper, just at a time when the Chinese government was creating a massive bureaucracy, commissioning censuses, collecting a huge variety of taxes and reporting on conditions in a vast and varied land mass, meant that the central government could easily and cheaply amass and use a vast amount of paper. Even though the majority of the tens of thousands of paper documents collected in Cave 17 were Buddhist, they were not all sutras, for there are even accounts of special funerals held for animals such as donkeys, horses and dogs, not just because they had been loved but because in Buddhist belief, all animals represent a soul in the hierarchical cycle of rebirths.[11] One of the manuscript copies of the Diamond Sutra brought back by Stein was dedicated to a beloved animal: 'Humbly, on behalf of my old ploughing ox, that its soul may be reborn in the Pure Land...'[12]

There were also a number of secular papers: legal documents including wills, contracts, arrangements for the repayment of debts, the record of a nun bartering 'a three-year-old black cow, quite unmarked' for a quantity of wheat and millet, local government regulations and proclamations and letters, both official and private, all of which reveal the widespread use of paper in the area in the fifth to tenth centuries.[13]

Paper was indubitably invented in China, even if the exact date of its discovery remains unknown. That the manufacture of paper was transmitted from China to Europe through the Arabs is also clear. A traditional story is that the secret of paper-making was only known to the outside world after some Chinese paper-makers were captured by the victorious Arabs at the Battle of Talas River in 751 and taken to Samarkand where they established a paper manufactory. However, finds of paper in the deserts by Sven Hedin and Aurel Stein make it quite clear that paper was already known and used throughout Central Asia by the fourth century. The most famous pieces of evidence are the 'Sogdian letters' of 313–14, found by Stein near Dunhuang in 1907.[14] Apparently abandoned by a fourth-century postman, the letters were written by a Sogdian woman living in Dunhuang who seems to have been left penniless by her absent husband, 'I would rather be a dog's or a pig's wife than yours!' Paper did eventually make its way to Europe, brought by the conquering Arabs to Spain by the tenth century and Italy, through Sicily, by the twelfth century.[15] Ironically, despite the survival of early paper in Central Asia, it was regarded at first with suspicion in Europe and considered unsuitably fragile for important documents. And though the invention of paper and its transmission westwards is easily documented, the invention of woodblock printing is another matter altogether.

Though the technology of paper-making was described as early as the second century and illustrated in the *Tiangong kaiwu* ('The Exploitation of the Works of Nature'), there was no detailed written description of the process of woodblock printing in Chinese until an article based upon an oral account by a printer was published in 1947.[16] In the *Tiangong Kaiwu* (1637) a variety of technologies such as porcelain production, bronze and iron casting and the manufacture of cinnabar were described. All involved the transformation of an unlikely raw material into a remarkably different product: lumpy clay into translucent porcelain, stiff, spiky bamboo into smooth paper and earthy ore into bronze bells. The simple carving of a wooden printing block offered no such obvious transformation and was almost completely ignored in Chinese literature. Such passing references that did exist to copying were frequently so vague that it was not possible to tell what form of reproduction was involved, whether hand copying by scribes or woodblock printing.

One obscure reference to printing in traditional Chinese sources that was taken up by Stanislas Julien (in 1874) and other western writers was an account of the activities of the Sui emperor Wen in 593. Through a misunderstanding of a couple of terms, they proposed that in 593 Emperor Wen ordered that texts be carved on wooden blocks and published.[17] Scholars now agree that the account does not refer to printing but to an imperial order to recarve worn-out (three-dimensional) images and to collect classic texts. The misunderstanding was clarified in 1919 but the chance discovery of the Diamond Sutra with its date of printing and subsequent similar finds in the Far East have led scholars to search for further references in traditional texts. However, the terminology used to describe imperial patronage in the form of commissioning multiple copies of religious works for wide distribution, as practised by the Sui and Tang emperors, remains vague and it is virtually impossible to know whether copies were manuscript or printed.

With its elegant frontispiece and exquisitely carved and spaced characters, it is clear that the Diamond Sutra was the product of a mature industry whose precise origins are, as yet, unknown. Though it might be assumed that since paper was invented in China, woodblock printing was, too, other earlier examples of printing have been found elsewhere in the Far East.

A hundred years before the printing of the Diamond Sutra, an earlier printing enterprise was undertaken in Japan under the patronage of the empress Shotoku who ordered the printing of a million 'charms' (*dharani*), and the manufacture of small wooden pagoda-shaped containers in 764–70. The short Buddhist text on Empress Shotoku's 'charms' came from 'The Great Spell of Unsullied Pure Light', translated into Chinese just before 705 by a monk of Sogdian origin, Fazang. The short sutra seems to have been associated with funeral ritual in India and promised great benefit to those who copied it. As the title suggests, it invoked the goddess Pure Light, the future female ruler of Buddhist prophecy, which may have influenced its selection by the Japanese empress.[18]

Adding a certain confusion to the origin of woodblock printing, a different woodblock print of the same text was found in 1966 in a pagoda in a Korean temple

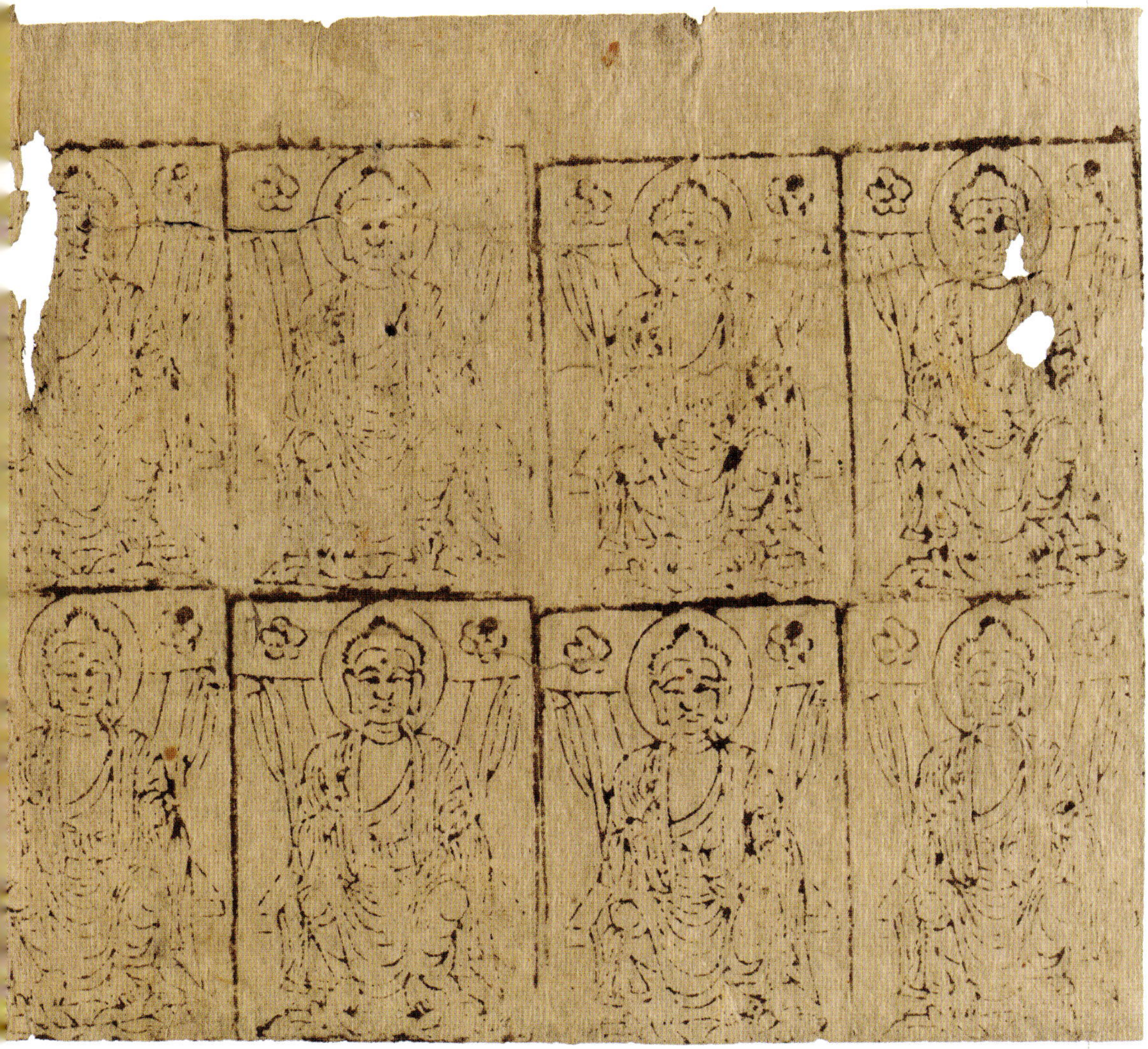

whose construction was completed in 751. Both the Japanese and the Koreans at the time used the Chinese script, and the Korean *dharani* even incorporates some of the special 'taboo' characters invented by the Chinese empress Wu (625–705) and used during her reign, 690–705. The use of these special characters does not necessarily imply that the *dharani* was produced between 690 and 705 for they continued to be used long after the death of the empress, nor does it necessarily imply that the

ABOVE *Small stamped images of the Buddha may indicate one of the ways that woodblock printing began. Quite a number of sheets of repeated images such as these have been found in Cave 17 and many of the caves at Dunhuang have walls decorated with repeated Buddha images made by puffing red chalk through the holes stamped around the outline of a Buddha image on paper. Creating a stamp with a Buddha image enabled rapid reproduction of the image, instantly earning merit.*

無垢淨光經
相輪陀羅尼

dharani was an imported product, printed in China, for China's cultural dominance of East Asia at the time was such that almost anything Chinese might be followed, and Koreans could well have copied the Chinese taboo characters.[19]

Wherever it originated, and China seems the most probable place of invention, early printing, whether in China, Korea or Japan was associated with religious ritual, most prominently with Buddhist practice. The Buddhist stress on the significance of relics and on the replication of Buddhist images and the repetition of the words of the Buddha to attain merit must have provided a strong impulse towards its use. In Japan, the technology remained within the Buddhist temples until the fourteenth century.[20] In China, however, the technology was soon adopted in the secular world. Liu Pin, writing in about 880, just over a decade after the printing of the Diamond Sutra, reported: 'Once when I was in Sichuan I examined in a bookshop a schoolbook printed from wooden blocks.'[21] Indeed in Cave 17, alongside the woodblock printed Buddhist works, examples of secular printing were found. These included several calendrical almanacs, one datable to AD 877 and another, undated but probably also ninth century, fragment which states that it was produced in the eastern market of the imperial capital. These are particularly interesting, for throughout China's imperial history the production of the calendar was an imperial prerogative, so these privately printed versions were illegal.[22]

The first detailed descriptions of the process of woodblock printing were published by Protestant missionaries in 1820 and 1838. William Milne (1785–1822) and William Henry Medhurst (1796–1857) were investigating the most efficient and economic method of publishing and distributing the Chinese translation of the Bible. Milne described how the regular blocks of hard grained wood such as pear or jujube were smoothed with rice paste to fill in any cracks. The paper inscribed with the hand-written text was then placed face down on the sticky rice paste surface and rubbed. It was then dried and the paper rubbed off leaving 'a clear impression of each character'.[23] Medhurst described the process of block carving. First all the blank spaces were cut away. 'The workman then engraves

OPPOSITE *In 764 the Japanese empress Shotoku (718–770) ordered the production of 'a million charms' or* dharani *to be placed in specially made pagoda-shaped wooden containers for distribution to temples. These small strips of paper, probably printed from metal plates, antedate the production of the Diamond Sutra by just over a century. However, the use of metal and the comparatively small size of the* dharani *set this enterprise apart from the Diamond Sutra, indubitably produced from wooden blocks and many metres longer, as well as being illustrated.*

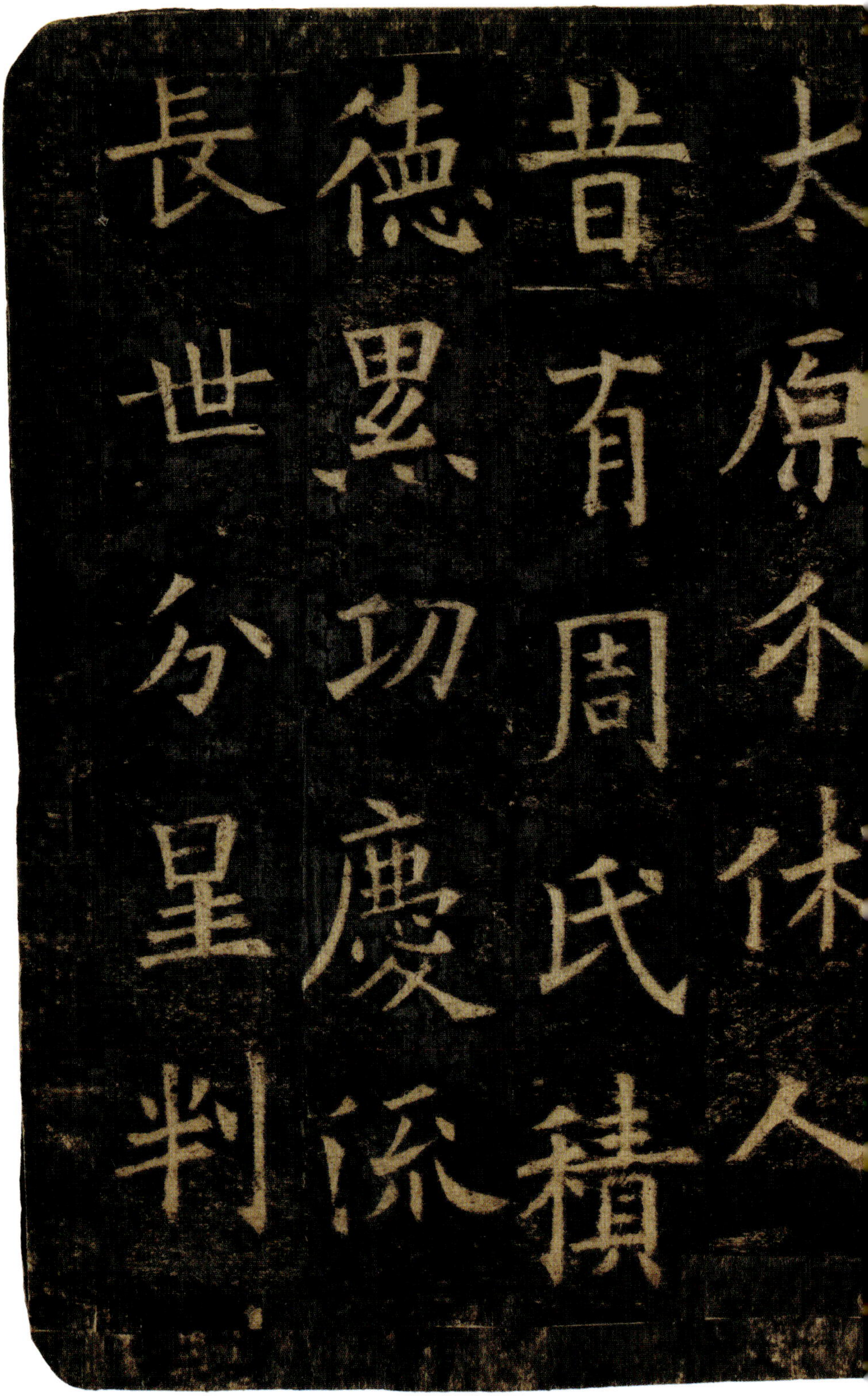

ABOVE AND OPPOSITE *Rubbing made of a eulogy celebrating a Buddhist master in the Huadu monastery written and inscribed by the celebrated scholar and imperial calligrapher Ouyang Xun (557–645). Ouyang Xun's calligraphy on paper was subsequently inscribed in stone. To provide copies for students of calligraphy, rubbings were taken from such stone carved slabs by pasting paper*

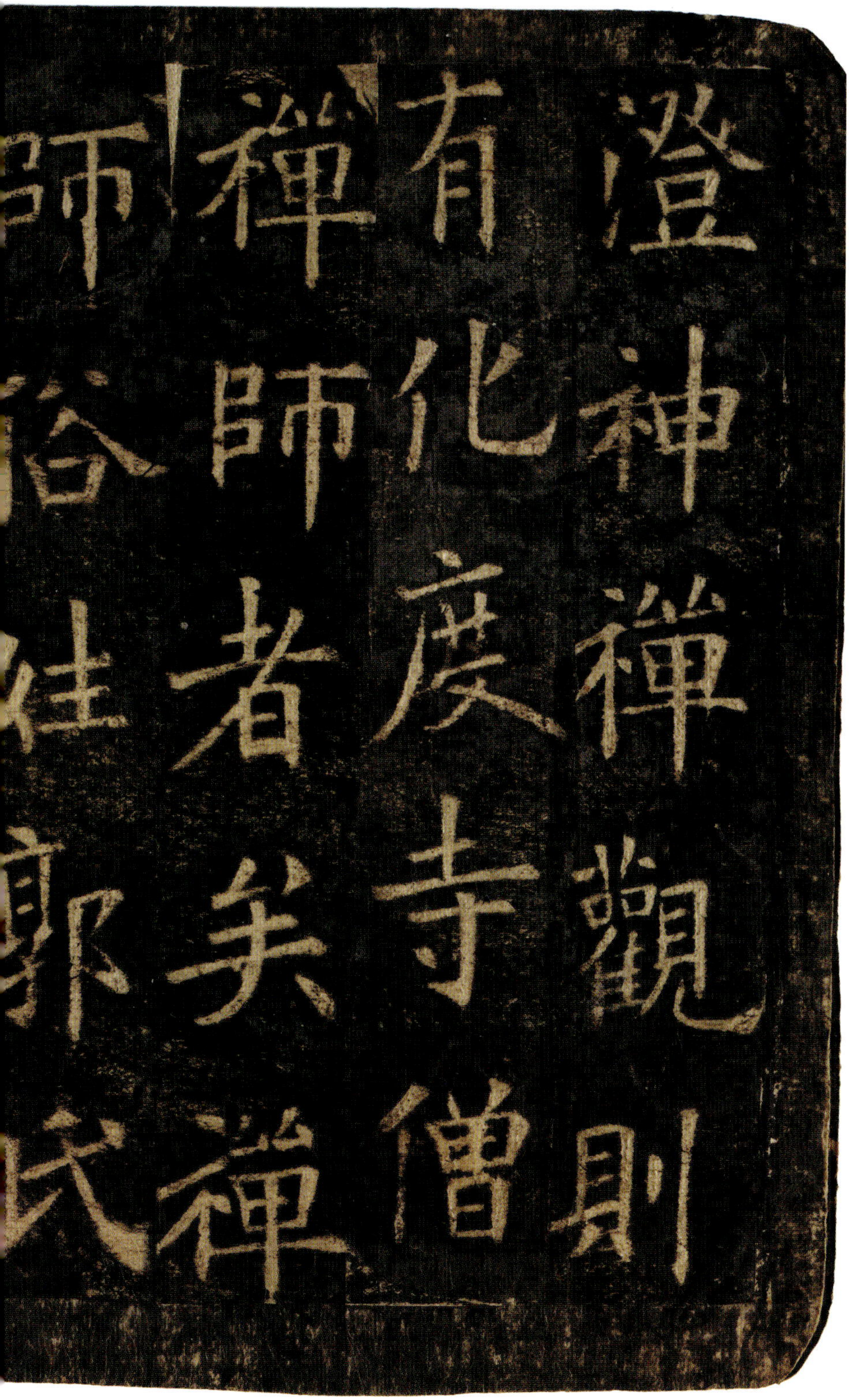

on them and then applying ink with a soft pad to take up the image. Here the text has been cut into strips and pasted into a pocket-sized booklet for convenience. The Confucian Classics were carved in stone in 175–83 by imperial order during the Han dynasty, and the practice of taking rubbings of such authorised texts is thought to have been another inspiration in the development of woodblock printing.

all the strokes which run horizontally, then the oblique, and afterwards the perpendicular ones, through the whole line which saves the trouble of turning the block round for every letter [or character].'[24]

A block-cutter could cut on average 150 characters per day and any errors were easily and quickly corrected by cutting out the mistaken character, carving a replacement and inserting it in the right place.[25] The process of printing from the prepared blocks was simple. The block was held firmly in place on a table and water-based ink applied to the raised surface with a brush. A sheet of paper was placed on the ink surface and lightly pressed with a rubbing pad. The paper was removed and dried and the process repeated.[26] Medhurst observed that two printers with separate blocks could print 2000 sheets a day and that it was possible to take between 15,000 and 30,000 impressions from the average woodblock but that those of very fine wood, carefully looked after, might last for 40,000.

From the beginning, text and illustration were easily combined in woodblock printing. The Diamond Sutra has a separate illustration at the beginning, but single prayer sheets also found in Cave 17 beautifully combine text and image. Though some suggest that, like paper, Far Eastern woodblock printing technology was transferred to the West, it is more likely that European printing, certainly benefiting from the transmission of paper, was independently developed. Simple woodblock printing of the Far Eastern type was not used for long in Europe, being quickly replaced by printing with movable type pioneered by Johannes Gutenberg in Mainz in the mid-fifteenth century. Movable type was suited to an alphabetic system of writing but the Chinese script, with its tens of thousands of different characters, required an enormous font of type which was complex to store and retrieve. As Medhurst observed (with the printing of the Bible in Chinese in mind), 'of xylography [woodblock printing] the advantages are – that it is suited to the nature of the Chinese language ... it is adapted for printing in different forms and sizes of the character. It requires no complicated machinery, or expensive apparatus. The blocks, once cut, need no further correction; though they are capable of it if necessary. New editions may be frequently printed without trouble...'[27] And though western missionaries, with their European background, eventually chose to cast metal movable type characters for their printing enterprise, woodblock printing survived in China for over 1000 years, well into the twentieth century and is still used for illustrated works such as New Year Prints.

ABOVE *A woodblock carved with four pages of the 'Impartial Power' section of the* Yin zhi jin jian *('A Mirror of Hidden Good') shows how the characters appear in reverse. When rubbings were taken from stone inscriptions, the characters appear the right way round. When woodblocks were produced for printing, however, the text was first inscribed by a skilled calligrapher on a sheet of fine paper which was placed face down upon a block of fine-grained wood so that the characters are carved in reverse, only to appear the right way round when the print is taken. The block is carved on both sides and two pages of text appear on each side with the (outer) margin in the centre, where the title text reaches the top of the block. The printed sheet was then folded along the centre line and the two outer sides of the sheet stitched into the spine. Where mistakes were made, the block-cutter simply gouged out a small square and then slotted in a replacement. A square awaiting a replacement character can be seen near the top right hand corner.*

CHAPTER FIVE

A JOURNEY

AFTER LEAVING the Caves of the Thousand Buddhas at Dunhuang with his cases of manuscripts and paintings, Stein first camped nearby at Anxi for the summer of 1907, where Jiang made a start on identifying some of the manuscripts. Having spent the winter travelling through the mountains to the north and inspecting the Great Wall at Jiayuguan, he turned back westwards. Stein camped in Khotan (Hetian) for the summer of 1908 where the finds from his entire second expedition were finally packed for the journey to London via India. On 15 July 1908 Stein noted, 'The packing is at last all done ... There are 30 cases with manuscripts and other written records on wood, etc. Jiang has got only through one-third of the Thousand Buddha Caves texts.'[1]

It was not until January 1909 that the cases of manuscripts reached England, and they were first stored in rooms in the Natural History Museum whilst Stein fought for better accommodation. The British Museum offered a space which provoked condemnation from Stein: 'The basement room ... apparently hitherto used for the storage of old newspapers' had 'light wholly insufficient', threatening the 'constant strain' of having to work by artificial light. 'Neither during my official career in India nor in the course of my explorations have I been called to work in what without exaggeration may be called a sort of cellar.' He was not only concerned about the comfort and health of his paid assistants but also the constant stream of academic visitors that he was expecting from all over Europe. 'It would be physically impossible to find space for them to work in the confined basement room quite apart from the consideration that they would be fully justified in refusing to give their (gratuitous) labours in a locality unfit for serious work.'[2] Stein was, however, compelled to accept the half-basement, although he continued to press for improvement.

The team of workers who would continue the numbering and classification work that Jiang and Stein had begun in China was led by Fred Andrews who had been introduced to Stein by Rudyard Kipling's father, Lockwood Kipling, in India. Fred Andrews, then Vice-Principal of the Mayo School of Art in Lahore, took photographs, sketched Stein's three-dimensional finds and patterns on ancient silks and acted as a general support for Stein when the latter was away on his expeditions.[3] Andrews was paid by the India Office to number and describe more than 25,000 manuscripts and other finds, as were junior assistants who included John Percival Droop, H.G. Evelyn-White, C.L. Woolley (who was later to become

famous for his excavations at Ur) and Miss F.M.G. Lorimer who stayed from 1910 to 1922, and because of her efficiency was known to Stein and his friends as 'the Recording Angel'.[4]

Stein was right to assume that European scholars would be keen to see his finds, despite uncomfortable conditions, and the most enthusiastic was his rival in the race to Dunhuang, Paul Pelliot. Pelliot had returned from China in the autumn of 1909, and soon afterwards, the distinguished French Indologist Emile Senart wrote to Stein to inform him that Pelliot would be visiting London shortly and hoped that Stein would allow him to see the manuscripts. Pelliot himself seemed

ABOVE *Dunes near Khadalik photographed by Stein. The type of terrain over which Stein passed varied from high mountain passes to the rather unending flatness of the central deserts. He recorded his journeys in meticulous detail, both with pen and camera, noting, too, the position from which photographs were taken and the technical aspects such as shutter speed.*

keen to avoid meeting Stein, which rather worried Fred Andrews. It was not difficult to avoid meeting Stein in the British Museum, for he disliked London and, when in England, spent most of his time staying with friends in Oxford. After Senart's polite letter, properly addressed to Stein, Pelliot seems to have directed his enquiries not to Stein or Andrews, but to Lionel Giles, the Assistant Keeper for Chinese Books and Manuscripts in the British Museum. As Stein's

ABOVE *The wind-eroded Great Wall was photographed by Stein near Anxi where he camped after leaving Dunhuang. The photograph shows parts of the Wall, possibly of similar date to the Han dynasty beacon towers he investigated in the area, and demonstrates how structures made of tamped earth or pisé could last for many hundreds of years in the dry desert. Stein was remarkable in the wide variety of his interests, often reflected in his photography.*

manuscripts were not handed over to the British Museum until after the end of the First World War, they were not, technically, anything to do with Giles at the time, despite the fact that they were temporarily accommodated in the British Museum. Pelliot may not have been aware of the distinction and he may have preferred to correspond with a fellow Sinologist, but it bothered Andrews who wrote to Stein on 9 April 1910:

> Today I heard from Giles that Pelliot will be at the British Museum next week and he (Giles) has made a selection of Chinese manuscripts to show him. I am sorry Pelliot should be coming before your return, and I should like a brief line from you as soon as possible advising me as to what you should like him to see, of the general collection. You will know exactly why I ask this of you. He will naturally be anxious to see much, but it would have been so much better for him to have waited for you.[5]

Stein replied on 13 April 1910:

> As to Pelliot it seems astonishingly strange that no information about his visit should have reached me direct. I do not think that the selected specimens will repay his visit unless it is quite a flying one, and, of course, without previous intimation you could not be expected to have more manuscript cases opened and contents arranged for examination ... If Pelliot desires to go through manuscripts not yet unpacked and inventoried, it certainly ought to be done only in the Oriental Manuscripts Department [here Stein is also muddying the waters over ownership and control of the documents] and under their care. Below in the cellars there is neither room nor need for attendance.[6]

Stein's wariness about Pelliot, well founded since Pelliot felt Stein had betrayed him by winning the race to Dunhuang, was gradually dispelled as he acknowledged Pelliot's expertise and the speed with which he worked. Stein was always very keen to see the manuscripts he had collected properly catalogued by specialists, and annotated for publication in his own excavation reports (where he was careful to acknowledge their contributions). In the case of his second expedition, he was also anxious to have the best selection of manuscripts and paintings made for an exhibition in the British Museum planned for 1914 and knew that Pelliot was best placed to choose the most significant Chinese documents from Dunhuang, not just because of his Sinological expertise but because he had been working on the Dunhuang manuscripts that he, himself, had brought back for the Bibliothèque nationale in Paris.

Apart from selecting dated manuscripts and documents with descriptions for eventual publication in Stein's detailed report on his second expedition, *Serindia* (which did not appear until 1921), Pelliot made a selection of items for the 1914 exhibition and, in the autumn of 1910, offered to produce a catalogue of the Chinese documents Stein had brought back from Dunhuang.[7] Two unlined cases of documents from Dunhuang were dispatched to Pelliot in Paris in January 1911, a time of year when it might have been prudent to use cases with a protective lining (and they were not returned until 1919).[8] In 1913 Pelliot admitted that because of the burden of work, he could not complete the catalogue, but Stein himself had got what he wanted from Pelliot, the identification of the most significant documents for his exhibition and publication.

It seems clear that it was Pelliot who realised the true significance of the Diamond Sutra as the world's earliest dated printed book. Though Stein had made a note of it in Khotan on 11 July 1908, he did not expand upon its unique qualities at the time. 'Extracted from [the bundle numbered] ciii well printed Chinese roll dated 860 AD [sic]'. Its full inventory number, Ch. Ciii.0014, indicates that it came from the Caves of the Thousand Buddhas (Ch), and that it was the fourteenth scroll in bundle number ciii; the 00 indicates that the full number was assigned in London, after 1909. In *Serindia*, Stein stated, 'When objects had been marked by me merely with the place of discovery and numbers were subsequently added at the time of unpacking at the British Museum, two zeros precede the number.'[9] Stein had been unaware of the real significance of the fact that it was printed and frequently got the date wrong. It was wrongly listed, not just in his notes, but in his first, popular, account of the expedition, *Ruins of Desert Cathay* (1912). However, in the exhibition catalogue of 1914, the right date was finally published and this was almost certainly due to Stein's old rival Pelliot's informed appraisal.[10]

OPPOSITE *Stein not only made detailed surveys of the land he crossed which were elaborated into full maps on his return to India, but he also took many hundreds of photographs and developed the glass plates on the spot. Witness this view of the ruins of Miran seen from the west, a plate that was somewhat spoiled during processing, hence the spot on the left.*

CHAPTER SIX

A RESTORATION

AUREL STEIN was above all concerned that his Central Asian finds should be examined by the best linguistic specialists to discover the content, and his somewhat careless attitude to conservation was characteristic of his time. In his day, the postal services were frequent and reliable and he often posted unique manuscripts to scholars all over Europe so that they could study them at their leisure. Rudolf Hoernle in Oxford received a packet of paper fragments in 1907 which had been sent by George Macartney, British Consul in Kashgar, to J.Ph. Vogel of the Office of the Director General of Archaeology in Simla, who then posted them to Hoernle, and Stein authorised the dispatch of some 200 Dunhuang manuscripts to Paul Pelliot in Paris in 1911 in unlined cases, courtesy of Thomas Cook and Sons.

Posting unique manuscripts would be unthinkable today, and their condition and conservation are of prime importance to museums and libraries. The history of the conservation of the Diamond Sutra illustrates the changing attitudes to the care of manuscripts in the British Museum and British Library during the 100 years since the Diamond Sutra arrived in London in 1909. Looking at early photographs, it is clear that the sutra had already been damaged over a thousand years ago and repaired with patches on the back before it was deposited in Cave 17. The earliest surviving photograph is that included in Stein's *Ruins of Desert Cathay* in 1912 (fig. 1). Plate 191 shows the frontispiece with a severe water stain running along the entire sheet, and the rolled-up portion of the sutra shown on the left clearly reveals two major patches. In the photograph Stein included in *Serindia* (1921), which was prepared over a decade (with interruptions to its production partly due to the First World War), both the water stain and the patches are less prominent. There are, unfortunately, no records of the treatment of the Diamond Sutra from 1909 to the 1960s, so following the process is only possible by looking at old photographs, examining the sutra itself and considering events.

It is likely that some conservation work was undertaken to prepare the Diamond Sutra for its first display in the exhibition of Stein's finds held in the British Museum in 1914. Removal of the patches on the back would have been carried out with the intention of protecting the sutra from further damage and, perhaps, making it lie flatter. Such early patches were applied to areas of damage, most characteristically along the centre of the scroll. Chinese scrolls were rolled up and closed for storage by having a narrow silk tie (attached to the thin stave at the right hand end of the scroll) wrapped tightly around them. It is very common to find damage along the centre of a scroll caused by rubbing or excessive tightening of the tie. Patches applied to manuscripts and documents during the Tang period were often not very suitable: the paper was often of a different type to that of the original, often heavier and coarser, and the liberal application of paste, or worse, glue, could cause further damage to the fragile scroll. Today, we try to maintain the

Fig. 1 *The photograph of 1912 shows items as they were when they first arrived in England, probably selected by Paul Pelliot who, as a Sinologist, was better equipped to judge the collection than Stein. At the bottom is the Diamond Sutra, showing a stain running across the frontispiece, clear evidence of early patches on the left-hand side, as well as the original wooden roller in place on the left. Above is one of the many printed prayer sheets found at Dunhuang, all later than the Diamond Sutra, probably locally produced in the tenth century but attractive to Stein's European audience because of their illustrations. At the top, less glorious in black and white, is the wonderful yellow-dyed, blue-silk tied copy of the Gem Heap sutra.*

appearance of a scroll as we find it and, as far as possible, retain old patches as part of the history of the scroll, but in the past it is probable that 'inappropriate' early repairs were removed because they were seen as damaging.

The photograph of the scroll reproduced in *Serindia* shows a less prominent water stain. It is likely that some effort was made to remove it, probably by washing, immersing the scroll in hot water or, more seriously, by bleaching. Both treatments would have had a bad effect on the yellow dye that was so commonly found in the paper used for Buddhist texts, whether manuscript or printed, in China. The dye, made from the bark of the Amur cork tree, imparts a yellow tinge to the paper, a colour associated with Buddhism and seen in the saffron robes of many monks, but it is also a powerful insecticide which protected precious documents from becoming worm-eaten. Though the colour can be quite strong, the dye is easily soluble in water and it is likely that washing or bleaching the frontispiece of the Diamond Sutra may have removed much of the original colour.[1]

We do not know when the photograph reproduced in *Serindia* was taken, certainly before 1921, perhaps as early as 1914, but, though it shows traces of the old patches, it also shows that the Diamond Sutra was still unlined. The question of lining has been a difficult one to resolve. All the manuscripts and printed documents found in Cave 17 were unlined, for they were 'books' and documents, not traditionally lined. However, once such ancient documents were removed from their context, regarded as precious ancient relics rather than working texts, it was common, particularly in Japan, to mount them, backing them and enclosing them in a frame of fine silk, as if they were paintings. Paintings in the Far East were always mounted and framed in silk and the same treatment was applied, by extension, to significant texts, as can be seen in the sets of the empress Shotoku's charms acquired in Japan. Even as late as the mid-1970s, when curators and conservators in the British Library had reached the conclusion that wherever possible, non-intervention was the best method of conserving the Dunhuang documents, Japanese delegations in particular criticised their conservation condition, feeling that they should be respectfully mounted. The conclusions of the British Library's conservators and curators today remain the same: the Dunhuang collection should be treated as a collection of documents, not paintings, and preserved, as far as possible, in their original form and format.

It appears, however, that in the early decades of the twentieth century a decision was made at the British Museum to back the Diamond Sutra. This may have been because of the apparent fragility of the scroll, a fragility that probably seemed more serious when the early repairs were removed, for removal seems to have skinned the back of the paper, making it even thinner. The treatment of the water stain may also have affected the paper.

Most of the conservation of the Dunhuang documents, which consisted of backing fragile scrolls with sturdy manila paper or pasting fragments onto dark brown sugar paper, was carried out in the British Museum bindery where the conservators were much more familiar with European papers and European book formats. It seems likely, however, that the Diamond Sutra, singled out for its fine frontispiece and therefore associated with 'art' rather than pure text, may have been treated slightly differently. It seems that sometime after the *Serindia* photograph was taken, the scroll was given its first backing of fine Japanese paper.[2]

The backing appears to have been quite sensitively applied and the paper chosen with some care. It is likely that this backing may have been applied by a Japanese scroll mounter who worked in the British Museum under Laurence Binyon. Binyon (1869–1943), the poet best known for his First World War lines 'They shall grow not old as we that are left grow old,/ Age shall not weary them nor the years condemn,/ At the going down of the sun and in the morning,/ We shall remember them', worked as an Assistant Keeper in the British Museum's Department of Prints and Drawings, where the Sub-Department of Oriental Prints and Drawings was created in 1909, the year that Stein's finds from his second expedition arrived in London. Though he wrote on Chinese art as well, much of Binyon's training in the subject was through Japan, through Japanese friends and advisors, through the Japanese art magazine *Kokka* and through the collections of Far Eastern paintings, mostly amassed in Japan, that were beginning to be acquired by the British Museum. Thus it was logical that he should have employed a Japanese scroll mounter and probable that he, Binyon, was responsible for overseeing the first backing.[3]

The Diamond Sutra, together with all the other Dunhuang documents from Stein's second (and the third expedition of 1913–16) was handed over to the British Museum in 1919. Lionel Giles (1875–1958) was placed in charge of the collection and he 'was able to begin sorting, examining and cataloguing them one by one. It was no light task, even in a physical sense, for the total length of the sheets which had to be constantly unrolled and rolled up again must have amounted to something between ten and twenty miles.'[4] Giles's description of constant rolling and unrolling illustrates one of the great problems of conservation for any backing, however skilfully applied, is liable to create unevenness and sometimes cracking, particularly in a scroll that must be unrolled and rolled for inspection and storage. Though Giles himself admits to constant rolling and unrolling, he does not seem to have welcomed visitors, and two distinguished specialists from the National Library of China, Wang Chongmin and Xiang Da, who spent 1936–7 in London, were particularly bitter about Giles's treatment. In a whole year, he only allowed Xiang Da to see 496 scrolls (out of a possible 6980), thus avoiding considerable rolling and unrolling.[5]

During the Second World War, the Diamond Sutra was moved to the National Library of Wales at Aberystwyth for safe-keeping (fig. 2). It is difficult to tell exactly when it was moved there. The first evacuation of 171 cases (containing 6000 books and manuscripts) from the British Museum's Department of Oriental Printed Books and Manuscripts was on 24 August 1939, and another mass evacuation of 'all remaining Oriental manuscripts', numbering 20,000, took place after dozens of incendiary bombs fell on the British Museum in May 1941. The Diamond Sutra was almost certainly in the first load, for when Lionel Giles spoke to the China Society in London in October 1941, giving 'a short history of the Stein collection of Chinese manuscripts in the British Museum', he mentioned that his catalogue, although not yet printed, 'had been completed some years ago, just before the manuscripts were removed from the Museum for safety'.[6]

Though the war made it impossible for conservation work to be carried out on the manuscripts packed away for storage in Wales, it is clear that, wartime excepted, over the decades between 1920 and 1960, more and more backings were applied to the Diamond Sutra, always with the intention of smoothing out creases and cracks but, almost inevitably, worsening its condition. The story of the restoration of the Diamond Sutra is told by the conservator.

Fig. 2 *The National Library of Wales, Aberystwyth, where Stein's collection of Chinese and other manuscripts and documents from Dunhuang, including the Diamond Sutra, spent the Second World War. With mountains in the background, the imposing pale stone building looks rather an impressive target.*

FOLLOWING THE FOUNDATION of the British Library (from the British Museum Library) in 1972, and the creation of the Oriental Manuscripts and Printed Books department (OMPB), a new conservation studio was established with the aim of developing specialisms and expertise in core Asian collections. One area that was singled out for conservation work was the Stein collection.

As mentioned earlier, many Chinese scrolls within the collection had, in the previous 60 years, been subject to western methods of, and materials for, repair, stemming from the long-established bookbinding tradition of the British Museum bindery. Whilst western-style books were successfully conserved in this way, 'books' in other formats fared less well as there were inevitable compromises. This was now the time to reappraise the approach to the conservation of Asian objects, learning traditional techniques from the East and acquiring, if possible, more compatible repair materials from eastern sources.

In 1974, 1975 and 1979 three study tours to China were undertaken: the first by Peter Lawson, head of the new conservation studio, who went together with other representatives from the British Museum and the V&A as part of a cultural visit; the second by Howard Nelson, Assistant Keeper of the Chinese collections, who was specifically concerned to observe

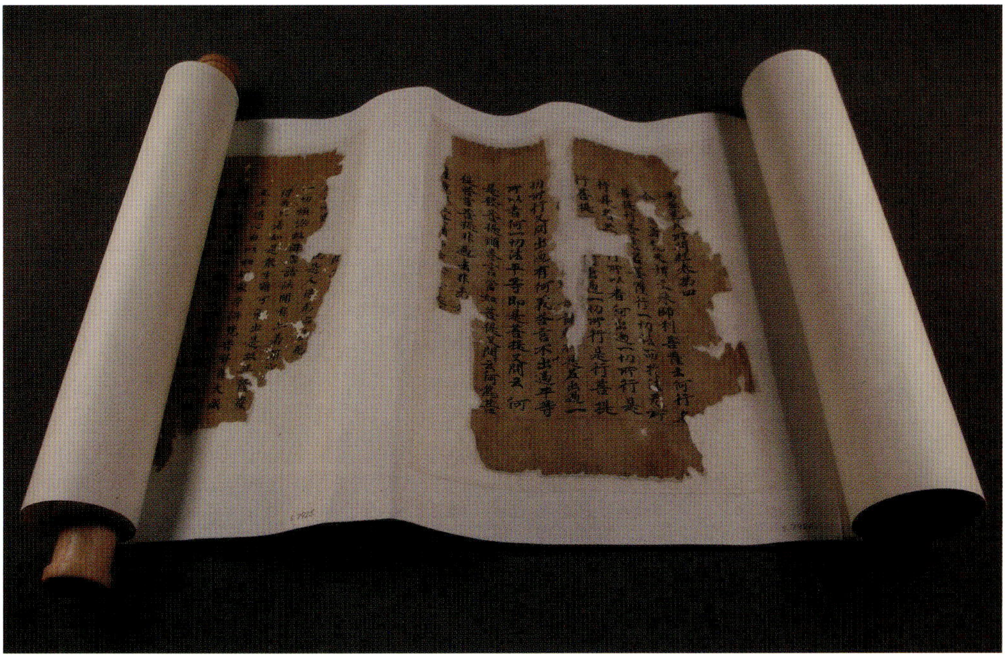

Fig.3 *An example of one of the first group of ten fragments mounted in the style of a hand scroll, complete with beechwood knobs to protect the top and bottom of the scroll.*

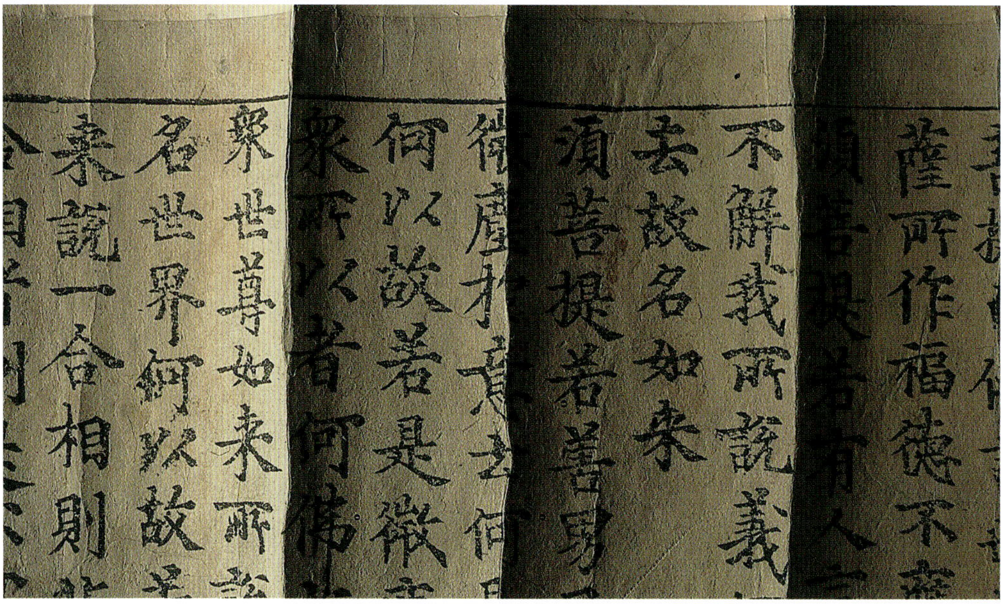

Fig. 4 *Vertical creases have a tendency to form the closer the panels are to the inner core of the scroll. Damage through repeated use can weaken the paper, which in turn may lead to vertical splitting.*

Chinese scroll conservation methods and storage options; and the final tour was again made by Peter Lawson who also purchased materials for the studio in London.

It was fortunate that extra funds for two additional conservators were soon found, thus enabling the studio to expand and allowing the newly enlarged team to put into practice what had been learnt in China. Initially, these new techniques and materials were applied to the Stein paper fragments, groups of ten fragments being mounted on paper so as to form a continuous scroll (fig. 3, previous page). The focus was then on the Diamond Sutra, whose existing lining was now showing characteristic vertical creasing, forming ridges with a likelihood of imminent splitting (fig. 4). The team had a solution: to undertake strip repairs on the verso of the creases and adding a lining, using Chinese paper (fig. 6, overleaf).

It is easy to understand the logic of this approach to the Diamond Sutra, which followed the long-established and highly skilled East Asian scroll mounting tradition that used a variety of hand-made paper and other materials developed specifically for scroll conservation. Tempting though this method might have seemed, Stein hand scrolls, now accepted in the West as 'documents' to be read and studied rather than 'objects' to be displayed, needed to function differently from traditionally mounted scrolls which may be hung and viewed. It soon became apparent that the

Fig.5 *This shows the deep undulations on the frontispiece, due in part to the differing expansion and contraction rates in the paper linings and heavy adhesives.*

new lining to the Diamond Sutra, rather than providing stability, caused more problems especially during the rolling and unrolling operation, creating new fractures. Clearly, this was not the answer to the long-term preservation of the sutra or indeed other Dunhuang scrolls (fig.5).

Through the 1980s, conservators, with the full support of curatorial colleagues, developed a method of minimum intervention similar to restoration principles used in the (western) Prints and Drawings department, adding only what was required to a missing or fragile area, not necessarily filling all gaps if they were stable or aesthetically acceptable, and using the very best Japanese and Chinese papers, equipment and techniques.

Whilst this hybrid approach of western principles and eastern materials and techniques is well suited to scrolls in their original condition, it was not necessarily appropriate for the hundreds of scrolls that had been lined from the 1920s onwards, the Diamond Sutra being the prime example.

In 1987, a decision was made to set up a long-term project with two broad aims. The first was to understand the nature and the reason for the fading of the horizontal stain across the frontispiece and the background dye; this would include looking into the pH (to check the acidity of the paper – level of acidity being one of the key indicators of paper degradation), the fibre composition of the scroll and other tests using made-up samples.[7] The second was to restore the

Fig.6a *In the photograph of the Diamond Sutra in* Serindia *(1921) the stain on the frontispiece is less prominent than in* Ruins of Desert Cathay *(1912) Fig 1. The wooden roller seems to have been removed and the patches on the verso of the scroll are neater, suggesting that some conservation work had been carried out although the scroll, at this time, was still not lined.*

Fig. 6b *This image was taken in 1978. It shows the new white Chinese paper lining, but also the 1950s manila border. The seemingly flat and stable appearance of the sutra masked the inherent tensions within the scroll.*

Fig. 7 *Following conservation, this scroll is now stored on a larger diameter roller, making it far less likely to form creases than if it were tightly rolled around a narrow roller.*

Diamond Sutra to as close as possible to its 'original' condition. The conservation would consist of 'peeling away' up to five paper linings, the removal of the glue and paste residues that had built up over the course of the relinings – this was the most problematic task – and, most importantly, the realignment of the frontispiece.

In 1990, links were established with Kenneth Seddon, Professor of Inorganic Chemistry at Sussex University, latterly at Queen's, Belfast, to explore the chemical constituents of berberine, the yellow dye used on Dunhuang scrolls and possibly to develop a solvent that would allow the removal of the adhesive without dissolving the dye.[8]

In parallel with this research, a trial was undertaken in-house to find a way to remove the linings and adhesives using various methods, from ultrasonic moisture to super-heated steam. Lessons learnt from this joint research enabled the team carefully to remove the linings and the adhesive residues from two similar printed scrolls (fig. 7), thus paving the way to commence work on the Diamond Sutra in 2003.

The first phase was to remove the old edge repairs that had been carried out around 1950: overly strong, unattractively coloured manila paper on the top and bottom margins, and light, thinner Chinese paper on the side edges (fig. 8). Removal of these was difficult as sutra paper was dyed with berberine which was very light-sensitive and water-soluble. Using a controlled application of water and alcohol mix directly on to the border, it was possible to release the margins slowly (fig.9). A total of 11 metres worth of border paper was removed in this manner. During this time – a period of six months – exploratory tests were carried out on the linings: when the single lining of one of the panels was removed a multitude of previously hidden vertical creases were exposed (fig.10).

Additionally, a number of non-destructive analytical tests were undertaken such as measurements of paper thickness, surface pH spot-testing of panels, observation of fibre distribution within panel sheets and examination of adhesives under a polarising microscope. One of the test results revealed that the frontispiece had, surprisingly, five linings, explaining the reason for its rigidity (fig.11).

Fig.8 *The combination of two contrasting paper types with different texture and tones was aesthetically unattractive and disturbed the visual presentation of the sutra. In addition, the differing expansion and contraction rate of the manila border exacerbated the distortion of the scroll.*

Fig.10 *The creasing of the scroll, as shown here in a photograph taken under raking light, originally occurred when the sutra was repaired in antiquity (pre-twelfth century). The application of thick glue and heavy paper patches caused the paper to contract.*

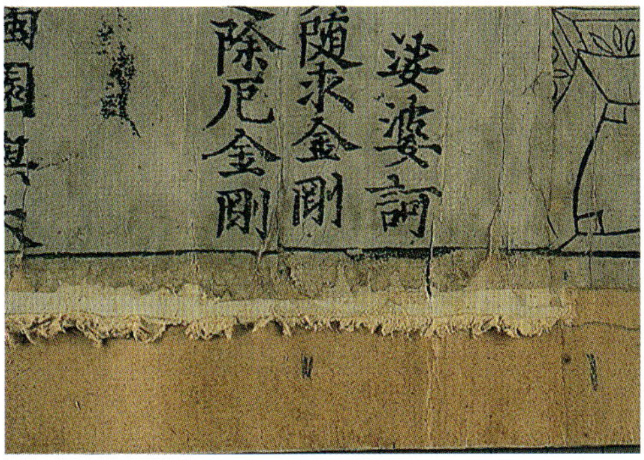

Fig.9 *The paper was first carefully thinned to allow the moisture to penetrate (the outer layer was quite waterproof) and soften the adhesive so the paper could be released and then the adhesive residues removed.*

Fig.11 *A 1cm² area of the sutra was carefully moistened and layers were lifted and separated. This opening up enabled the testing of adhesives, paper types and paper quality. It was also the first opportunity to investigate the paper of the frontispiece.*

The success of the first phase enabled a structured repair programme to be formulated between the Head of the Chinese Section and the Head of Paper Conservation at the Library. A decision was made to fully remove all linings from the scroll and separate the scroll into its component panels. The latter operation was necessary primarily because the scroll was found to have been separated previously and rejoined inaccurately.

In June 2006, the second phase began with the removal of the linings using controlled ultrasonic vapour via a tube to create a microclimate of 85 per cent humidity which released the adhesive bond from the lining paper (figs 12 and 13). A fibre-optic light, a cold light source, was placed underneath the object to highlight areas of damage (fig. 14). The removal of adhesive residues and linings was vital to the conservation of the sutra because they, together with repair

Fig. 12 *The most complex and challenging area of lining removal was the separation of the multiple sheets on the verso of the frontispiece. This image shows the painstaking removal of the outermost lining (1970s Chinese paper). Enough moisture had to be applied to soften the adhesive but not to saturate the sutra paper.*

Fig. 13 (above) *Following the removal of all the linings, numerous patches of paper of varying quality were exposed. Applied over areas of damage, these crude repairs contributed to the uneven thickness and distortion of the scroll. Removal followed the same approach as that developed for the lining removal, but with the added difficulty of the weak and damaged scroll paper clinging to the old repair.*

Fig. 14 *Scroll panel backlit within its controlled environment.*

paper patch remains firmly lodged on the surface, had led to areas of stress and distortion: they were physically pulling the weak areas of the original paper apart (figs 15 and 16). To remove the adhesive without affecting the yellow dye has been the greatest challenge to date.

Apart from the essential tools used for paper conservation such as brushes, knives, small scissors and tweezers, various other equipment was used – fine dentistry tools and modified clay modelling spatulas for the initial removal of the heavy deposits,

Fig. 15 (above) *Distortion of paper before removal of adhesive residues (verso)*

Fig. 16 *Distortion and fracturing of paper before removal of adhesive residues (recto)*

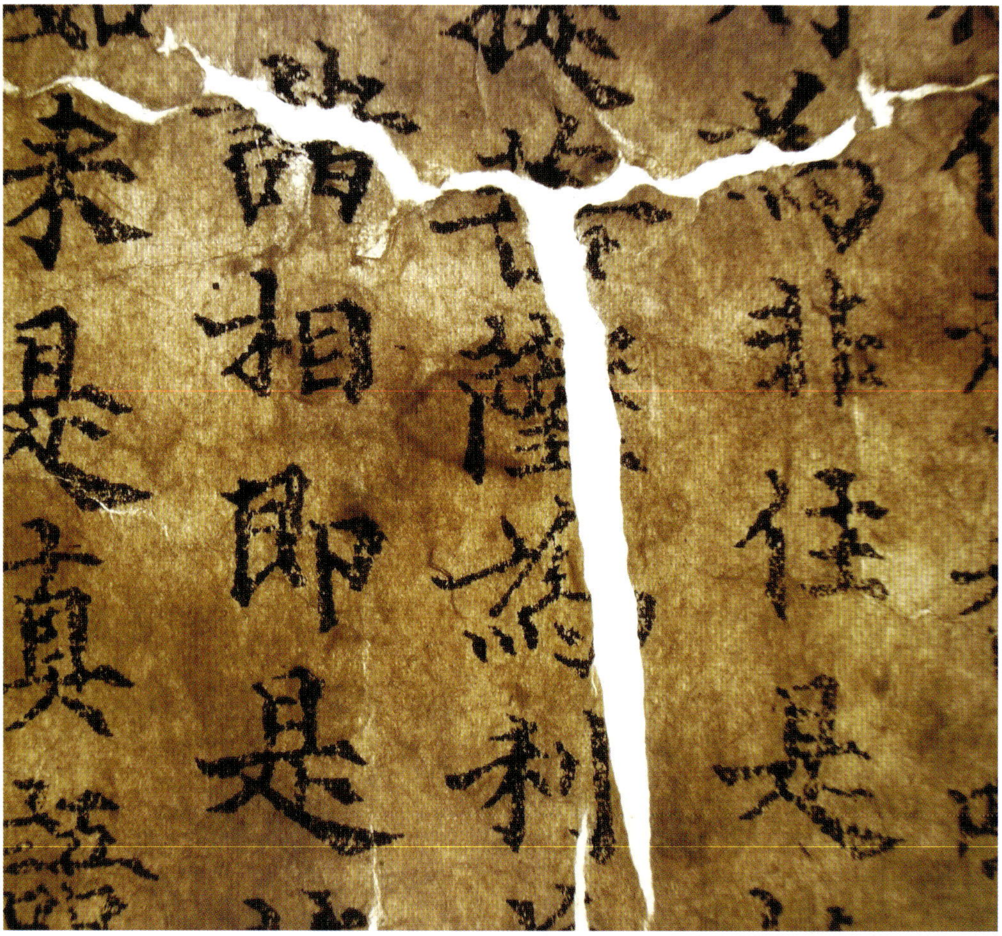

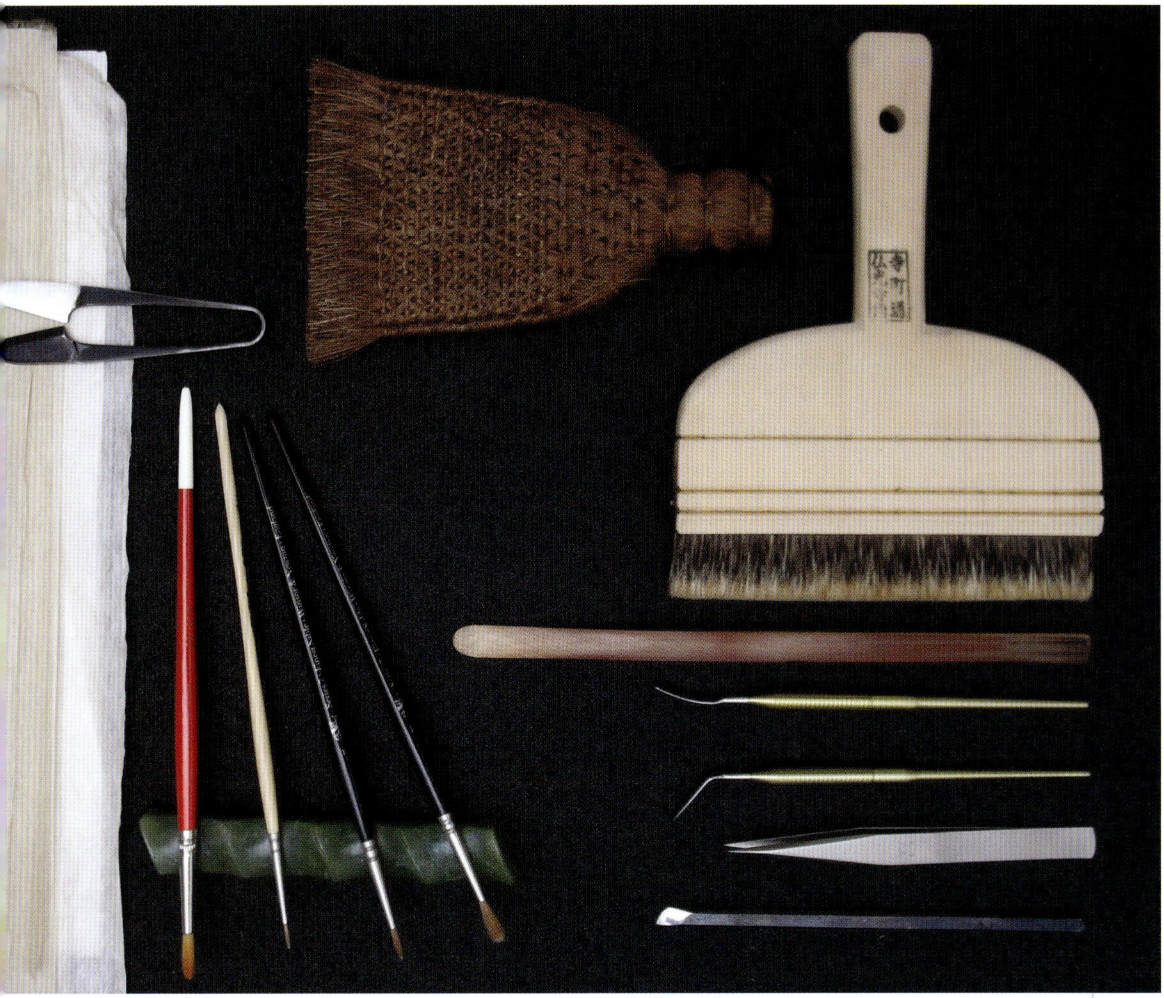

Fig. 17 *Tools and materials used for conservation. Clockwise from left: dyed Japanese paper mulberry papers (kozo-shi); Japanese scissors; Chinese smoothing brush; Japanese paste brush (nori-bake); spatulas; English sable hair brushes.*

followed by surgical precision tweezers and cotton wool for use when the adhesive was fluid enough to be rolled off the surface as a result of the ultrasonic vapour treatment (fig.17).

The completion of this laborious task, which took 18 months, was rewarded by the return of paper flexibility and character, and the original sheet formation such as fibre distribution and faint laid lines from the paper mould and texture could now be seen. However, this work exposed new problems, namely the fragility of paper due to extensive fracturing and the uneven thickness of the sheets (fig. 18, overleaf). This discovery went some way to explaining the challenges past conservators encountered

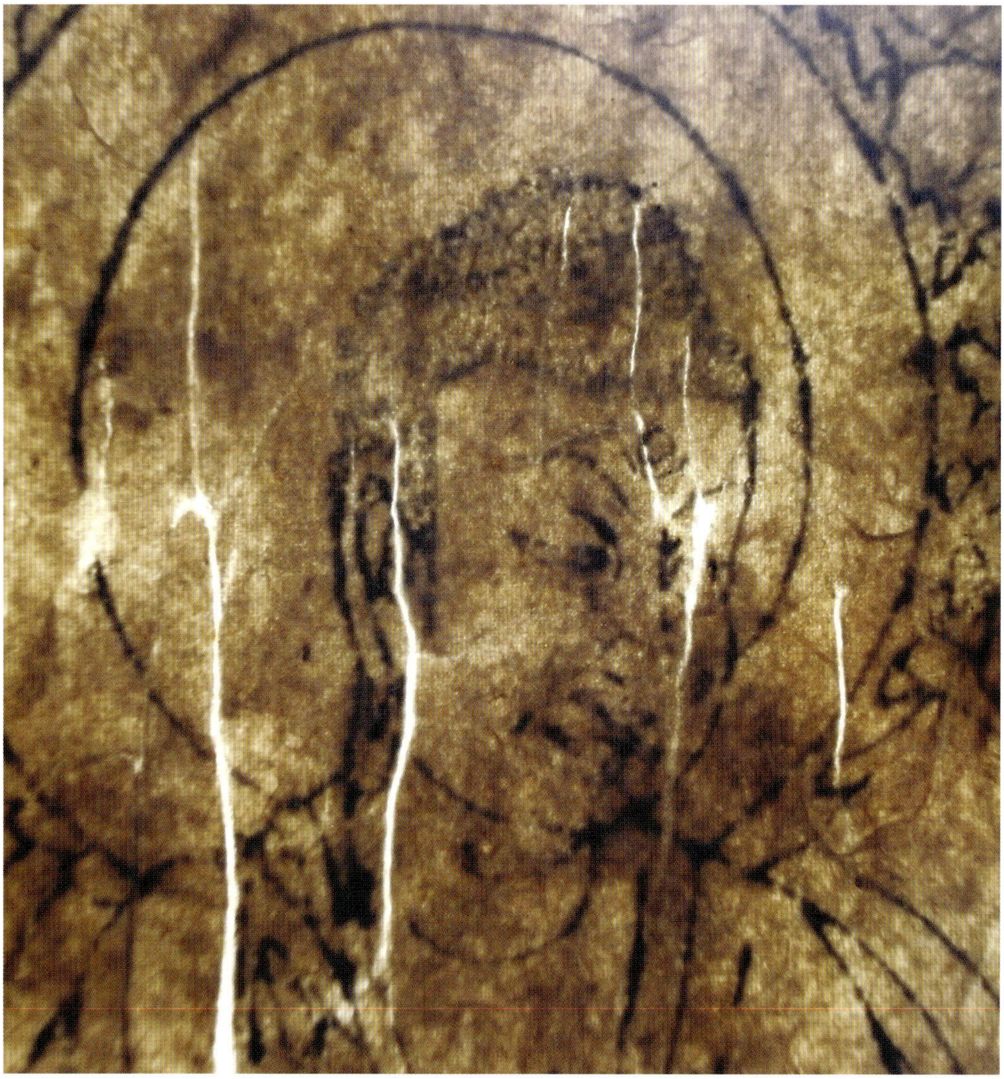

Fig. 18 *Extensive fracturing has been exposed following the removal of the linings and patches. Extreme care had to be taken when removing these final traces of old lining and adhesives from this area of the frontispiece.*

when attempting to align the text, not to mention the frontispiece image on which the distortion was most apparent.

Realignment was a slow and exacting process in itself (fig. 19). The problem arising from correcting misalignment in text and image was that it could only be carried out in a humid atmosphere when the paper expanded to draw the fractures together. Any drying during this critical period would have resulted in the newly matched joints separating. Once correctly aligned, they were very carefully reinforced using thin, dyed Japanese kozo (mulberry-fibre) paper strips with a feathered edge which gave a discreet,

Fig. 19 *Digital representation of a rough working sketch used in the realignment around a Bodhisattva's face on the frontispiece.*

Fig. 20 *A repair paper infill is being added to a small area of loss on the frontispiece. The paper is tone-dyed to a colour that is compatible with the sutra, with similar thickness and density. A starch-based adhesive is used to secure the infill to the front.*

a. b. c.

Fig. 21 (above) *Three-part image of realignment of an area from the top-left corner of the frontispiece; a. before remounting in the British Museum, 1911. b. after remounting in the British Museum, 1914. c. aligned following 2009 conservation work.*

blending appearance as opposed to a sharp, cut edge (fig. 20). The aim of the strips was to use the absolute minimum of repair paper on the back of the scroll to give the maximum strength. The repaired areas then underwent controlled drying using very light weights placed at strategic points to prevent further movement. Constant monitoring of the work ensured the sheet dimensions returned to the original size without any distortion of the text or image.

After more than 1000 hours of exacting work, finally completed in 2010, the sutra can now be seen the way it was intended; the frontispiece, in particular, now presents a complete and flowing image instead of our eyes following a series of disjointed lines, which had created a worryingly fragile appearance (fig. 21).

It was extraordinary to find that after 1100 years and much human intervention, the impression of the block print, the three-dimensional evidence of the actual printing process itself, was still present in places after the scroll linings were removed. It is only now that the Diamond Sutra can be fully viewed and handled without the masking of the linings. This will open up future areas of research, especially in the area of early printing (fig. 22) and paper-making for printing (fig. 23), as this sutra shows a high degree of maturity in these important technologies.

One final, important, decision remains to be made: the Diamond Sutra is a scroll, a continuous length of text formed by the joining of panels, in this case seven including the frontispiece. During earlier conservation treatments, the scroll was separated into its component panels, as indeed was the procedure this time. The question is whether to reassemble the sutra as a scroll, with all the limitations of this format, or keep the sheets flat and unattached, a safer method of storage, access and preservation but one that compromises its original form.

Fig. 22 *Raman (spectroscopy) microscope probe head above a panel. This is one of the advanced techniques used for pigment and ink analysis.*

Fig. 23 *Polarised light image of paper mulberry fibre taken from the edge of the Diamond Sutra.*

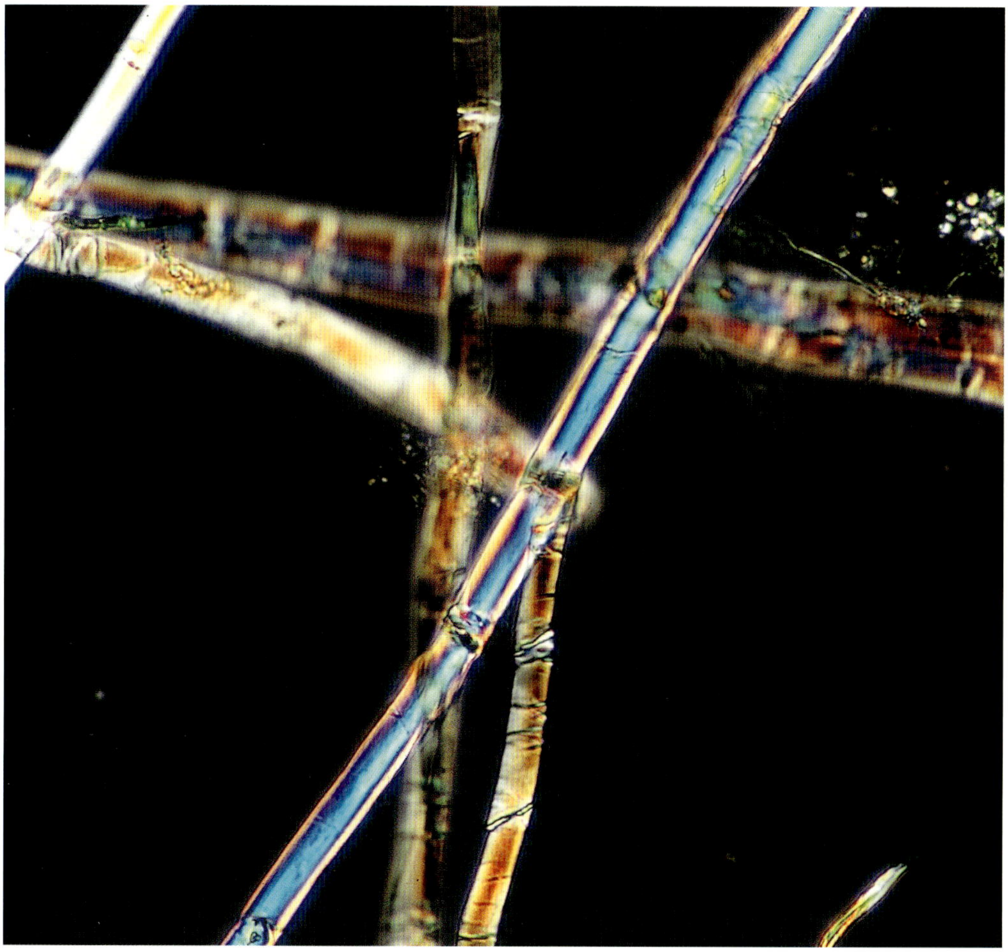

NOTES

INTRODUCTION

1 See Peter Hopkirk, *Foreign Devils on the Silk Road: The Search for the Lost Cities and Treasures of Chinese Central Asia*, London, John Murray, 1980 for the background and P.R. Harris, *A History of the British Museum Library*, London, British Library, 1998, pp. 554-7.

2 In China the scroll format for paper books developed out of the earlier use of thin slips of bamboo or wood as writing materials. These were joined together and rolled for storage and the format was copied with the advent of paper. By the beginning of the Song dynasty (960–1279), new formats were emerging and the use of folded paper leaves to form books became more common. The scroll is a cumbersome format, particularly for works of reference. See Tsien Tsuen-hsuin, *Written on Bamboo and Silk: The Beginnings of Chinese Books and Inscriptions*, Chicago, University of Chicago Press (2nd edn), 2004.

3 Shu-ling Chern, 'The Diamond Sutra in Chinese Culture before the Sung', PhD thesis, School of Oriental and African Studies, University of London, 2000, p. 102.

4 See Frances Wood, *The Silk Road*, London, British Library, 2003, chapters 10–14.

5 Susan Whitfield, *Aurel Stein on the Silk Road*, London, British Museum Press, 2004, pp. 44–5.

CHAPTER ONE

1 Aurel Stein, *Ruins of Desert Cathay: Personal Narrative of Explorations in Central Asia and Westernmost China*, London, Macmillan, 1912, vol. 2, p. 20.

2 For the German expeditions, see A. von Lecoq, *Buried Treasures of Chinese Turkestan* (1928), reprinted by Oxford University Press, 1985, and for the Pelliot announcement, J.L.L. Duyvendak in Hartmut Walravens, *Paul Pelliot: His Life and Works – A Bibliography*, Bloomington, Indiana University Press, 2001, p. xix.

3 Letter from Rudolf Hoernle to Sir Thomas Holderness, October 1878, copied to Stein, Bodleian Library, Stein Mss. 278/137–142.

4 Paul Pelliot, *Carnets de Route*, Paris, Les Indes savantes, 2008, p. 409, my translation.

5 Stein to Allen, Bodleian Library, Stein Mss. 28/32.

6 Stein, *Ruins of Desert Cathay*, vol. 2, pp. 24–5.

7 Aurel Stein, *Serindia: Detailed Report of Explorations in Central Asia and Westernmost China*, Oxford, Clarendon Press, 1921, p. 801.

8 Ibid., p. 802.

9 Ibid., p. 803.

10 Ibid., pp. 805, 808.

11 Ibid., p. 813.

12 Wang Jiqing, 'On the Photography of Wang Jiayan and his Family', *IDP Newsletter*, 10, Spring 1998.

13 Stein, *Serindia*, p. 818.

14 Aurel Stein, *Sand-buried Ruins of Khotan: Personal Narrative of a Journey of Archaeological and Geographical Exploration in Chinese Kurdistan*, London, T. Fisher Unwin, 1903, vol. 2, p. 188.

15 Arthur Waley, *Ballads and Stories from Tun-huang*, London, 1960, p. 237.

16 Philippe Flandrin, *Les Sept Vies du mandarin Français*, Monaco, Editions du Rocher, 2008, p. 167, my translation.

17 Paul Pelliot, 'Une bibliothèque médiévale retrouvée au Kan-sou [Gansu]', *Bulletin de l'Ecole Française d'Extrême-Orient*, vol. VIII, 1908, p. 502.

18 Flandrin, *Sept Vies,* p. 189ff.

19 Bodleian Library, Stein Mss. 4/46v.

20 Published in Shanghai by the American Presbyterian Mission Press. There is a copy on the reference shelves in the British Library as it remains useful in an old-fashioned way.

21 Stein, *Sand-buried Ruins*, vol. 2, p. 26.

22 Stein, *Serindia*, p. 802.

23 Stein, *Sand-buried Ruins*, vol. 2, p. 191.

24 Ibid., vol. 2, pp. 192–3.

25 Ibid., vol. 2, p. 194.

CHAPTER TWO

1 Li Xianlin [chief editor], *Dunhuangxue da cidian,* Shanghai, Shanghai cishu chubanshe, 1998, p. 350.

2 Paul Pelliot, 'Une bibliothèque médiévale retrouvée au Kan-sou [Gansu]', *Bulletin de l'Ecole Française d'Extrême-Orient*, vol. VIII, 1908, p. 506.

3 Rong Xinjiang, 'Ye Changchi: Pioneer of Dunhuang Studies', *IDP News* 7, Spring 1997: http://idp.bl.uk/archives/news07.

4 Ibid.

5 Lin Shitian and Saren Gaowa, 'Guojia tushuguan Liu Tingchen jiu cang Dunhuang yishu', *Dunhuang Tulufan yanjiu*, 11, 2008 (Shanghai), p. 489.

6 The Tanguts were a group who lived on the borders of China and Tibet and formed an empire in the area in the tenth century stretching from northern Tibet northeastwards, to the contemporary border of Mongolia which included Dunhuang. The Tangut empire was destroyed by the Mongols in the early thirteenth century, leaving only some extraordinary stepped stupas in Ningxia and sites such as Kharakhoto revealing paintings and documents in their own extraordinary script. See Ruth Dunnell, *The Great State of White and High*, Hawaii, University of Honolulu Press, 1996.

7 Pelliot, 'Une bibliothèque médiévale', p. 506.

8 Aurel Stein, *Serindia: Detailed Report of Explorations in Central Asia and Westernmost China*, Oxford, Clarendon Press, 1921, p. 814.

9 *Dunhuangxue da cidian*, p. 61.

10 Lukas Nickell, ed., *Return of the Buddha: The Qingzhou Discoveries*, London, Royal Academy of Arts, 2002, p. 16.

11 See Arthur W. Hummel, *Eminent Chinese of the Ch'ing Period*, Washington, U.S. Government Printing Office, 1944, p. 726.

12 Many of these tiny pieces, carefully cut into squares smaller than a postage stamp, have been found in the Stein collection. They would have been burnt and, as ash, mixed with water to be taken as medicine, with all the magic that words might convey.

CHAPTER THREE

1 Mark Edward Lewis, *China's Cosmopolitan Empire: The Tang Dynasty*, Cambridge, Mass., Bellknap Press, 2009, p. 217.

2 For the wealth and activities of Chinese Buddhists at the time, see Lewis, *China's Cosmopolitan Empire*, pp. 214–29.

3 I have relied heavily on the late Wladimir Zwalf's catalogue *Buddhism: Art and Faith*, London, British Museum, 1985.

4 Or. 8210/P.11 is a printed fragment; see Lionel Giles, *Descriptive Catalogue of Chinese Manuscripts from Tunhuang in the British Museum*, London, British Museum, 1957, p. 279, no. 8084.

5 http://en.wikipedia.org/wiki/Kumarajiva and Zwalf, *Buddhism*, p. 77.

6 Published in the *Journal of the Royal Asiatic Society*, 1864–5.

7 Nicholas Poppe, *The Diamond Sutra: Three Mongolian Versions of the Vajracchedika Prajnaparamita. Texts, Translations, Notes and Glossaries*, Wiesbaden, Harrasowitz, 1971 (Asiatische Forschungen, vol. 35), p. 1.

8 Shu-ling Chern, 'The Diamond Sutra in Chinese Culture before the Sung', PhD thesis, SOAS, University of London, 2000, p. 85. She gives an interesting account (p. 123) of the 62 character problem in the Chinese translation of the Diamond Sutra. 62 characters, essentially yet another question and answer about the non-existence of 'beings' which 'existed during the mid-6th century to AD 682 … but went missing before Emperor Xuanzong published his commentary in AD 735. Then they were somehow recovered before … 822'.

9 Paul Harrison and Shogo Watanabe, 'Vajracchedika Prajnaparamita', in Jens Braarvig, *Buddhist Manuscripts in the Schoyen Collection*, vol. 3, Oslo, Hermes Publishing, 2006, p. 142. Harrison and Watanabe were working from two sixth- to seventh-century manuscripts from Gilgit.

10 Translation from the Chinese by Charles Muller at http://www.acmuller.net/bud-canon/diamond_sutra.html: Muller's sections 11 and 12.

11 Lightning mysteriously disappeared from the Khotanese translation; see R.E. Emmerick, 'The Concluding Verses of the Khotanese Vajracchedika', in Lewis Lancaster (ed.), *Prajnaparamita and Related Systems: Essays in Honour of Edward Conze*, Berkeley Buddhist series, 1977, p. 83.

12 A.C. Graham, *Disputers of the Tao: Philosophical Argument in Ancient China*, La Salle, Open Court, 1989, p. 85.

13 Professor Paul Harrison, see http://tibeto-logic.blogspot.com/2009/10/paul-harrison-on-diamond.html. The Diamond Sutra is chanted very beautifully on the British Library's 'Turning the Pages' digitised version. The chanting was specially recorded by the Foguang Temple.

CHAPTER FOUR

1 Jeannette Mirsky, *Sir Aurel Stein: Archaeological Explorer*, University of Chicago Press, 1977, p. 46.

2 Rudolf Hoernle, 'Who was the Inventor of Rag Paper?', *JRAS*, 1903, p. 697.

3 Bodleian Library, Stein Mss. 205, fol. 128.

4 Tsien Tsuen-hsuin, *Paper and Printing*, part 1 of vol. 5, *Chemistry and Chemical Technology*, in Joseph Needham (ed.), *Science and Civilisation in China*, Cambridge University Press, 1985, p. 40.

5 Hans Bielenstein, 'The Restoration of the Han Dynasty', *Bulletin of the Museum of Far Eastern Antiquities*, Stockholm, 1954, no. 26, p. 9.

6 Tsien Tsuen-hsuin, *Written on Bamboo and Silk: The Beginnings of Chinese Books and Inscriptions* (2nd edn), University of Chicago Press, 2004, p. 149.

7 Tsien, *Paper and Printing*, p. 38.

8 Tsien, *Written on Bamboo and Silk*, pp. 146–7, fig. 23.

9 Denis Twitchett, *Printing and Publishing in Medieval China*, London, Wynkyn de Worde Society, 1983, p. 11.

10 Tsien, *Paper and Printing*, p. 35.

11 Danielle Eliasberg, 'Pratiques funéraires animales en Chine', *Journal Asiatique*, vol. 280, 1992, p. 125.

12 British Library, Or. 8210/S. 5544.

13 Lionel Giles, *Six Centuries at Tunhuang: A Short Account of the Stein Collection of Chinese Manuscripts in the British Museum*, London, China Society, 1944, is the best overall description of the variety of documents in the collection.

14 Susan Whitfield and Ursula Sims-Williams, *The Silk Road: Trade, Travel, War and Faith*, London, British Library, 2004, pp. 148–9.

15 Tsien, *Paper and Printing*, pp. 298–9.

16 Ibid., p. 195.

17 The mistakes are set out neatly by Arthur Waley in 'Note on the Invention of Woodcuts', *New China Review*, vol. 1, no. 4, 1919, pp. 412–15.

18 T.H. Barrett, *The Woman Who Discovered Printing*, London, Yale University Press, 2008, p. 93. He argues that despite a lack of clear reference, this sutra may provide evidence for printing in China under the empress Wu (690–705), thus pushing it back before the Japanese and Korean examples.
The full name of the short *dharani* is Rasmivimalavisuddhaprabhadharani and is T 1024 in the *Taisho Tripitaka*.

19 T.H. Barrett, *Woman Who Discovered Printing*, p. 94.

20 Peter Kornicki, *The Book in Japan: A Cultural History from the Beginnings to the Nineteenth Century*, Honolulu, University of Hawaii Press, 2001, pp. 122–4.

21 Waley, 'Note', p. 414. Illegally printed calendars, some from Sichuan, were amongst the fragments Stein brought back from Cave 17; see Twitchett, *Printing and Publishing*, p. 25.

22 British Library, Mss. Or. 8210/P. 6 and Or. 8210/P.12. See Susan Whitfield, 'Under the Censor's Eye: Printed Almanacs and Censorship in Ninth-Century China,' *British Library Journal*, vol. 24, no. 1, Spring 1998, pp. 4–22.

23 William Milne, *A Retrospect of the First 10 Years of the Protestant Mission to China*, Malacca, 1820, quoted in Joseph McDermott, *A Social History of the Chinese Book: Books and Literati Culture in Late Imperial China*, Hong Kong University Press, 2006, p. 17.

24 William Henry Medhurst, *China: Its State and Prospects with Especial Reference to the Spread of the Gospel*, London, 1838, quoted in McDermott, *Social History*, 2006, p. 18.

25 It is a common error to assume that a single mistake when carving a block would mean having to throw the whole thing away, which is far from accurate. For the mistaken view, see John Man, *The Gutenberg Revolution*, London, Review, 2002, p. 90.

26 Tsien, *Paper and Printing*, p. 200.

27 Medhurst, *China*, pp. 561–2.

CHAPTER FIVE

1 Bodleian Library, Stein Mss. 37, fol. 128.

2 British Museum archives, CE 32/23/23/2.

3 Jeannette Mirsky, *Sir Aurel Stein: Archaeological Explorer*, University of Chicago Press, 1977, pp. 43, 340–1.

4 See Helen Wang, 'Stein's Recording Angel – Miss F.M.G. Lorimer', *Journal of the Royal Asiatic Society*, Series 3, 1998, pp. 207–28.

5 Bodleian Library, Stein Mss. 38/23.

6 Bodleian Library, Stein Mss. 38/26.

7 British Museum archives, CE 32/23/35/2.

8 British Library, Or. 13114: correspondence with M. Pelliot.

9 Bodleian Library, Stein Mss. 205, fol. 551 and Aurel Stein, *Serindia: Detailed Report of Explorations in Central Asia and Westernmost China*, Oxford, Clarendon Press, 1921, p. xv, footnote 16.

10 *Guide to an Exhibition of Paintings, Manuscripts and Other Archaeological Objects Collected by Sir Aurel Stein KCIE in Chinese Turkestan*, London, British Museum, 1914, p. 57.

CHAPTER SIX

1 Ken Seddon and Peter Gibbs, 'The Dunhuang Diamond Sutra: A Challenging Problem for Scientific Conservation Techniques', in Susan Whitfield and Frances Wood, *Dunhuang and Turfan: Contents and Conservation of Ancient Documents from Central Asia*, London, British Library, 1996, pp. 59–69.

2 Mark Barnard and Frances Wood, 'A Short History of the Conservation of the Dunhuang Manuscripts in London', in Susan Whitfield and Ursula Sims-Williams, *The Silk Road: Trade, Travel, War and Faith*, London, British Library, 2004, pp. 97–104.

3 John Hatcher, *Laurence Binyon: Poet, Scholar of East and West*, Oxford, Clarendon Press, 1995, p. 166. For Binyon's clever manipulation of the division of paintings and manuscripts between the British Museum and New Delhi (profiting from the First World War), see Frances Wood, 'Two Thousand Years at Dunhuang', in Whitfield and Wood, *Dunhuang and Turfan*, pp. 3–4.

4 Lionel Giles, *Six Centuries at Tunhuang: A Short History of the Stein Collection of Chinese Manuscripts in the British Museum* (lecture delivered to the China Society in October 1941), London, China Society, 1944, p. 6.

5 Wang Chongmin, afterword in *Dunhuang yishu zongmu suoyin*, Beijing, Shangwu yinshuguan, 1962, p. 544. In the light of Giles's long years of access to the collection and his refusal to allow proper access to Chinese visitors, Wang Chongmin is particularly scathing about Giles's catalogue of the manuscripts, published in 1956 after his retirement; see Wood, 'Two Thousand Years at Dunhuang', pp. 5–6.

6 P.R. Harris, *A History of the British Museum Library 1753–1973*, London, British Library, 1998, pp. 552–3 and Giles, *Six Centuries at Tunhuang*, p. 6.

7 Kumiko Matsuoka, 'An Investigative Study of the Frontispiece of the Diamond Sutra', in Whitfield and Wood, *Dunhuang and Turfan*, pp. 20–6. See also Sandy Ryan, 'Beyond the Pale', Conservation Science Research Project thesis for De Montfort University with the British Library, 1999. The thesis covered the history, application and identification of bleaches and bleach residues used in conservation using modern, but similar quality samples to those found in Dunhuang.

8 Peter Gibbs, 'Conserving the Dunhuang Diamond Sutra', BSc thesis, University of Sussex, 1992; Peter Gibbs, 'Pre-10th century Chinese Paper: A Study in Scientific Conservation Techniques', PhD thesis, The Queen's University of Belfast, 1995.

INDEX

PICTURE CREDITS

INTRODUCTION

pp.7–8 British Library, Or.8210/P.2, the Diamond Sutra

p.11 Library of the Hungarian Academy of Sciences, Stein Photo 3/6 (19)

CHAPTER ONE

p.14 British Library, Photo 392/26 (323); p.16 British Library, Photo 392/27 (376); p.18 Musée Guimet, Paris, AP 8186. Photo RMN/Ollivier; p.19 British Library, Photo 392/26 (322); p.20 British Library, Photo 392/27 (587); p.23 British Library, 2259.f.4, fig.188; page 25: British Library, Or.8210/S.351; p.26 British Library, Photo 392/28 (803); pp.28–9 British Library, Photo 392/28 (746)

CHAPTER TWO

p.33 British Library, Or. 8210/S.253; p.35 British Library, Photo 392/26 (238); p. 39 British Library, Or. 8210/ S. 5720

CHAPTER FOUR

pp.59–61 Song Yingxing, *Tiangong kaiwu*, 1637, British Library (reprint) 15226.b.19; p.65 British Library, Or. 8210/ P. 18; p.66 British Library, Or. 78.a.11; pp. 68–69 British Library, Or. 8210/ S. 5791; p.71 British Library, Or. 14251

CHAPTER FIVE

p.75 British Library, Photo 392/26 (160); page 76 British Library, Photo 392/26 (334a); p.79 British Library, Photo 392/26 (240)

CHAPTER SIX

p.83 *Ruins of Desert Cathay*, fig. 191, British Library 2259.f.4; p.86 © National Museums Liverpool (Stewart Bale Collection, Merseyside Maritime Museum). By permission of the National Library of Wales; p.90 British Library, OIT. 950, *Serindia* (1921) by Aurel Stein, vol IV, p.100

·Лик· Златоуста

МАСТЕРСКИЕ ДЕКОРАТИВНО-
ПРИКЛАДНОГО ИСКУССТВА
«ЛиК»

2004
Москва
ИНТЕРБУК-БИЗНЕС

ЛИК ЗЛАТОУСТА

МАСТЕРСКИЕ ДЕКОРАТИВНО-
ПРИКЛАДНОГО ИСКУССТВА
«ЛиК»

УДК 762.11(470.55)(084.1)
ББК 85.153(2)6я6
Л56

Авторы статей

Е. В. Тихомирова
Галерея авторского оружия «Русские палаты»

З. А. Малаева
Всероссийский музей декоративно-прикладного и народного искусства

С. В. Гнутова
Центральный музей древнерусской культуры и искусства им. Андрея Рублева

Художник

Д. Е. Дацко

Слайды предоставлены Мастерскими
декоративно-прикладного искусства «ЛиК»

Отпечатано в типографии «Гореньски Тиск», Словения

ISBN 5-89164-147-X

Город Златоуст известен во всем мире как российский центр, где на протяжении без малого двух столетий зародилось, достигло расцвета, пережило «смутные» времена и вновь возродилось искусство златоустовской гравюры на металле. Отрадно сознавать, что этот альбом выходит в свет в год 250-летия со дня основания Златоуста. Более того, мы, организаторы и ведущие художники Мастерских декоративно-прикладного искусства «ЛиК», рассматриваем это издание как наш скромный дар любимому городу к его юбилею.

Златоуст стал для нас, Александра и Нины Лохтачевых, Григория Мануша, по-настоящему родным, а златоустовская гравюра на металле — делом всей жизни. Возрождению и развитию традиций этого уникального искусства мы отдали немало времени, труда, душевных сил. Вспоминается, что трудности, стоявшие перед нами в период становления Мастерских «ЛиК», казались непреодолимыми, но они не испугали наш маленький творческий коллектив единомышленников, наоборот, открыли в нас новые качества и дарования — человеколюбие и терпимость, ответственность и упорство, педогогический талант.

Красота, подаренная людям, опыт и знания, переданные ученикам, — в этом видим мы свой посильный вклад в духовную и культурную жизнь современной России.

За годы существования Мастерских «ЛиК» более 200 человек освоили тонкости ремесла, получили возможность познакомиться с богатой историей русского изобразительного искусства. Среди них — не только квалифицированные мастера, но и руководители, ведущие художники многих фирм. Творческая и производственная «судьба» этих людей состоялась — не в последнюю очередь — благодаря работе на нашей, теперь уже старейшей, если говорить о новейшей истории Златоуста, фирме.

Изделия Мастерских получили высокую оценку в нашей стране и за рубежом со стороны государственных деятелей, выдающихся представителей культуры и искусства, а также Русской Православной церкви, в частности Патриарха Московского и Всея Руси Алексия II.

Низкий поклон златоустовцам, которые поддерживали меня и оказывали всяческое содействие на разных этапах становления «ЛиКа». С их помощью в Златоусте удалось создать систему обучения будущих мастеров — от начальной школы до высшей.

Я бесконечно благодарен друзьям-художникам Нине Лохтачевой и Григорию Манушу за их веру в мои организаторские и творческие способности, неустанный совместный труд, моим ученикам — за то, что они проявляют и в искусстве, и в бизнесе лучшие человеческие и творческие качества в духе традиций Мастерских «ЛиК».

Выражаю искреннюю признательность коллективу издательства «Интербук-бизнес»: их высокопрофессиональная работа над этим альбомом, надеюсь, будет по достоинству оценена любителями искусства.

Искренне верю, что это издание станет точкой отсчета нового этапа в развитии златоустовской гравюры на металле, создаст предпосылки для совершенствования новых его направлений во славу нашего города, носящего имя Вселенского Учителя святого Иоанна Златоуста.

Художественный руководитель Мастерских декоративно-прикладного искусства «ЛиК», скульптор

Александр ЛОХТАЧЕВ

ХУДОЖЕСТВЕННОЕ ХОЛОДНОЕ ОРУЖИЕ

Появление в 1990 году первых образцов художественного оружия, выполненных в городе Златоусте Челябинской области в Мастерских декоративно-прикладного искусства «ЛиК» («Лохтачев и Компания»), для многих стало полной неожиданностью. В то время трудно было себе представить, что эти изделия вполне официально изготовлены не на государственном заводе, а на частной фирме, и созданы они мастерами по их собственным художественным эскизам в новой современной манере, но с сохранением традиций златоустовской оружейной школы. Оказалось, что пока московские и тульские мастера-оружейники делали первые, еще очень робкие шаги по легализации своей деятельности, мечтали о свободном творчестве и возрождении славы русского оружейного искусства, создатели златоустовской фирмы «ЛиК», опираясь на свой профессиональный опыт и веря в будущее своего дела, приступили к выпуску авторского коллекционного оружия.

Мастерские декоративно-прикладного искусства «ЛиК» явились первой современной производственной мастерской по созданию художественного оружия в постсоветский период российской истории. Деятельность этого предприятия послужила примером для многих, ныне успешно действующих оружейных фирм не только Златоуста, но и других исторических центров развития этого вида искусства. Изделия Мастерских «ЛиК» — мечи, палаши, сабли, кинжалы, кортики, ножи — представляют собой впечатляющие авторские разработки в области современного оружейного искусства. Наиболее интересные в художественном отношении образцы дают возможность по достоинству оценить мастерство и талант златоустовских мастеров-оружейников.

Уральский город Златоуст завоевал мировую известность еще в XIX веке. В 1815 году была открыта Златоустовская оружейная фабрика, которая на протяжении почти двух столетий являлась основным центром производства холодного оружия в России. С первых лет существования

1. Кортик «Урны Санкт-Петербурга» (фрагмент). Из серии «Петербургские мотивы». 1997

фабрики особое внимание здесь уделялось изготовлению украшенного, художественного оружия. Эта деятельность златоустовских оружейников XIX столетия сыграла важнейшую роль в отечественной культуре. Были созданы произведения оружейного искусства, которые заняли достойное место среди памятников мирового уровня. Яркая, своеобразная стилистика златоустовского художественного оружия определила формирование в XIX столетии новой своеобразной оружейной школы, существенно отличавшейся от старейших отечественных школ — московской и тульской. Отличительной особенностью художественного оружия Златоуста стала неизменная и последовательная разработка нового для русского оружейного искусства вида художественного творчества — знаменитой златоустовской гравюры на металле.

Одним из важнейших достижений златоустовской оружейной школы явилось формирование такой системы промышленного производства, в которой создание художественных изделий занимало бы достойное место, а творческие таланты мастеров могли с успехом реализовываться. Подобные процессы в отечественной художественной промышленности, характерные для России первой половины XIX века, получили наиболее полное развитие среди особых, редких художественных производств. Так происходило в Вятке на фабрике мещан Макаровых по обработке капокорня (изделия этой фабрики были представлены на Промышленной выставке в 1833 году). Так создавалась наиболее крупная из русских кружевных мануфактур — фабрика Протасовой близ Мценска. Однако внедрение художественного процесса в отрасль военной промышленности было необычным явлением. Эта новая для российской практики организация государственной оружейной фабрики с наличием в ней художественного производства явилась одной из причин обращения к опыту таких крупнейших оружейных центров Западной Европы, как Золинген и Клингенталь. Созданный с помощью немецких мастеров особый цех украшенного оружия на Златоустовской оружейной фабрике был, по сути дела, уникальным в российской истории. Начиная с 1816 года Златоуст с успехом выполнял все правительственные и многочисленные частные заказы на изготовление художественного оружия. Благодаря развитию в этом центре производства украшенного оружия оружейные мастера художественной специализации выделились в особую профессиональную группу. Их образовательная подготовка существенно отличалась от ранее существовавшей в русской оружейной практике. Если московские оружейники XVII века, в том числе художники («знаменщики»), проходили так называемую школу ученичества, которая была основана на обучении у мастера в течение 5–7 лет всем практическим навыкам, то в начале XIX века профессиональная подготовка художественных кадров строилась на

2. Набор «Охотничий»: нож и кинжал. 1999

совсем иной основе. Существовавшая в этот период российская система академического образования позволила получить наиболее талантливым заводским ученикам оружейной фабрики высшее профессиональное образование в Петербургской Академии художеств. Кроме того, широко использовались возможности самой Златоустовской оружейной фабрики. В заводской школе одаренная молодежь проходила подготовку по рисованию и живописи. Под руководством известных на фабрике рисовальщиков, художников-самородков, в заводской «чертежне» ученики совершенствовали свои навыки в области рисунка и композиции. В библиотеке оружейной фабрики хранилась новейшая для того времени литература по истории, мифологии и прикладному искусству. Арсенал давал возможность изучать традиции русских художников-оружейников по образцам тульских изделий. Златоустовские оружейники направлялись в Тулу и Петербург «для ознакомления со вкусом». Действующая на оружейной фабрике уникальная система подготовки мастеров художественной специализации сыграла прогрессивную роль в развитии отечественного оружейного искусства, явилась тем необходимым условием, благодаря которому получила мощное развитие природная одаренность Бушуевых, Бояршиновых, Тележниковых, П. Уткина, С. Фетисова, Л. Лукина и многих других талантливых златоустовских мастеров.

Созданию атмосферы творческого подъема способствовала деятельность директора оружейной фабрики П. П. Аносова. Его собственные разработки получения легендарной булатной стали являются примером соединения ремесла, науки и искусства.

Художественное оружие Златоуста — это яркое, своеобразное явление в истории русского искусства. Оно получило широкое признание и высокую оценку не только благодаря оригинальности декора, выполненного прославленной златоустовской гравюрой на стали. Стилистическое развитие художественного оружия с первых лет своего существования удивительно точно уловило общие тенденции развития отечественной культуры. Это позволило оружейному искусству Златоуста уже в первой половине XIX века выйти за рамки замкнутости и обособленности этого вида декоративно-прикладного искусства. Оно распространило отработанные на оружейных формах художественные методы и приемы на изготовление самых разнообразных бытовых предметов из стали. Система декорирования оружия послужила основой златоустовской художественной школы. Прочные традиции этой школы помогли сохранить своеобразие златоустовского стиля в самые сложные исторические периоды отечественной культуры. В 1920–1980-е годы на Златоустовской фабрике не прекращались поиски новых форм и нового содержания, оттачивалось владение техническими навыками, шлифовалось качество исполнения, осваивались новые и традиционные технологии.

Оружейные памятники в советское время создавались достаточно редко. В стране отсутствовал свободный рынок дорогостоящего художественного оружия. Только по специальным государственным заказам на фабрике изготовляли подарочное, почетное наградное, мемориально-юбилейное холодное оружие. Изобразительный ряд и композиционное решение этих изделий продолжали традиции яркой выразительности. Оформление предметов строилось по определенной, заданной тематике: это традиционные сцены охоты, растительные орнаменты, уральские пейзажи, пафосные исторические изображения и характерные сюжеты социалистического реализма. Однако как бы ни были мастера талантливы и целеустремленны в своих поисках, их оружейное творчество несло черты идеологической запрограммированности обязательных художественных решений и было строго лимитировано, ограничено рамками государственных заказов и законодательных норм.

Для дальнейшего развития отечественного оружейного искусства требовались новые условия. Они появились в конце 1980-х годов благодаря кардинальным социально-экономическим изменениям в нашей стране.

Именно в этот период был в полной мере востребован богатейший исторический опыт златоустовской оружейной школы. В 1990 году профессиональные художники супруги Александр и Нина Лохтачевы, а также их коллега и единомышленник Григорий Мануш организовали Мастерские декоративно-прикладного искусства «ЛиК».

3. Набор «Морской»: кортик и компас. 1999

N
30
60
E
120
150
S
210
240
W
300
330

По словам златоустовского исследователя и искусствоведа С. Куликовских, художники-организаторы видели задачу будущих Мастерских в том, чтобы «не только сохранить самобытное уникальное искусство украшения изделий из металла, но вернуть былую славу русского оружия, возвратить златоустовской гравюре на металле ее исконное назначение — украшать предмет, будь то кубок или кинжал, клинок офицерской сабли или подсвечник, поднос или предмет церковной утвари». Очевидно, что основным стимулом появления мастерских явилась возможность свободного воплощения творческой фантазии и собственных художественных образов, композиций, форм. Основатели фирмы — зрелые профессиональные художники — осознавали проблему создания новых художественных изделий в соответствии с эстетикой и возможностями новейшего времени. Александр Лохтачев как главный идеолог «ЛиКа» убежден, что общественная потребность сегодняшнего дня заключается в сохранении богатейших исторических традиций Златоуста и приумножении лучших достижений самобытной российской культуры. У Мастерских «ЛиК» есть все основания, чтобы стать первым звеном в деле создания в Златоусте крупного художественного центра со своими производственными мастерскими, научно-исследовательскими и учебными институтами, культурно-просветительными учреждениями.

Сегодняшняя первоочередная задача — сделать все возможное для того, чтобы появилось больше изделий, достойных славных традиций Златоуста, чтобы активно развивалась определенная социальная, общественная и культурная среда Златоуста как центра уникального художественного промысла. И чем больше в городе появляется новых мастерских, тем шире поле деятельности художественно одаренных, ищущих людей.

Для развития таланта и мастерства местных умельцев требуется определенная профессиональная подготовка.

4. Сабля (фрагмент). 2000

И здесь «ЛиК» нашел свое место в общем процессе, обратясь к историческому опыту, существовавшему на Златоустовской оружейной фабрике в XIX столетии. Первоначально при мастерских была организована школа подготовки кадров. Опытные художники «ЛиКа» стали преподавателями. Они старались передать молодежи все технические приемы златоустовской гравюры на стали. Затем, в 1995 году, на базе Мастерских «ЛиК» был открыт филиал Челябинского (ныне Южно-Уральского) государственного университета по специальности «технология художественной обработки материалов». В основе образования лежат классические для любого художника, в том числе в области декоративно-прикладного искусства, дисциплины — рисунок, композиция, живопись. Студенты осваивают академический рисунок с гипсовых слепков и с натуры, изучают историю искусств. Параллельно идет обучение традиционному златоустовскому мастерству. Для этого используются богатые возможности, которые предоставляет производственная деятельность Мастерских. Таким образом талантливая молодежь получает высшее образование, а также традиционную для Златоуста и ныне востребованную специальность «инженер-художник».

Огромное желание возродить славу родного города проявляется в том, что для многих направлений деятельности «ЛиКа» характерна ярко выраженная общественная направленность. В основе одного из наиболее крупных общественных проектов «ЛиКа» лежит разработка и создание памятников-символов современной российской истории. В 1995 году проводились торжественные празднования 50-летия Победы в Великой Отечественной войне (1941—1945). В честь этого знаменательного события по заказу правительств Российской Федерации и города Москвы коллективом Мастерских «ЛиК» были созданы монументальные произведения — Щит и Меч Победы и Мечи «Памяти и Благодарности» народам стран-участниц антигитлеровской коалиции — Англии, Франции, Америки и России. Щит и Меч Победы установлены во вводном зале мемориального комплекса на Поклонной горе в Центральном музее Великой Отечественной войны. Мечи «Памяти и Благодарности» были вручены на торжествах в Москве президентом России Б. Н. Ельциным Джону Мейджору, Франсуа Миттерану и Биллу Клинтону.

Для художников «ЛиКа» обращение к теме государственной символики явилось необычайно интересным творческим проектом. Руководитель авторского коллектива Александр Иванович Лохтачев использовал исторический опыт богатейших златоустовских традиций по созданию памятного оружия в честь Отечественной войны 1812 года. Однако современные художники, пытаясь усилить смысловую нагрузку, применили несколько иные приемы для выражения идеи воинской славы и силы, могущества и непобедимости народа в борьбе с иноземными захватчиками. Щит и Меч Победы создан по законам памятника монументально-декоративной скульптуры. В основу концептуальной идеи взят традиционный для государственной символики образ меча. Его схематичные, сильно стилизованные формы напоминают крест. Детали укрупнены, скульптурная форма рукояти меча, обрамленная дубовыми листьями, увенчана крупным навершием в виде развевающихся знамен. В центре перекрестья горит огромный горный хрусталь безукоризненной огранки. Монументальность памятника соответствует масштабности самого события. Меч имеет высоту 2,15 метра, а щит в диаметре — 95 сантиметров. Большие объемы и большие пространства памятника заполнены плотным набором знаковых изображений. Среди них символы духовной веры народа, в том числе древнеславянские языческие образы солнца (ярило), а также образы Христа и святого Георгия Победоносца. В фигурных картушах — знаменательные даты славных побед русского народа. В изобразительном ряде присутствуют аллегорические образы классического искусства — трубящие ангелы как символы гения Славы и Ника — богиня победы. Образ Матери России, изображение герба Советского Союза, форма щита из шестнадцати лепестков по числу союзных республик воспринимаются как дань памяти всему советскому народу, победившему в Великой Отечественной войне. Российский герб — знак настоящего времени и нынешнего поколения. Так язык старых и новых символов, сохраняющих для современных авторов и художников большую значимость и емкое содержание, выразил идею патриотизма и гражданственности.

Элементы национальной символики использованы при создании Мечей «Памяти и Благодарности» народам Франции,

Англии, Америки — стран, вошедших в антигитлеровскую коалицию. На мече Франции помещена старая национальная эмблема — галльский петух, символ боевого духа. Для английского меча избран один из самых почитаемых символов — образ святого Джорджа, поражающего змия не копьем, а мечом. Американским символом стала статуя Свободы. На всех мечах присутствует изображение советского ордена Победы, которым были награждены и главнокомандующие союзными войсками. Все мечи имеют надписи: «Народу Франции (Англии, Америки) благодарная Россия». Меч, предназначенный России, выполнен как уменьшенная копия меча Победы с Поклонной горы. Авторы проекта создания символических мечей, посвященных победе в Великой Отечественной войне, — А. И. Лохтачев, Н. В. Лохтачева, Г. И. Мануш. Авторский коллектив попытался решить одну из наиболее трудных художественных задач — совместить детализацию изобразительного ряда и масштабность общих форм, цельность основной композиции с богатым многообразием деталей. О неоспоримой удаче мастеров говорят высочайший уровень и качество изделий. Исполнение каждого элемента и его оформление рассчитано не только на общее восприятие памятника, но и на детальный осмотр. Особая тщательность и ювелирная отточенность, характерные для многих изделий Мастерских «ЛиК», проявились здесь особенно ярко.

В основе художественного оформления мечей-символов лежит традиционная златоустовская гравюра на металле. Если в обычной гравюре инструментом мастера служит стальная игла, в златоустовской гравюре рисунок наносят лаком с помощью кисточки, а детали догравировывают иглой по лаку. Затем производят травление, при котором не покрытая лаком поверхность подвергается химической обработке кислотами и щелочами. В этом процессе происходит совмещение искусства гравера и живописца. Именно поэтому так важно участие в работе профессионального художника. Так работали все мастера Златоуста начиная от Ивана Бушуева. Ныне технология усложнилась. Больше уделяют внимания дополнительной гравировке резцом контура рисунка после травления, что, естественно, повышает чистоту изображения. Используют не только кислотное, но и электрохимическое травление, а также совмещение обоих видов, что дает интересный результат. Травлением чаще оформляется фон орнамента. При этом различные материалы, будь то латунь или бронза, дают разные виды фонов. Применяется травление и для нанесения самого орнамента. Дополнительный эффект создается благодаря многоуровневому травлению. Мастерские «ЛиК» в совершенстве овладели секретами златоустовской гравюры на металле. Эта классическая техника лежит в основе оформления каждого изделия и содержит ряд необходимых операций: рисовку кистью, гравировку иглой по лаку, травление, гравировку резцом.

В традициях златоустовской художественной школы большое внимание уделяется цветовому решению изделия. Очевидно, мастера «ЛиКа», взяв за основу двухцветность памятников периода высокого классицизма, придерживаются строгой цветовой гаммы, состоящей из белого и желтого цвета. Белый цвет достигается никелированием, желтый — с помощью техники гальванического золочения. Строго говоря, в распоряжении художников «ЛиКа» четыре тона: при покрытии никелем травленой плоскости металла получается серый матовый фон, а гладкой плоскости — серый блестящий. Золочение также дает два тона — желтый матовый и блестящий. Одна из самых сильных сторон техники златоустовской гравюры на металле — полирование, доведение поверхности до зеркального состояния. В мастерских используют и ручную, и механическую полировку, доводя гладкость и блеск металла до совершенства.

Изделия, выполненные в «ЛиКе», с их традиционными способами художественной обработки и разнообразием применения златоустовской гравюры на металле, подчинены идее сохранения уникального ремесла, бесценного исторического наследия российских мастеров. Творческий коллектив стремится продолжить преемственность высокого качества и чистоты изделий, достигаемых благодаря мастерству исполнителей. Образцовые, эталонные памятники современного златоустовского искусства создаются художественными приемами, выполненными вручную и при отказе от тиражных технологий. Не случайно, высокой похвалой звучат отзывы отечественных и зарубежных специалистов и ценителей современного искусства: мастера «ЛиКа» безукоризненно владеют приемами художественной обработки металла.

Важнейшей производственной программой «ЛиКа» является создание художественного клинкового оружия. Во всем объеме предметов декоративно-прикладного искусства, выпускаемых мастерскими, половину составляют образцы оружия. Такой выбор приоритетного для Златоуста направления деятельности вполне оправдан и исторически закономерен. Истоки златоустовской художественной школы лежат в производстве художественного оружия, и все виды художественной обработки металла рождались, оттачивались и совершенствовались на оружейных образцах. Именно искусство изготовления художественного оружия способствовало развитию и процветанию самого города Златоуста как крупного промышленного и культурного центра.

За прошедшие годы в Мастерских «ЛиК» создано большое количество образцов художественного оружия. В настоящее время его выпуск составляет свыше 300 единиц в год. Для сравнения любопытно вспомнить известные исторические сведения об объемах производства Златоустовской оружейной фабрики в начальный период ее существования. За первые два года (1816–1817) ведущие мастера фабрики Вильгельм Николай Шаф с сыном Людвигом украсили немногим более 100 сабель и шпаг. В следующем году русские ученики Шафов за два месяца 1818 года украсили уже 300 сабель и шпаг. В 20-е годы XIX века, когда потребность в украшенном оружии была наиболее высокой в связи с празднованием юбилея Отечественной войны 1812 года, выпуск достигал 2500 штук в год. Такие объемы производства художественного оружия фактически удовлетворяли потребность всей страны в период активного использования холодного клинкового оружия.

В наше время роль и место предметов оружия в жизни общества кардинально изменились. Наиболее прочной традицией осталось изготовление украшенных сабель, шпаг, палашей в качестве дорогих подарочных экземпляров. В последние годы получило развитие и коллекционное оружие, которое рассматривается как памятник современного искусства. Авторы-создатели художественного оружия отмечают, что нынешние заказчики и коллекционеры становятся все более взыскательными, профессионально подготовленными, умеющими по достоинству оценить не только качество исполнения работы, но и оригинальность художественных замыслов, талантливость их воплощения. Златоуст (как никакой другой отечественный центр) с первых лет существования в нем оружейной фабрики в начале XIX столетия прославился созданием подарочного, коллекционного, наградного, призового, охотничьего и другого украшенного оружия. Эти богатейшие традиции, заложенные Иваном Бушуевым и другими основателями златоустовской школы художественного оружия, продолжаются стараниями многих современных мастерских, которым создание подарочных и коллекционных изделий дает возможность продемонстрировать в полной мере свои творческие и профессиональные возможности.

Среди современных лидеров златоустовской художественной школы Мастерские «ЛиК» сохраняют свой высокий авторитет не только в области исполнительского мастерства. «ЛиК» — это прежде всего лаборатория профессионального творчества. Инициаторы создания Мастерских «ЛиК», его организаторы и ведущие художники Александр и Нина Лохтачевы, Григорий Мануш определяют творческое кредо предприятия. За более чем десятилетний период работы создано значительное количество произведений декоративно-прикладного искусства. Особый интерес представляют концептуальные взгляды и накопленный опыт ведущих художников «ЛиКа» в области современного художественного оружия. Этот вид творчества в настоящее время переживает стадию своего становления, выработку теоретических подходов и оценочных критериев.

Для творческого коллектива «ЛиКа» неоспоримым является следующее. Чтобы постичь тенденции, проявляющиеся в современном оружейном творчестве, необходимо выявить их связи с тенденциями, господствующими в других направлениях искусства. Все виды творчества взаимодействуют между собой и оказывают друг на друга влияние уже потому, что преследуют единую цель — создание среды обитания современного человека. Художественному оружию отводится та же роль, что и любому другому памятнику искусства. Создание предметов художественного оружия подчиняется общим законам, по которым создаются произведения искусства, и в этом смысле не имеет каких-либо специфических особенностей. В то же время художественное оружие как произведение может рассматриваться в разных аспектах. Пластика оружейной формы то существует в качестве оригинального дополнения интерьера, то служит доминантой внутреннего убранства в качестве самодостаточного художественного произведения. Таковы традиции применения украшенного оружия как необходимого атрибута оформления разнообразных церемоний или как украшения дворцовых и усадебных интерьеров. Это специфическое прикладное предназначение художественного оружия как памятника искусства в современных условиях приобретает одно из наиболее актуальных и перспективных звучаний и самое главное — дает возможность и дальше развиваться этому виду творчества. Художественной задачей мастеров «ЛиКа» является создание современных оригинальных изделий, в том числе оружия, соответствующих эстетике сегодняшнего дня. Это не реставрация или копирование старых оружейных форм. Важно почувствовать переход от исторического опыта к современным образцам, но в то же время пытаться сохранить прославленные традиции златоустовского стиля. Вклад художников «ЛиКа» в дальнейшее развитие этого искусства состоит в том, что они отыскали у старых мастеров элементы ремесла, которые смогли использовать для создания новых современных художественных образов. И в этом опосредованном обращении к опыту прошлого, бесспорно, проявляется ориентация мастеров и художников «ЛиКа» на приемы классического декоративно-прикладного искусства.

Так, творчество прославленного Ивана Бушуева привлекает современных художников не только потому, что он является родоначальником златоустовской гравюры на стали. Он явился создателем своеобразной, неповторимой пластики отечественного (златоустовского) холодного оружия. Современные мастера «ЛиКа» изучают традиции авторского поиска пластических законов, характерных для классического златоустовского оружия. Необходимо ощутить его «скелет», найти ту свободу линий, которая составляет оружейную формообразующую пластику. Разработка формы холодного, особенно длинноклинкового, оружия становится одним из основных элементов в выборе средств его украшения. Данная концепция отражает характерные особенности творческого мышления А. И. Лохтачева. Он трансформирует художественные взгляды профессионального скульптора на оружейное искусство. Ему интересно не только исполнить оружейный образец в плоскости, но и попытаться и этот тип изделий соотнести с объемным пространственным образом. Третье измерение он выражает не через детали, а через всю концепцию произведения, создавая интересный изобразительный эффект. Такой подход объясняет особое пристрастие художника к работе с «длинномерами» — оружием крупных форм

5. Ножны охотничьего ножа. 1998

(сабли, палаши, мечи). Так, своеобразной визитной карточкой А. И. Лохтачева можно считать оригинальное решение сабли под названием «Офицерская». Совершенно отчетливо ощущается, как завораживает плавное движение изогнутых линий сабельного эфеса, как стремительно пытается вырваться из замкнутой формы широкий мазок лепестковых изгибов боковых дужек гарды, как естественно и логично обрамлены сабельные ножны изящными контурами крупных деталей оправы. В этой работе, несомненно, созданной под влиянием творчества И. Бушуева, видится попытка А. И. Лохтачева осмыслить архитектонику лучших произведений прославленного мастера. Не случайно, узнаваемые формы этой сабли были использованы для воссоздания скульптурного памятника И. Бушуеву, воздвигнутого на привокзальной площади Златоуста.

Одним из наиболее важных направлений современного искусства А. И. Лохтачев считает творческие поиски взаимосвязей разных видов декоративно-прикладного искусства, в частности, освоение архитектурно-пространственной среды с учетом возможностей интерьерных композиций. С этих позиций разрабатывались многие художественные проекты. Наиболее ярко они проявились при создании Щита и Меча Победы. Эти памятники несут не только огромную смысловую нагрузку, раскрывая авторское видение темы патриотизма. Они смогли занять почетное место в общем интерьерном решении торжественного вводного зала Славы мемориального комплекса на Поклонной горе.

Совершенно в иной манере спроектирован Александром Ивановичем Лохтачевым кинжал «Уреньга». Форма этого изделия не имеет аналога в традиционных златоустовских образцах оружия. Однако, используя приемы стилизации скульптуры малых форм, автор моделирует очертания оправы кинжальной рукояти и пытается создать с помощью собственного художественного языка образ неповторимой красоты самого протяженного в Челябинской области горного хребта Уреньга, у основания которого раскинулся Златоуст. К теме родной природы А. И. Лохтачев обращается постоянно. Одной из ранних работ был кинжал «Златоуст» (1994),

6. *Кинжал «Урал». 1999*

позже появились кинжалы «Урал» (1999), «Тайга» (2001). В 2002 году закончена одна из самых удачных работ этого замечательного мастера — оружейный комплект, состоящий из кинжала и двух ножей. Комплект посвящен горной цепи, состоящей из Большого, Среднего и Малого Таганая. В 1826 году П. П. Аносов, потрясенный красотой уральской природы близ Златоуста, написал: «Увидев в первый раз всю картину Таганая, я долго оставался неподвижным». Гордому величественному Уралу посвятил свою авторскую работу А. И. Лохтачев — кинжал и ножи, оправленные серебром и драгоценными камнями, с великолепными по красоте клинками из современного материала, выполненного по технологии дамасской стали.

В этих вещах авторская идея потребовала использования не только приемов формообразования, но и дополнительного подкрепления в виде активного изобразительного декора. Исторический опыт златоустовской оружейной школы заложил основы чуткого совмещения пластики общей формы предмета и его оформления. Будущий владелец златоустовского художественного оружия мог не только оценить красоту своеобразных оружейных форм, но и любоваться искусством гравюры с разнообразными изображениями, орнаментом, сюжетами.

Единство формы и содержания — отличительная черта многих памятников оружейного искусства Златоуста. Современные оружейные формы, созданные в Мастерских «ЛиК», приобрели тонкую изысканную декоративность благодаря творческой энергии и таланту главного художника мастерских Нины Владимировны Лохтачевой. В своей работе она стремится познать законы орнаментального искусства и продемонстрировать все многообразие этого мощного, одного из наиболее интересных в оружейном искусстве художественного приема, подчеркнуть его поистине неограниченные возможности. Стараниями Н. В. Лохтачевой сохраняется ярко выраженная стилевая особенность художественного почерка Мастерских «ЛиК» — увлечение орнаментом. Этот факт и важен, и интересен, так как среди современных создателей авторского оружия очень мало художников, которые бы специализировались в этой области, умели бы работать с орнаментом, сохраняя его гармонию, определенный строй и ритм в сложных, своеобразных оружейных формах. В изделиях «ЛиКа» орнаменту отводится совершенно особая роль. Он служит не только для обрамления сюжетных изображений. Во многих работах орнамент доминирует, превращаясь в основной мотив декора. Для орнаментики большинства изделий присущ крупный, отчетливо читаемый, свободно расположенный сочный рисунок. Композиционное построение рисунка рассчитано на сохранение достаточного объема свободного фона, проработка которого, как правило, подчеркивает некую монументальность узора. Основными мотивами орнамента являются стилизованные листья аканта, изогнутые лепестки и завитки, трехлепестник, розетки, фигурные рамки и щитки. Например, в декоративный рисунок ножа «Восточный» Н. В. Лохтачева включила свой любимый цветочный орнамент, который широко распространен в восточном искусстве. В одном из вариантов сабли «Офицерская» опробован прием контрастного сочетания золоченого крупного аканта и плотного переплетения мелких серебристых изогнутых завитков на углубленном матовом фоне. Бесконечное разнообразие и неповторяемость композиционного построения орнаментального декора является отличительной особенностью работ «ЛиКа». Большой интерес вызывают разработки Н. В. Лохтачевой вариантов характерных национальных орнаментов. Так, авторское прочтение восточного узора предложено для оформления своеобразной арабской формы кинжала типа джамбия. Мотивы узбекского орнамента украшают характерную узбекскую форму ножа типа пчак. Для воплощения художественного замысла художник использует весь богатый арсенал изобразительного ряда, традиционного для этого вида изделий, — геральдические символы, воинские атрибуты, мифологические и сказочные образы, изображения животных и др.

И наконец, развитие златоустовских оружейных традиций невозможно представить себе без необходимой практичности, утилитарности, функциональности любого образца оружия. Первые русские мастера Златоустовской оружейной фабрики начала XIX столетия жили и работали в то время, когда общая культура восприятия предмета оружия была иной. В России очень долго сохранялось особое, священное отношение к оружию, которое в общественном сознании имело глубокий символический смысл: оружие карало и убивало, защищало и охраняло, утверждало силу и могущество, демонстрировало власть, богатство и общественное положение. Очевидно, это понимание особого места предмета оружия в жизни общества способствовало тому, что оружейные мастера прошлого никогда не создавали украшенные оружейные сувениры или оружейные безделушки. Понятие оружейного сувенира пришло к нам совсем недавно, из традиций европейской культуры. Златоустовское украшенное оружие XIX века прославилось не только замечательной художественностью образцов, но и великолепными функциональными достоинствами. Безусловно, этому способствовала традиционно существовавшая на Златоустовской оружейной фабрике тесная связь процесса декорирования предмета со всем комплексом оружейного производства. Собственно говоря, сам цех украшенного оружия являлся лишь звеном в общей заводской цепи.

Значительное место в объеме художественных работ занимало оформление состоящих на вооружении образцов офицерского оружия — кавалерийских и пехотных сабель и шпаг, кирасирских и драгунских палашей, драгунских и казачьих шашек. Эти образцы были профессионально сконструированы и изготовлены в соответствии с боевыми требованиями. Для мастера Златоустовской оружейной фабрики, работающего над созданием украшенного оружия, вопросы надежной и удобной оружейной конструкции и рациональной технологии изготовления, качества клинковой стали и оптимальной формы рубяще-колющего действия оружия, были столь же близки, как и проблемы художественного творчества. Этот опыт промышленного оружейного производства строевого оружия был смоделирован мастерами и при работе с нестроевыми, произвольными образцами сабель, шпаг, палашей, шашек, кортиков, ножей. Соблюдался неписаный закон оружейного производства — красота декора, форм оружия, используемые художественные технологии и материалы должны лишь подчеркивать функциональные оружейные достоинства. Эту особенность развития оружейного искусства стремится учесть в своих творческих работах Г. И. Мануш. В своем лице он совмещает работу художника по проектированию образца оружия, его дизайнерского решения и возможности универсального мастера, умеющего выполнять любую технологическую операцию. Однако в его прочтении темы функциональности оружия на первом месте стоит взгляд современного художника, работающего в области оружейного творчества. Он обладает замечательным талантом отличного рисовальщика и графика. Используя свои широкие знания в области истории оружия, Г. И. Мануш является автором изобразительной концепции многих оружейных проектов. Ставя задачу использовать предмет оружия для выражения авторских художественных образов, он применяет весь арсенал приемов, наработанных традициями златоустовской оружейной школы. В отличие от оружейных художников прошлого Г. И. Манушу важно не просто украсить, оформить, декорировать образец холодного оружия. Главное внимание он уделяет вопросу гармонии внешних форм и декоративного оформления оружия. В этом, как считает художник, суть эстетики оружейного дизайна, уровень которого и предопределяет рабочие достоинства предмета оружия. Такой творческий подход продиктовал разработку и создание целой серии разнообразных охотничьих наборов, а также охотничьих гарнитуров, объединенных оригинальной разнообразной компоновкой. Например, по мотивам исторических образцов был спроектирован комплект «Былина», включающий тесак и нож. При этом в конструкцию ножен тесака с внешней стороны включена дополнительная полость для ножа. Разработки оригинальных оружейных комбинаций представляются весьма интересным и перспективным направлением. Они позволяют художнику и мастерам экспериментировать с пространством и плоскостью, взглянуть с дополнительной точки зрения на характерный строй, особую архитектонику оружейного предмета.

Не менее важна тематика оформления оружейных образцов определенного функционального назначения. Форма и изобразительный ряд должны создавать единый художественный образ. В выборе сюжетов художественного решения предмета оружия существовали сложившиеся многовековые исторические традиции. Мастера «ЛиКа» придерживаются этих классических канонов и в своих тематических разработках отдают предпочтение понятным и близким к назначению предмета оружия сюжетам.

Тема под условным названием «офицерское оружие» является важнейшей. В основе формообразования этой группы предметов лежит моделирование традиционных в XIX веке видов уставного офицерского оружия. В Мастерских «ЛиК» создали обобщенный стилизованный образец кавалерийской офицерской сабли, пехотной офицерской сабли, кирасирского офицерского палаша, морского офицерского кортика. Художественный ряд этих изделий построен на создании знаковой системы декора, передающего символический образ благородства и достоинства русского офицера. В рамках этой тематики уделено должное место и наградному, почетному, памятному оружию. Так же, как и другие художественные мастерские Златоуста, «ЛиК» активно развивает традицию изготовления памятных, юбилейных кортиков. Например, в серию адмиральских и офицерских морских кортиков включен кортик с использованием черного дерева. Он посвящен трагической гибели подводной лодки «Курск».

Создание авторского оружия, не регламентированного ни своей формой, ни декоративной разработкой, всегда представляло огромные возможности для творчества и свободного полета фантазии мастеров-оружейников «ЛиКа». С этой точки зрения вызывает интерес тема охотничьего оружия. Охоте посвящены традиционные охотничьи наборы разной комплектации, варианты охотничьих мечей и ножей, нож «Сокол», охотничий кортик «Олений» и др. Близкой для художников-«ликовцев» оказалась тема царской охоты, которая вдохновила на создание нарядных кортиков и ножей. Декоративное решение этих изделий построено на использовании изображений животных в обрамлении разнообразного по характеру растительного орнамента.

Одна из ранних работ Александра и Нины Лохтачевых — кинжал «Рюриковский», выполненный в 1993 году. Этот кинжал бережно сохраняется в выставочной коллекции и демонстрируется в ассортиментном кабинете Мастерских «ЛиК». Обратившись к страницам древнерусской истории, художники уже на первых этапах своей деятельности заявили еще об одной важной программной установке своего творчества.

Развивая тему древнерусских сказаний, в мастерских с увлечением создают многочисленные вариации тесака «Былина», ножа «Серебряное копытце», используя для выражения замыслов богатый орнаментальный ряд, набор различных материалов — кости, перламутра, цветных пород дерева, янтаря и драгоценных камней.

Особое внимание к восточному оружию — давняя традиция златоустовской оружейной школы. Истоки этого явления лежат в признании огромного вклада культуры Востока в историческое развитие оружейного искусства, в том числе холодного клинкового оружия. Ни одна из европейских культур не дала миру такого многообразия надежных и практичных, удобных и рациональных, разумных и устойчивых оружейных форм и технологий. В периоды наивысшего развития златоустовской оружейной школы XIX века местные мастера постоянно расширяли свой опыт благодаря изучению многовековых традиций восточных оружейников. Это изучение шло в разных направлениях. П. П. Аносов и его последователи посвятили многие годы раскрытию секретов и тайн восточного булата, сыграли большую роль в теоретическом и практическом освоении процесса получения высококачественных сталей. За два последних столетия тема булата, имеющего восточные истоки, получила еще одну историческую родину — Златоуст. Современные златоустовские мастера столь же уважительно относятся к традициям восточной культуры: национальным формам, системе декоративного оформления. Также не остается без внимания тема булата и дамасской стали. Художники «ЛиКа», осуществляя поиски общей стилистики современных изделий, стремятся найти наиболее удачное художественное решение в применении узорчатых клинков из дамасской стали. Один из первых вариантов — кортик «Уреньга», в котором использован гладкий, не украшенный дамасский клинок с волнистым узором. В одном из вариантов сабли «Восточная» осуществлена попытка визуального соединения художественного строя кованого узорчатого дамасского клинка и полированной рукояти, для чего на верхнюю части клинка насечена продольная серебряная орнаментированная полоска. Более традиционным и сложным является прием, использованный в кортике «Адмиральский», в котором пята клинка украшена золоченым ажурным растительным узором, выполненным в технике травления. Одной из последних разработок в этом направлении является использование нового металла — современного композиционного материала, выполненного по дамасской технологии. Производители назвали его «нержавеющий булат». Этот металл пошел на изготовление клинков для комплекта «Таганай» и шпаги «Парус». Он обладает великолепными декоративными качествами, изысканным узором и красивой цветовой тональностью. Однако авторы комплекта «Таганай» внесли дополнительный художественный штрих в оформление красивого дамасского клинка — золоченую сужающуюся орнаментальную полосу по центру, усилив вертикальную ось всего изделия.

Разработка каждой тематической группы требует от художников решения различных творческих задач. Однако в создании художественного оружия существуют приемы, соблюдение и профессиональное исполнение которых и предопределяет высокий уровень всего изделия. Методика обобщения и осмысления разнообразных творческих подходов продолжает оставаться главным стержнем деятельности художников «ЛиКа». Вот как, например, о композиционном соединении сюжета и орнамента рассуждает Г. И. Мануш. По его мнению, многие мастера удачно справляются с оформлением плоскостной поверхности клинка, но объемные детали оружия, имеющие сложную конфигурацию, зачастую грешат тем, что орнамент и сюжет существуют сами по себе. В своих эскизах и готовых предметах Г. И. Мануш постоянно предлагает разные варианты решения этой задачи, то затейливо вписывая сюжетное изображение в орнамент, то ограничивая его рамочными контурами. В этом смысле изучение исторического наследия оружейного искусства, считает Г. И. Мануш, служит безграничным источником для творческих находок. Так, в традициях украшения восточного оружия наиболее полно воплотилось сочетание национальных форм с изысканностью декора, в котором даже затейливость и красота восточного шрифта играет роль необычного, оригинального орнамента. Для современных создателей коллекционного оружия особый интерес представляет опыт златоустовских умельцев прошлых лет. Лучшие работы такого мастера, как И. Бушуев, можно назвать примером умелого соединения сюжета, орнамента

7. Палаш «300 лет Санкт-Петербургу» (фрагмент). 2001

и детальной проработки, единства основной композиции с богатым многообразием деталей, ни одна из которых не выпадает из ансамбля. Интересное художественное решение использовано на златоустовских ножах и кинжалах, выполненных в 1880–90-е годы. На оправы рукоятей и ножен были нанесены в рамочной окантовке — по образцу живописных полотен — реалистические изображения леса, уральских сопок, растительного и животного мира, пейзажей и панорам. Рамки имели разную конфигурацию и оставляли на изделиях значительные по площади гладкие поверхности. Этим сохраняется чистота рамочных контуров, и предмет не перегружается излишним декором.

Творческая составляющая деятельности Мастерских «ЛиК» продолжает развиваться. Художниками разработан богатый арсенал изделий, состоящий из более чем 120 новых оружейных образцов, в основе которых — 40 базовых сертифицированных моделей клинков. В число образцов входит длинноклинковое и короткоклинковое оружие: сабли, палаши, шпаги, шашки, охотничьи кортики и кинжалы, ножи, кортики офицерские и адмиральские, кортики лесничих, тесаки, национальные формы холодного оружия (мачете, джамбия, ятаганы), а также топоры.

Изготовлением оружия в «ЛиКе» занимаются две мастерские. Автор изделия — это создатель и разработчик идеи, ее проектировщик. В эскизе рисуется форма будущего изделия. При создании художественного образца важная роль отводится художественному совету, на коллективное обсуждение которого автор выносит изобразительную концепцию будущего изделия. Модельный мастер изготавливает базовую модель в пластилине и передает ее

8. Тесак и нож в ножнах «Былина». 2001

в мастерскую, где делают первый образец в материале. Здесь клинок, рукоять и ножны проходят полный объем слесарной, столярной работ, полировки и заточки клинка. На изготовление клинка идут высококачественные марки стали. Из этой мастерской выходят практически готовые изделия, но без декоративного оформления. Затем изделие поступает в другую мастерскую, где вновь разбирается. На этом этапе в работу включаются высококвалифицированные слесари-сборщики, полировщики, художники, граверы, закрепщики камней, которые при непосредственном участии автора, по его эскизам исполняют все необходимые художественные работы — гравюру на металле, никелирование, золочение, заключительные полировочные работы. Такая организация создания художественных изделий построена по принципу четкой специализации мастеров, каждый из которых наиболее профессионально выполняет свою задачу. Безусловно, эта производственная модель восходит к опыту Златоустовской оружейной фабрики.

В Мастерских «ЛиК» используют разные приемы воплощения нового художественного замысла. Для каждой удачной модели художник стремится продумать несколько вариантов оформления. Богатая авторская фантазия помогает создать большое разнообразие художественных изделий. Один из примеров — изящный нож «Серебряное копытце». Он имеет несколько вариантов оформления за счет применения разных материалов — кости, перламутра, цветного дерева, в каждом из которых достигается новый декоративный эффект. Несколько иной прием использован теми же авторами (Г. И. Мануш, Н. В. Лохтачева) при создании ножа «Царская охота» и ножа «Охотничий». Оба изделия выполнены по единому художественному эскизу, но смысловые акценты, отраженные в названиях изделий, авторы попытались передать различными декоративными приемами. Обе работы посвящены теме охоты в русской истории, и поэтому форма ножей и их декоративное оформление традиционны и близки по стилистике практичным, надежным и прочным русским охотничьим ножам. Характер орнамента один и тот же, в обоих случаях внимание привлекает нарядное, крупное плетение оригинальной золоченой оправы длинных кожаных ножен. При этом в одном случае гладкий дамасский клинок и небольшая крестовина на рукояти подчеркивают традиции функционального применения ножа на охоте, а в другом — изящный орнамент на клинке и нижней гайке рукояти придает дополнительную роскошь этому ножу. Примером интересного авторского художественного проекта является создание сабли «Восточная» в двух вариантах на базе одной и той же модели клинка восточной формы (работа творческого коллектива в составе А. И. Лохтачева, Н. В. Лохтачевой и Д. А. Лохтачева). Авторы проекта стремятся передать свое видение восточной красоты с ее непременными атрибутами изысканности, нарядности, богатства. Два варианта сабли отличаются применением разных материалов и разным цветовым решением. В первом варианте использован клинок, выкованный из традиционного для Востока материала — дамасской стали с крупным волнистым узором. Этот ценный клинок из дамаска оправлен в нарядную оправу, соединяющую в себе золотой ажурный орнамент и блеск белой зеркально отполированной поверхности. Изогнутая рукоять исполнена из светлого дерева, что закрепляет общую теплую тональность цветового решения сабли. Декоративное убранство дополняют граненые топазы, горный хрусталь, цирконы изысканных оттенков.

Соединение в оружии металла и камня — сравнительно новый для художников «ЛиКа» элемент художественного решения. Наиболее глубокие традиции применения драгоценных камней имеет восточное оружие. Используя этот опыт, художники «ЛиКа» часто помещают крупный камень в завершение рукояти. Например, исключительной красоты голубой топаз «Титаник» весом 248,8 карата украшает нож «Восточные мотивы». Благодаря талантливому ювелиру-граверу и огранщику В. В. Блинову огранка драгоценных и полудрагоценных камней, уральских самоцветов занимает все более заметное место при оформлении коллекционного оружия. Во втором варианте сабли «Восточная» камню также отведена большая роль. На изготовление рукояти пошел замечательной красоты агат серо-синего перелива. Его дополняют крупные безукоризненной огранки топазы и цепочки мелких лазуритов и аметистов, украшающих оправы рукояти и ножен, выполненных из драгоценного металла — серебра. Строгое цветовое решение этой сабли создает впечатление особой тонкой изысканности, лишенной яркого мишурного блеска.

В оформлении обеих сабель использован любопытный художественный прием. Всю поверхность внешней стороны ножен украшает широкая орнаментальная полоса с растительным узором, которая композиционно разделена на части не только с помощью накладных фигурных обоймиц с кольцами для крепления поясной портупеи, но и разным техническим приемом исполнения орнамента. Устье и наконечник ножен украшены продольными накладками с прорезным ажурным орнаментом, а средняя часть ножен продолжает этот узор, выполненный в технике травления. Применение просечного ажурного узора, с одной стороны, еще более усложнило общий декоративный строй сабли, с другой — внесло элемент изящности и легкости.

Поиски новых художественных решений предопределили новое направление в работе с авторским оружием — более активное использование серебра и, соответственно, обращение к новым приемам обработки этого металла: чеканке, штамповке, резьбе. Даже никелирование в последнее время все чаще заменяется покрытием серебром. Освоение нового материала началось в 1997 году. Сначала художники и мастера повторили в серебре некоторые изделия, выполненные в латуни: кортики «Адмиральский» и «Корабельный», охотничий меч, кортики «Царская охота». Следующим этапом стало более активное сочетание серебра с драгоценными камнями, удачно дополняющими в особо ценных образцах общее цветовое решение. Так был выполнен изысканный и тонкий по художественному замыслу оружейный комплект «Таганай», в котором авторы отразили свое восхищение природой Южного Урала. Сабля «Восточная», отмеченная дипломами Всероссийского конкурса ювелиров на приз «Признание Петербурга» (2002 и 2003), блестяще продемонстрировала возможности современных мастеров Златоуста. Одна из последних работ — шпага «Гардемарин», посвященная 300-летию Санкт-Петербурга, предложила совершенно новое авторское прочтение оружейных форм с использованием драгоценных металлов и камней. Удивительно легкая пластика серебра вдохновила художников на создание современного фантазийного образца, наделенного необычайно яркой выразительностью. Возможно, это новое авторское направление, разработанное А. И. Лохтачевым, получит дальнейшее развитие и оформится в значительное явление современного декоративно-прикладного и ювелирного искусства.

Думается, не случайно именно творческая разработка темы Петербурга, проникнутая особым уважением к этому великому городу, послужила толчком для появления нового, оригинального художественного взгляда. Эта тема занимает совершенно особое место среди художественных проектов Мастерских «ЛиК». Столичное искусство и культура оказывали огромное влияние на развитие златоустовской художественной школы на протяжении всей ее истории. В Санкт-Петербурге находился Департамент горных и соляных дел, непосредственно ведавший Златоустовской оружейной фабрикой, и оружейные мастера, граверы, художники чутко следили за вкусами петербургских законодателей моды. В столицу посылали лучшие художественные работы и получали оценки, от которых зависело дальнейшее развитие златоустовского оружия. Историческая взаимосвязь между Петербургом и Златоустом сказалась и в том факте, что крупнейшую в России частную оружейную фабрику, проработавшую в столице до 1914 года, основал в 1823 году ведущий художник Златоустовской оружейной фабрики В. Н. Шаф. Очевидно, что историческая память тесных творческих и деловых контактов Петербурга и Златоуста сохраняется и поныне. Одним из излюбленных изделий многих современных златоустовских оружейных мастерских является кортик, посвященный Петру Великому. Свою интерпретацию этого изделия в 1996 году предложили и художники «ЛиКа». Однако Александр и Нина Лохтачевы не остановились на уже апробированном образце, а значительно расширили образный ряд этой тематики. Оригинальные авторские замыслы воплотились в легко узнаваемые скульптурные элементы кортиков «Фонари Санкт-Петербурга» и «Урны Санкт-Петербурга». Еще более насыщен художественный язык палаша «300 лет Санкт-Петербургу» (автор Н. В. Лохтачева). Строгая форма изделия заполнена богатым орнаментальным узором, подчеркивающим центральные изобразительные сюжеты знаковых архитектурных памятников Петербурга. Знаменитые на весь мир силуэты зданий Адмиралтейства, Главного штаба на Дворцовой площади, Биржи на Васильевском острове с Ростральными колоннами, Александровская колонна на Дворцовой площади составляют основу изобразительного ряда. Чередующийся мотив с очертаниями чугунных решеток Летнего сада выполняет роль рамочного контура в композиционном построении декора. В центральной части ножен — изображение фигуры ангела с крестом на шпиле Петропавловского собора и надпись: «Красуйся, град Петров, и стой неколебимо, как Россия». В оформлении клинка удачно использована оригинальная авторская находка — изображение гравюры петровского времени с панорамой старого города. Портрет Петра Великого, его монограмма, герб Санкт-Петербурга, российский государственный герб органично дополнили изобразительные символы, посвященные легендарному городу. Сияние крупного ограненного голубого камня на головке рукояти палаша завершает насыщенное декоративное убранство изделия.

Работа по созданию уникальных памятников продолжается. В наше время происходит бурное развитие российского оружейного творчества. Значительно оживился рынок современных образцов художественного оружия. Появилось большое число талантливых художников-оружейников. Любители и ценители современного художественного оружия получили возможность сделать свой выбор среди большого разнообразия изделий. В этом контексте не может остаться не замеченным подвижнический труд художественного коллектива златоустовских Мастерских декоративно-прикладного искусства «ЛиК», с честью выполняющего задачу сохранения высокой культуры златоустовского оружейного искусства. Оружейные изделия мастеров «ЛиКа» широко представлены на российских и международных выставках, по достоинству оценены отечественными и зарубежными специалистами. За выдающийся вклад в культурное и экономическое развитие России в 2003 году Мастерские «ЛиК» получили главную всероссийскую общественную награду — «Российский национальный Олимп».

Е. В. Тихомирова

9. Сабля «Восточная» (с фрагментами). 2003

10. **Палаш «300 лет Санкт-Петербургу» (с фрагментами). 2001** ►

Награжден дипломом I степени Всероссийского конкурса ювелиров «Признание Петербурга» и признан лучшим украшением года в номинации «Ювелирные произведения, посвященные 300-летию Санкт-Петербурга» (Санкт-Петербург, 2003).

Красуйся, град Петров, и стой неколебимо, как Россия...

САМОДЕРЖЕЦ ВСЕРОССИЙСКИЙ · ОСНОВАТЕЛЬ РУСКОГО ФЛОТА В 1696 Г. ·

300
САНКТ ПЕТЕР БУРГ

11. Трости. 2000

12. Палаш «Морской». 2000

14. **Сабля «Восточная»: авторский вариант (с фрагментами). 2001** ►
Лауреат Всероссийского конкурса ювелиров «Признание Петербурга» (Санкт-Петербург, 2002).

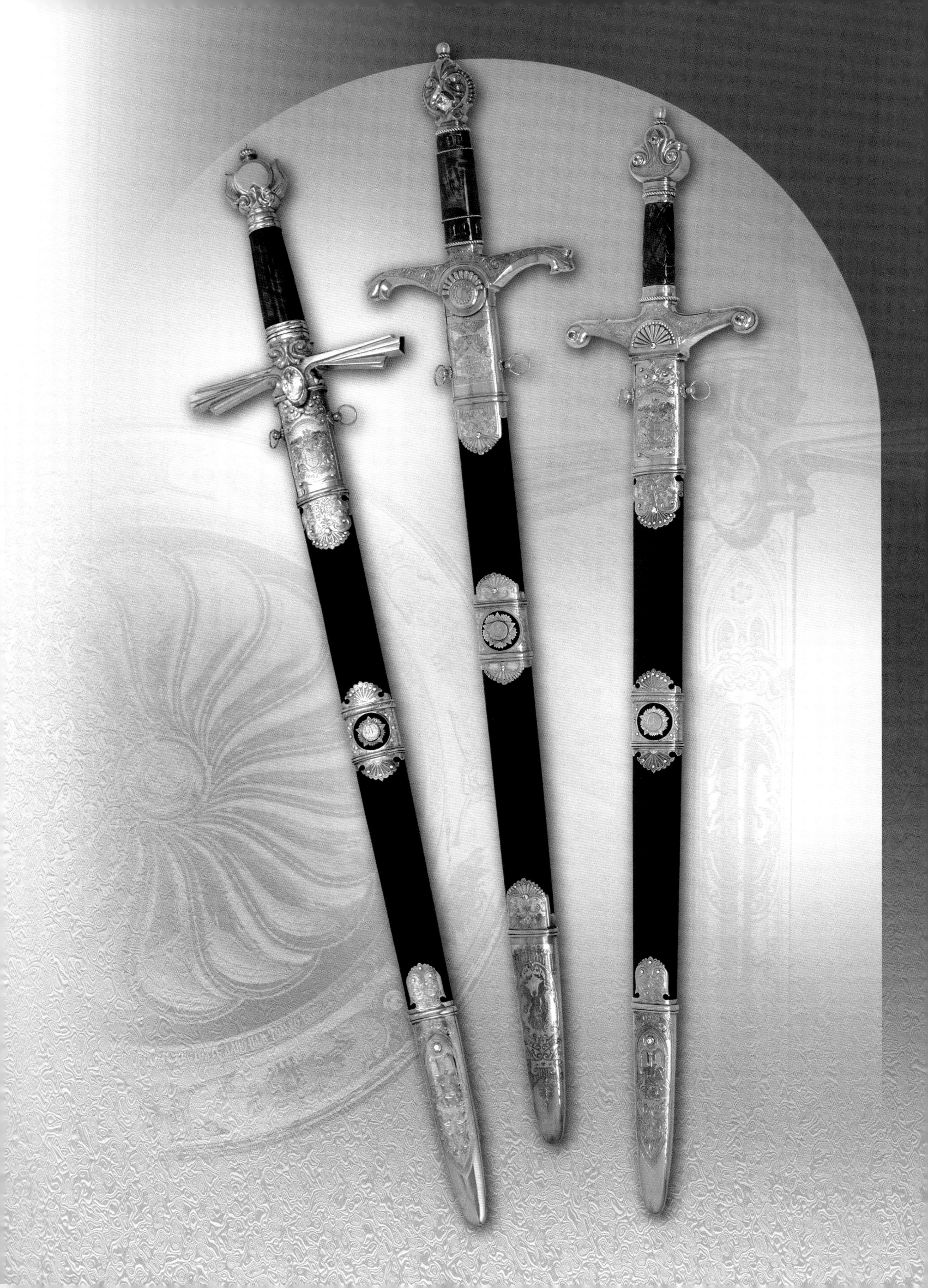

15—17. ***Мечи «Памяти и Благодарности народам стран-участниц антигитлеровской коалиции». 1995***
Созданы к 50-летию Победы в Великой Отечественной войне и вручены президентом России Б. Н. Ельциным Биллу Клинтону, Франсуа Миттерану и Джону Мейджору.

18. ***Щит Победы. 1995***
Создан к 50-летию Победы в Великой Отечественной войне.

19. ***Меч Победы. 1995***
Создан к 50-летию Победы
в Великой Отечественной войне.

ПОБЕДА
ПОБЕДА
РОССИЯ

20. Меч «Памяти и Благодарности народу Америки». 1995

ПОБЕДА
1945
ПОБЕДА

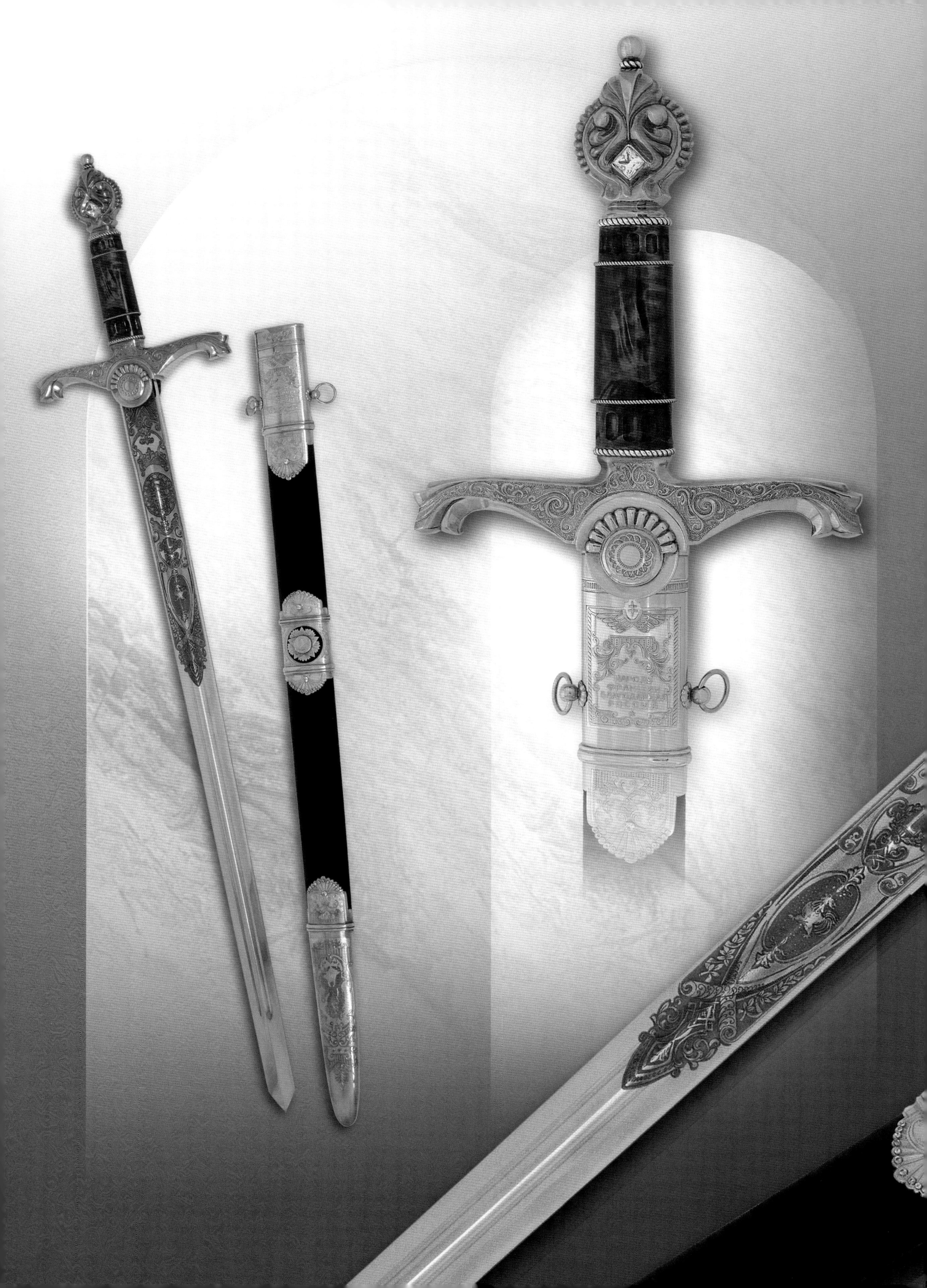

21. Меч «Памяти и Благодарности народу Франции». 1995

22. Меч «Памяти и Благодарности народу Англии». 1995

23. Сабля «Офицерская» (с фрагментами). 1997 ►

24. Тесак и нож в ножнах «Диана». 2002
Награжден дипломом выставки народных промыслов России (Тюмень, 2003).

25. Тесак и нож в ножнах «Былина». 2001
Отмечен дипломом выставки холодного оружия в Ханты-Мансийске (2001).

26. Эскиз тесака с двумя ножами. 1998

27. Нож «Мотивы Востока». 2002
Удостоен диплома 6-й выставки
«Клинок – традиции и современность»
(Москва, 2002).

28. Кортик «Олений». 1999

29. Эскиз кортика «Олений». 1996

30. **Шпага «Парус» (с фрагментами). 2003**
Экспонировалась на Международной ювелирной выставке «Junwex» (Санкт-Петербург, 2003).

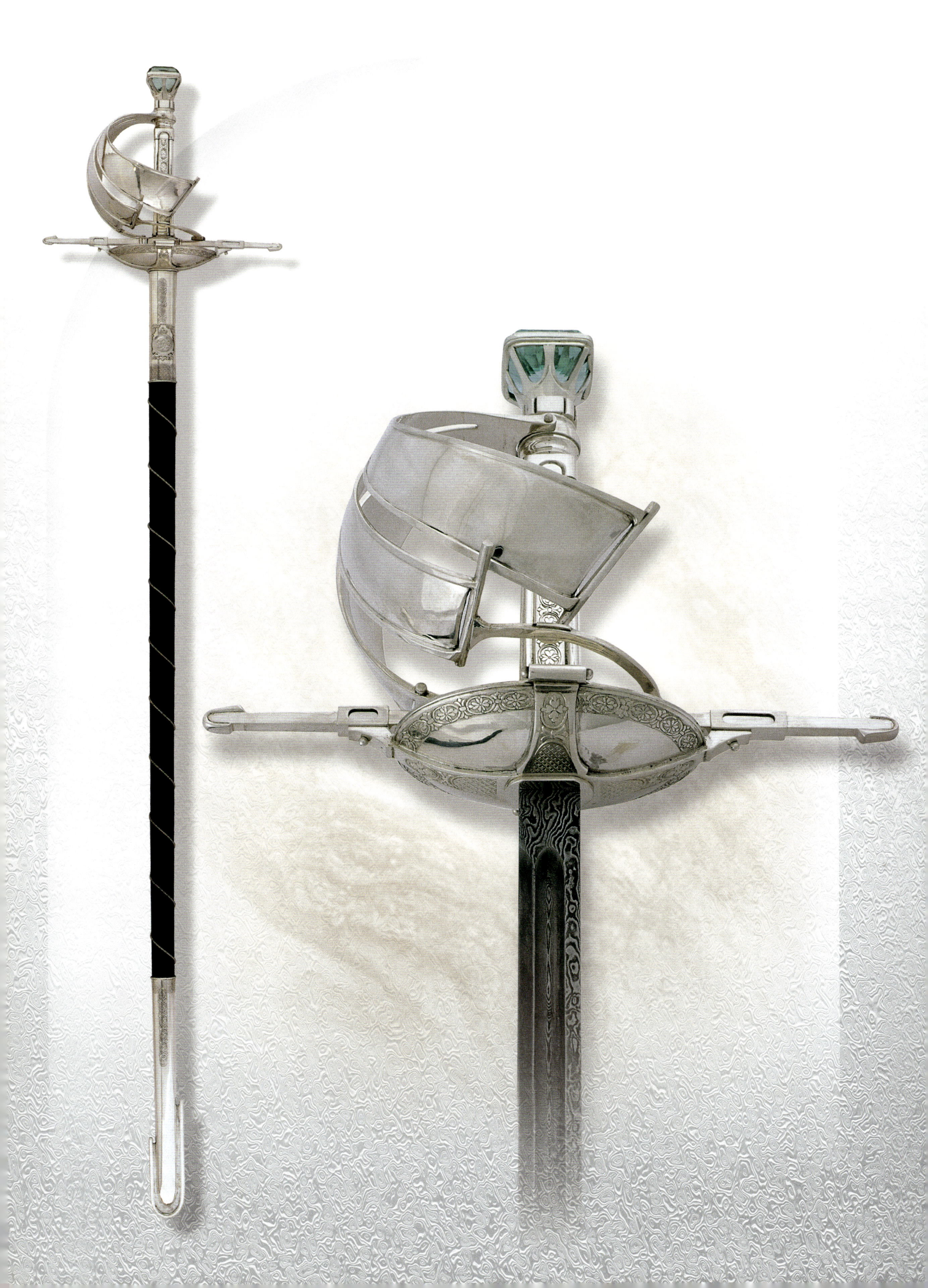

31. ***Сабля «Офицерская». 1997***

32. ***Сабля «Офицерская»: авторский вариант (с фрагментом). 2001***
Экспонировалась на выставке «Государственные символы России» (Москва, 2002). Мастерские «ЛиК» награждены дипломом за создание высокохудожественных произведений с изображением государственных символов Российской Федерации.

33. ***Сабля роты почетного караула. 1995***

34. ***Сабля (с фрагментами). 2000*** ►

Экспонировалась на 6-й выставке
«Клинок — традиции и современность»
(Москва, 2002).

35. Кинжал «Жар-птица». 2001

36. Нож «Золотое руно». 2000

37. Кинжал «Крест». 1994

38. Кортик «Адмиральский» (слева),
тесак и нож в ножнах «Диана», кинжал «Крест». 1998–2002

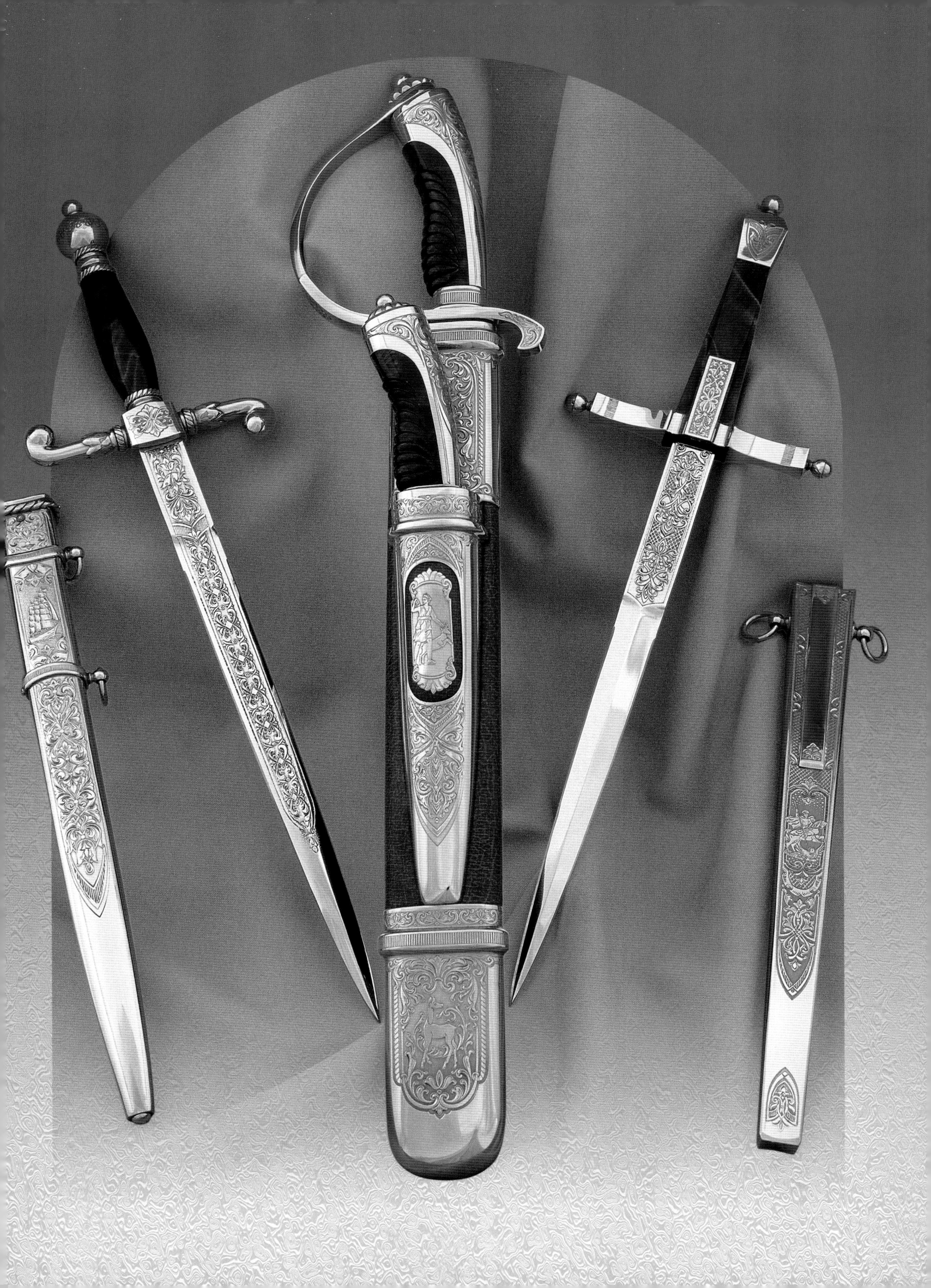

39. Кортик «Царская охота». 2001

40. **Кортик «Морской». 1999**

41. **Кортик «Адмиральский». 2000**
Экспонировался на Московской международной ювелирной выставке «Ювелир-2001».

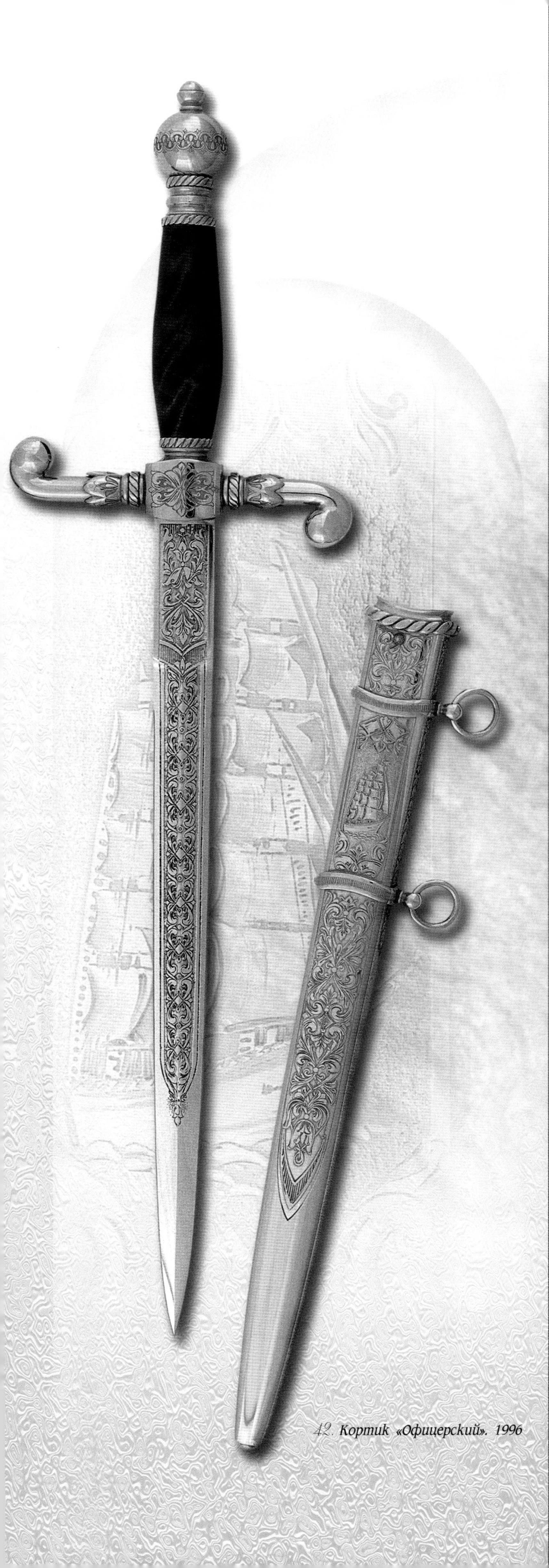

42. Кортик «Офицерский». 1996

43. *Нож «Русский» (с фрагментами). 2003*

44. *Нож «Сокол» (с фрагментами). 2001*

ЗЛАТОУСТ

45. Эскиз охотничьего ножа. 1998

46. Нож охотничий. 1998
Экспонировался на Московской международной оружейной выставке (Москва, 1998).

47. Нож «Охота». 2002

48. **Нож охотничий. 2001**

Отмечен дипломом выставки «Российские охотничье-спортивные товары-2001». Мастерские «ЛиК» награждены дипломом за художественно-дизайнерские разработки изделий.

49. Нож охотничий. 1998

50–53. *Ножи охотничьи «Серебряное копытце». 2001–2002*
Награждены дипломом выставки «Дни Челябинской области в Москве» (2001).

54. Эскиз длинного охотничьего кортика. 2002

55. Меч малый охотничий. 2001

56. Кортик охотничий. 2002

57. **Нож «Северный». 1994**

58. **Кинжал «Джамбия». 2002**

Отмечен дипломом на конкурсе ювелирных изделий «УралЮвелир» (Екатеринбург, 2002).

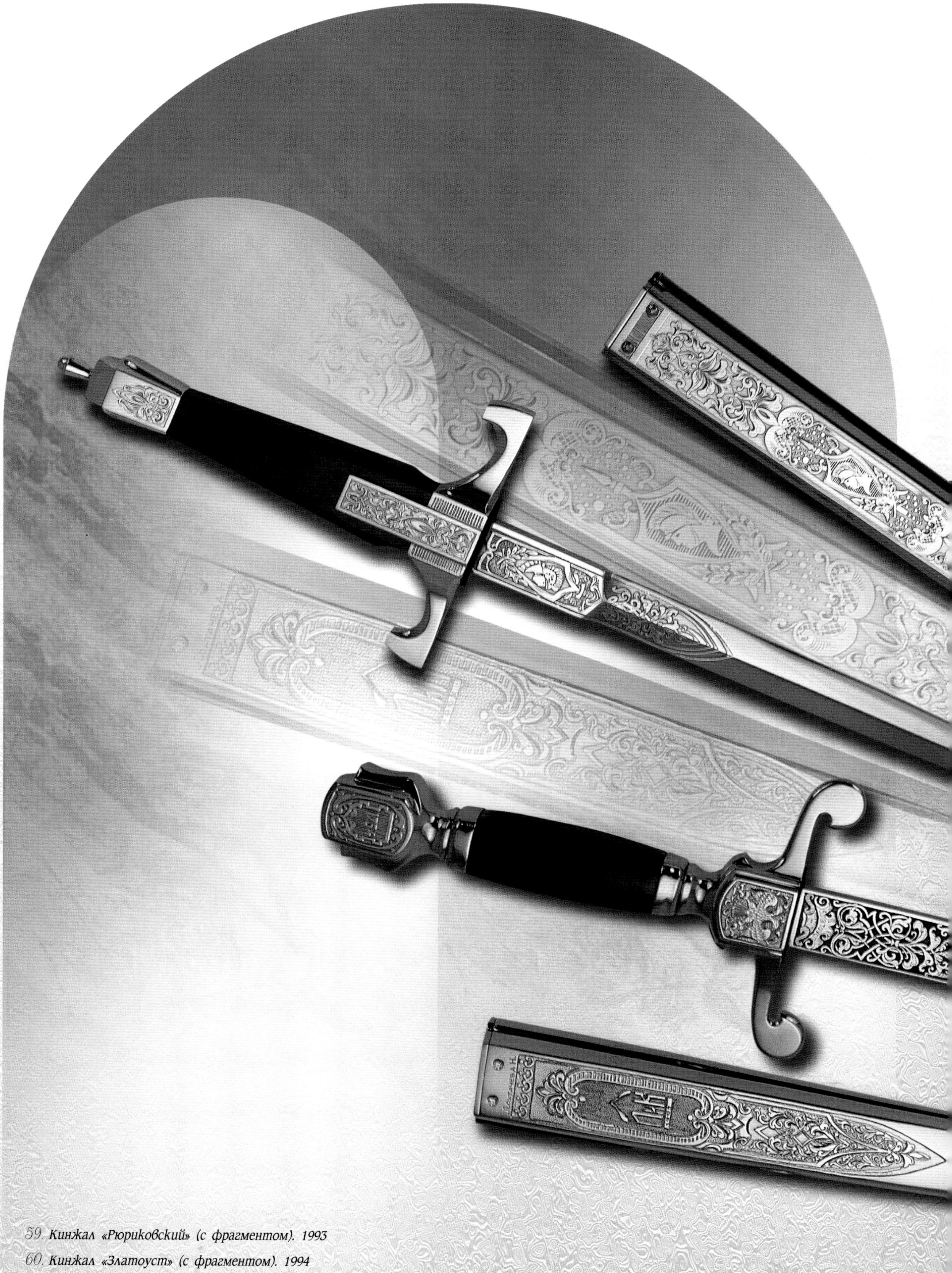

59. Кинжал «Рюриковский» (с фрагментом). 1993

60. Кинжал «Златоуст» (с фрагментом). 1994

61. Эскиз ножа «Волна». 1997

62. Нож «Волна». 2001

63. Нож «Морозко». 1998

64. Нож «Пчак». 1998

65. Нож «Восточный». 2002

66. ***Набор охотничий: нож и кинжал. 1998***
Отмечен дипломом III степени и признан лучшим украшением года в номинации «Художественное оружие» на Всероссийском конкурсе ювелиров «Признание Петербурга» (Санкт-Петербург, 2001).

67. *Кинжал «Уреньга». 1999*

68. **Кинжал «Урал».** 1999

За серию кинжалов, посвященных уральской природе, Мастерские «ЛиК» в 2000 году получили благодарность Министерства культуры РФ за творческий вклад в развитие российской культуры.

69. *Эскизы кинжала. 1999*

70. Кинжал «Урал». 2003

71. Нож «Сокол». 2003

*72. **Кортик «Фонари Санкт-Петербурга». Из серии «Петербургские мотивы». 1997***
Экспонировался на выставке «Народные художественные промыслы России» на Нижегородской ярмарке (Нижний Новгород, 1997).

*73. **Кортик «Урны Санкт-Петербурга». Из серии «Петербургские мотивы». 1997***

74. Кортик «Петр Великий». 1996

75. Кортик «Корабельный». 2000

76. Кортик «Памятный». 2001

77. **Кортик «Наградной». 1994**
Победитель конкурса в номинации «Среднеклинковые украшенные изделия» в рамках 5-й выставки «Клинок – традиции и современность» (Москва, 2001).

Златоуст 99г

78. *Эскиз ножа. 1999*

79. ***Кортик «Морской». 1996***
Экспонировался на выставке «Народные художественные промыслы России» на Нижегородской ярмарке (Нижний Новгород, 1996).

80. Набор «Таганай»:
кинжал и два ножа. 2000–2002
Экспонировался на 6-й выставке
«Клинок – традиции
и современность» (Москва, 2002).

81. Нож «Восточные мотивы». 1998

82. **Шпага «Гардемарин» (с фрагментами). 2003** ►

Экспонировалась на Международной ювелирной выставке «Junwex» (Санкт-Петербург, 2003).

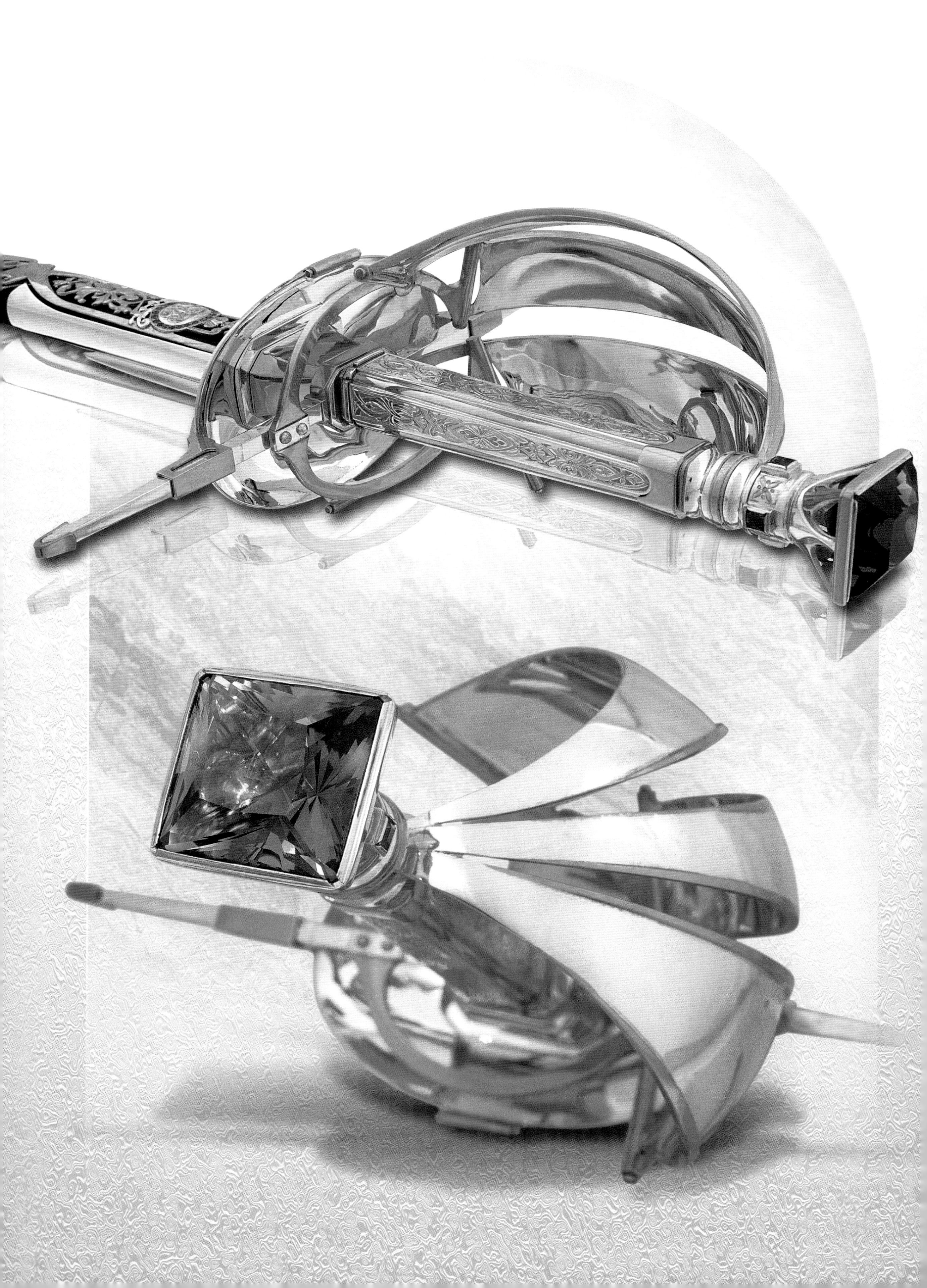

ДЕКОРАТИВНО-ПРИКЛАДНОЕ И ЮВЕЛИРНОЕ ИСКУССТВО

Общепризнанным отечественным лидером в производстве эксклюзивных предметов роскоши, выполненных в дорогой и чрезвычайно эффектной технике златоустовской гравюры на металле и представляющих современное авторское искусство, в настоящий момент являются широко известные в России и за рубежом Мастерские декоративно-прикладного искусства «ЛиК». Этому обстоятельству способствует целый ряд факторов социальной, экономической, культурной жизни России и в первую очередь — появление в стране респектабельного покупателя и не ограниченного в денежных средствах заказчика «высокого» эксклюзива; долгое и стабильное присутствие «ЛиКа» на свободном российском рынке художественной продукции, что свидетельствует о конкурентоспособности фирмы; грамотно выстроенная рекламно-маркетинговая политика, предусматривающая обязательное участие Мастерских в многочисленных российских и зарубежных выставках, ярмарках, форумах, конкурсах. Очень важным является и то обстоятельство, что Мастерские «ЛиК» расположены в городе Златоусте — традиционном центре русской художественной культуры. Мировую славу этот «город мастеров» на Южном Урале получил в первой половине XIX века, после того как была построена специальная фабрика по изготовлению холодного (белого) оружия при Златоустовском чугунолитейном заводе. Два талантливейших русских мастера-оружейника Златоустовской фабрики Иван Бушуев и Иван Бояршинов явились основоположниками оригинальной школы златоустовской гравюры на металле. Главной программной целью Мастерских декоративно-прикладного искусства «ЛиК» с самого начала их существования как независимого частного художественного объединения (с 1990 года) и до настоящего момента является сохранение и дальнейшее развитие культурных традиций Уральского региона как одного из крупных художественных центров Русского государства. Пожалуй, к числу важнейших задач, имеющих для коллектива Мастерских декоративно-прикладного искусства «ЛиК» нравственный, морально-этический и гражданский аспект, можно отнести создание в родном городе позитивной творческой атмосферы. Златоуст с давних времен славится школой высокого мастерства, позволяющей создавать оригинальные произведения русского декоративно-прикладного искусства. Именно школа в широком понимании этого слова может сыграть роль своеобразного «духовного катализатора», позволяющего обеспечить высокий уровень образования, культуры, профессионализма в любой сфере деятельности, и внимательное, чуткое отношение к такому виду художественной практики, как златоустовская гравюра на металле, являющейся национальным достоянием России.

Художники и мастера «ЛиКа» бережно сохраняют не только лучшие традиции самобытного оружейного искусства Златоуста, но и технологию производства дорогостоящих изделий из металла в технике златоустовской гравюры. Ими принципиально используются только характерные для старого Златоуста основные методы художественной обработки металла: рисовка кистью и гравировка иглой по лаку, травление, гравировка резцом, золочение и полировка. В работе художников умело синтезируются западноевропейские, восточные и национальные русские традиции декоративной обработки изделий из металла и в то же время присутствует бесконечное количество различных авторских новаций, проявляющихся в оригинальном дизайне предметов, орнаментальном декоре внешней поверхности, в использовании новых материалов, фантазийной огранке драгоценных и полудрагоценных камней, которые становятся неожиданным эстетическим акцентом привычных в своей утилитарной функции предметов. Ассортимент выпускаемых фирмой эксклюзивных произведений декоративно-прикладного и ювелирного искусства, среди которых можно видеть художественное холодное оружие, культовые изделия, ювелирные украшения, гобелены, камины, предметы сервировки праздничного стола и кабинетные вещи функционального назначения, великолепно демонстрирует широкий спектр художественных и технико-технологических приемов их высококачественной отделки, присущих искусству Златоуста XIX—XX веков.

Имена ведущих художников Мастерских декоративно-прикладного искусства «ЛиК» Александра, Нины и Дениса Лохтачевых и Григория Мануша стали известны российской общественности благодаря выполнению беспрецедентных в истории современной России заказов Правительств Российской Федерации и города Москвы по созданию к 50-летию

Победы во Второй мировой войне «Щита и Меча Победы» и четырех Мечей «Памяти и Благодарности» народам стран антигитлеровской коалиции. Фактом большой духовной значимости и историческим моментом в политической и культурной жизни страны стало воссоздание серебряной Дарохранительницы для храма Христа Спасителя. Поручение этого сложного и ответственного задания коллективу Мастерских «ЛиК» явилось заслуженным официальным признанием его первенства среди других художественных фирм

83. Ларец «Жемчужная свадьба». 2002

84. Кубок «Балет». 2001

и организаций, работающих сегодня в сфере декоративно-прикладного искусства, и позволило обрести почетный статус «Патриарших мастерских».

В результате успешной интеллектуально-творческой и организационно-производственной деятельности, направленной на создание новых и оригинальных видов изделий в художественном стиле и технике старинной златоустовской гравюры на металле, неустанных поисков экономически рентабельных и перспективных направлений в работе фирмы, Мастерские декоративно-прикладного искусства «ЛиК» имеют в числе своих заказчиков не только правительственные, церковные и крупные частные структуры и общественные организации, но и наиболее состоятельных покупателей и коллекционеров среди соотечественников. Подтверждением высокого авторитета и художественного рейтинга фирмы на современном российском рынке произведений декоративно-прикладного искусства на государственном уровне становятся строки из письма Министерства культуры Российской Федерации на имя организатора и генерального директора фирмы А. И. Лохтачева, в которых отмечается «высокое мастерство и виртуозность» художников и мастеров данного коллектива, подчеркивается их общий вклад как в «духовное возрождение Отечества», так и в «возрождение декоративно-прикладного искусства и народных промыслов России».

За 13 лет своего существования Мастерские «ЛиК», возглавляемые скульптором Александром Лохтачевым, реализовали в своей художественной практике восемь самостоятельных направлений авторской деятельности, из которых приоритетными являются производство художественного холодного оружия и вещей так называемого «партикулярного» характера, под которыми подразумеваются уникальные предметы дорогого, элитного обихода. В разряд последних попадают изделия для

85. Кубок «Золотое кольцо России». 2002

украшения интерьера и сервировки праздничного стола, подарочно-сувенирные и памятные предметы, призы и конкурсные награды. Основная продукция фирмы изготавливается из стали (клинковое оружие и трости), латуни, мельхиора, нейзильбера (предметы интерьерно-кабинетного назначения, сервировки стола и др.) с декоративной отделкой в традиционной технике златоустовской гравюры на металле. В художественном решении многих камерных вещей впервые для такого типа предметов используются ранее нехарактерные для искусства Златоуста уральские самоцветы. Наиболее перспективными разработками последних лет может считаться выпуск (с 1997 года) предметов культа, подарочных и памятных изделий и ювелирных работ, в том числе и украшений из дорогих материалов с традиционным для них широким применением ограненных камней и природных минералов. При изготовлении вещей этого ассортимента используются драгоценные металлы высокой пробы (серебро 925°, золото 999,9° и 750°) и иногда в сугубо эксклюзивном варианте — платина. Из ювелирных и поделочных камней наиболее часто используются благородные топазы, горный хрусталь, цитрины, цирконы, яшма, агаты, нефрит, малахит. Все полудрагоценные камни имеют великолепную фантазийную огранку, выполненную на высоком профессиональном уровне руководителем мастерской ювелирной огранки, художником-ювелиром и дизайнером Владимиром Блиновым.

В сферу художественно-производственных интересов Мастерских декоративно-прикладного искусства «ЛиК» входит выполнение индивидуальных заказов по изготовлению широко востребованных в наши дни каминов с применением уральского камня и гобеленов со светской и религиозной тематикой. С 1995 года мастерской гобелена руководит опытный художник-прикладник, участник многих художественных выставок Юрий Егаков.

Вся продукция Мастерских «ЛиК», входящая в прейскурантный перечень, представляет собой уникальные, коллекционные или эксклюзивные авторские изделия и относится к области современного декоративно-прикладного искусства. Эстетизм и необыкновенная красота златоустовской техники гравированного металла, высочайший уровень технического исполнения предмета в материале, использование ювелирных камней и драгоценных металлов при сохраняющейся функциональности многих вещей делают их модной и дорогостоящей принадлежностью современных частных и общественных интерьеров — кабинетов, гостиных залов, курительных комнат, домашних библиотек, солидных офисов, государственных апартаментов.

За последнее десятилетие ведущими специалистами и мастерами «ЛиКа» был создан целый ряд замечательных, можно сказать эксклюзивных, предметов быта и интерьера.

Впервые функциональные изделия (столовые приборы, подносы, ларцы, подсвечники и шкатулки) появились в ассортименте продукции Златоустовской фабрики в 1840-е годы при ее директоре Павле Петровиче Аносове (1797—1851), выдающемся инженере, металлурге и изобретателе. Характер златоустовской гравюры на металле в те годы отмечен сильным воздействием стилевых тенденций историзма, пришедшего на смену классицизму и придающего большое значение чисто орнаментальным композициям. В гравюре стали преобладать растительный и геометрический узоры.

86. Ювелирные камни фантазийной огранки. 1998

Изделия украшались пышным орнаментом типа «арабески», крупным рисунком из раковин, картушей, цветов, листьев аканта и лавра, на поверхности многих предметов появилась красочная древнеславянская вязь. С 1860-х годов в орнаментальную композицию вводятся памятные надписи и надписи-наставления назидательного характера, в декоре широко используется вошедший в моду восточный узор. В последней четверти XIX — начале XX века выпуск утилитарных бытовых предметов приобрел массовый характер, при этом все изделия фабрики имели ярко выраженную художественную индивидуальность.

Мастера Златоуста снова вернулись к сюжетному изображению, широко практиковавшемуся в период классицизма. Однако теперь, под влиянием «русского» стиля и его производного «неорусского» варианта, оно трактуется в реалистическом духе народной графики и представляет собой типичный лубок. На изделиях также появляются изображения российских полевых цветов и трав, колосья, ягоды земляники. Авторская фантазия особенно щедро проявляется в украшении таких необходимых в повседневной жизни предметов, как ножи и вилки. Ручки этих предметов декорируют цветочным узором, а на лезвиях ножей можно видеть лесные и сельские пейзажи, сценки охоты и рыбной ловли, изображения животных и птиц. Рисунки во многих случаях сопровождаются пословицами и поговорками типа «Мошна да тюрьма дадут ума», «Хлеб да вода — молодецка еда», «Бог на небе, царь на земле». Если столовые приборы делали на заказ, то в фигурном картуше помещали имя владельца. Использование гальванического метода никелирования, серебрения и золочения делало все стальные вещи похожими на дорогие серебряные изделия, которые были рассчитаны исключительно на вкусы зажиточного городского покупателя.

В советскую эпоху, начиная с 1920-х годов, в ассортимент фабрики вошли сувенирные топорики, рамки для фото, корпуса для часов, настенные тарелки и панно, настенные вешалки, полочки, портсигары и спичечницы, разнообразные лоточки, винные наборы и перекидные настольные календари. В 1930—1960-е годы при декорировании стальных предметов использовались как традиционные темы (орнаментальные композиции, пейзажи, изображение животного мира и охоты), так и кардинально новые, соответствующие духу эпохи — индустриальные пейзажи, сценки из колхозной жизни, советские символы, а также сюжеты по мотивам русских сказок и былин. В 1970—1980-е годы производство художественных изделий было поставлено на поток, и златоустовская гравюра на металле, постепенно упрощаясь в своих художественно-технических решениях и теряя статус предмета декоративно-прикладного искусства, была низведена до уровня рядового сувенира. Не погибнуть окончательно этому виду национального искусства удалось благодаря существованию в 1980-е годы в цехе № 16 на участке гравюры творческой группы художников, которые сумели сохранить уникальные художественные традиции своих предшественников и технику златоустовской гравюры на металле. Диапазон их творчества был достаточно широким, а владение профессиональными приемами стояло на уровне мировых критериев. Эти мастера выполняли оригинальные настенные панно с мягкими, лирическими пейзажами, подносы, лотки, охотничьи ножи и столовую утварь со сложным сюжетным и орнаментальным декором. Авторские работы этих мастеров не только демонстрировались на различных выставках декоративно-прикладного искусства, но и являлись предметом государственного (музейного) и частного коллекционирования.

Среди молодых художников, пришедших на фабрику в середине 1970-х годов и проработавших все последующее десятилетие, одной из наиболее талантливых и перспективных считалась Нина Лохтачева. Будучи активной продолжательницей художественных традиций Ивана Бушуева и Ивана Бояршинова, она являлась автором многочисленных разработок орнаментальных декоров и тематических рисунков, которые ею же были воплощены в материале, то есть в художественных изделиях из стали. В 1990 году Нина Лохтачева стала одним из трех организаторов первой частной художественно-производственной мастерской (ТОО «ЛиК») в городе Златоусте. С тех пор пройден долгий и многотрудный путь творческих свершений, поисков, находок.

87. Поднос «Птица Сирин» (слева), дарница, подносы декоративные. 1994—2000

Показательным моментом в деятельности Мастерских «ЛиК» всегда являлось именно успешное освоение новых видов материала при сохранении традиционной технологии златоустовской гравюры на металле, что позволило существенно расширить ассортимент художественно-бытовой и интерьерной продукции, особенно за счет объемных форм предметов. Переход в производстве заказных авторских работ эксклюзивного характера с подверженной коррозии жесткой стали на более мягкие и стойкие к негативным воздействиям атмосферы латунь и белые металлы, в том числе и серебро, явился подлинным «ноу-хау» ведущих художников фирмы: представителей старшего поколения — Александра и Нины Лохтачевых, Григория Мануша и младшей генерации в лице Дениса Лохтачева. Им же принадлежит удачная идея изготовления целого ряда авторских изделий — кубков, подносов, сервировочных предметов и других вещей — из драгоценного металла с использованием ювелирных камней. Выполненные из серебра со вставками из драгоценных камней, эти предметы попадают в разряд изделий современного ювелирного искусства при том, что они украшены в непривычной для современного покупателя дорогой и элитной технике златоустовской гравюры.

Каждый из ведущих художников Мастерских декоративно-прикладного искусства «ЛиК» — яркая творческая индивидуальность, имеющая собственную культурную программу, оригинальное видение художественной реализации творческих задач и их претворения в жизненную практику. Так, Александр и Денис Лохтачевы, Григорий Мануш неустанно трудятся над созданием новых видов и форм художественных изделий, проявляя в этом большую индивидуальную фантазию. В работу они вкладывают весь свой творческий потенциал и талант художника-творца, применяя в решении каждого нового предмета, его общем дизайне найденный ими пластический модуль. Александр Лохтачев, помимо создания многих таких чисто прикладных вещей, как подарочные кубки, подсвечники, сервировочные столовые предметы и подносы, работает и как скульптор, являясь автором произведений станковой пластики. Ему также принадлежит создание серебряного Гран-при «Ангел» для Государственного академического Малого театра (подарен Ярославскому драматическому театру им. Ф. Г. Волкова). Монументальное мышление позволило художнику создать очень лаконичный и торжественно-строгий образ или, вернее, символ духовной и преображающей силы искусства в виде фигуры ангела. Одновременно за счет использования позолоченного декора во внешней отделке подставки-постамента приз приобретает значение драгоценной вещицы и прекрасного образца камерной ювелирной пластики.

В художественном решении многих кубков («Балет», «Праздничный» и др.), ведерок для льда и шампанского («Столичное»), подносов («Российский»), как и многих других вещей, присутствует проверенная временем традиционная архитектоника формы, диктующая строгий ритм и геометрическую упорядоченность графического декора с включением российской символики (гербы), тематической миниатюры и изящного по чистоте рисунка растительного орнамента.

Одним из наиболее удачных и изысканно красивых интерьерных предметов, выполненных Александром Лохтачевым в соавторстве с Ниной и Денисом Лохтачевыми, является светильник-минора с символическим названием «Кристалл». Художественная форма этого ритуального предмета умело объединяет скульптурность и ажурную графику конструкции, поверхность которой украшена тонким орнаментом в виде виноградной лозы и изображением двух скорпионов. Одно из традиционных значений образа скорпиона — это преодоление смерти, которое подчеркивает историческое понимание миноры как мирового дерева, расцветающего «высшим светом» и достигающего своими лучами Бога. В предписании Книги Исход рекомендуется делать эти древнейшие светильники из драгоценного металла: «Он весь должен быть чеканный, цельный, из чистого золота». Минора «Кристалл», несмотря на то что выполнена из латуни, благодаря изысканной красоте техники златоустовской гравюры, использующей никелирование и золочение в художественной отделке предмета, воспринимается как драгоценное изделие декоративно-прикладного искусства. Фантазия мастеров, создавших этот предмет, подсказала нестандартное для такого светильника использование декоративного камня

88. Поднос «Букет» (фрагмент). 2000

89. ***Ларец. 2002***

90. ***Браслет «Снежная королева». 2002***

ручной огранки — горного хрусталя, который чрезвычайно усиливает художественную выразительность вещи. Существующая с 1999 года в Мастерской «ЛиК» технология работы с серебром позволяет изготавливать на заказ миноры из серебра и драгоценных камней. Использование в производстве целого ряда заказных и подарочных изделий дорогих металлов и камней дает возможность объективно рассматривать эти предметы не только как функциональные вещи дорогого быта или престижного интерьера, но и как образцы ювелирного искусства. Ювелирное дело как область приложения творческих способностей чрезвычайно занимает мысли всех трех организаторов и ведущих художников Мастерских «ЛиК». Возможности этой новой сферы деятельности активно стимулируют желание создавать подлинные произведения искусства или, выражаясь словами Нины Лохтачевой, порождают «творческую неуспокоенность и потребность выразиться в духовном плане», служат «гарантией будущих новых изделий и работ». Серьезной заявкой на лидерство в создании ювелирных эксклюзивных изделий стала композиция «Манхэттен» в виде двух крестов, выполненная Александром и Денисом Лохтачевыми и посвященная трагическим событиям в США 11 сентября 2001 года.

Эта памятная композиция сделана из дорогостоящих материалов — платины, золота, редкой формы природного жемчуга, бриллиантов и сапфиров. Впервые она была представлена на суд зрителя в сентябре 2002 года в Атриуме отеля «Балчуг Кемпински Москва» в рамках Международного салона украшений, предметов искусства и подарков класса люкс «Luxury-2002», организованного Золотым клубом (Москва). Нестандартная для ювелирного искусства тема и необычность ее ассоциативно-образного решения в материале привлекли внимание посетителей Салона и вызвали одобрительную реакцию со стороны законодателей высокой ювелирной моды.

Любое искусство вырастает из ремесла, из желания и умения человека создавать полезные и красивые вещи. И как это ни парадоксально, ремесленная основа составляет творческую базу искусства. Доскональное знание материала, технических особенностей его обработки, понимание его возможностей для выражения собственных художественных идей является краеугольным камнем креативного мышления художника. Металл всегда был одним из ведущих, классических материалов декоративно-прикладного искусства, который широко использовался в художественном творчестве и дал мировой культуре истинные шедевры человеческого мастерства. Наша жизнь и быт наполнены разнообразными предметами из металла, которые создаются художниками-профессионалами.

Одним из таких художников, увлеченных делом сохранения и дальнейшего развития искусства златоустовской гравюры на металле, является Нина Лохтачева. В ее творчестве орнаментальное украшение вещи занимает одну из главных позиций. Постоянной заботой Н. В. Лохтачевой как руководителя мастерской гравюры на металле всегда остается стремление создать новые варианты орнамента, оставаясь в рамках художественной традиции Златоуста. Содержанием большинства ее авторских композиций является искусно выполненный орнаментальный декор. В его основе лежит мотив растительного побега, который предстает в каждой новой вещи в виде стилевой реминисценции античных, древнерусских, восточных орнаментальных систем. Спецификой любого орнамента является повторяемость одинаковых элементов узора, и поэтому в задачу художника входит придумывание новых вариантов рисунка, создание каждый раз новой комбинации декоративной композиции.

94. Ключ символический. 1997

И другой, не менее важный, момент заключается в точном перенесении созданного орнамента из эскизного варианта, выполненного на бумаге, на плоскость объемного металлического предмета. Н. В. Лохтачева, в совершенстве владея сложной техникой златоустовской гравюры и обладая высоким уровнем мастерства, создает удивительно эффектные по художественному впечатлению и виртуозной технике исполнения образцы самых разных изделий, декорированные различными видами растительного орнамента.

Приоритет конструктивно-пластического решения художественных предметов ни в малейшей мере не снижает значения изобразительных элементов во внешней отделке изделий. Кроме того, в таком виде искусства, как златоустовская гравюра, создание вещи не мыслится без использования орнамента и сюжетных изображений, играющих не только эстетическую роль, но и имеющих гражданско-патриотическое, нравственное и национально-пафосное звучание. На многих подарочно-сувенирных, памятных и сервировочных изделиях, выполненных Ниной Лохтачевой, можно видеть различные композиции с изображениями сказочных птиц (поднос «Птица Сирин»), небольших компактных натюрмортов в духе старых златоустовских лубков (ведерко для шампанского), гербов (поднос «Саратовская губерния»), архитектурных объектов и памятников (декоративные кубки, поднос «175 лет Государственному академическому Малому театру России»). Некоторые ранние вещи начала 1990-х годов были выполнены художницей в классической манере златоустовской сюжетной миниатюры, например подарочный поднос «Ехал Ваня...».

Тонкий гравированный узор, словно старинное вологодское кружево, покрывает поверхность авторских изделий Нины Лохтачевой, поражая хитросплетением гибких линий и тугих завитков, тщательно выстроенного цветочного орнамента. Великолепны по своей художественной завершенности и высокому техническому уровню исполнения такие подносы, как «Подарочный», «Букет», поднос с изображением двух обручальных колец, входящий в комплект «Свадебный». Подарочные наборы «Винный», «Пиала», «Праздничный», декоративные тарелки, чайно-кофейные комплекты, подсвечники и многие другие вещи в исполнении Н. В. Лохтачевой всегда оригинальны по своему орнаментальному характеру, который всегда меняется даже при повторном заказе на изготовление одного и того же тредмета. Интересным ретроспективным решением отличается подарочный поднос «Поставщик двора Его Императорского Величества», выполненный художницей в духе русской старины. Его центральную часть украшает гербовая композиция с двуглавым царским орлом и лентой с «жалованной» надписью. В возрождении старинной традиции производства дорогих художественных предметов быта и интерьера большая заслуга лично Нины Лохтачевой и возглавляемого ею творческого коллектива Мастерских декоративно-прикладного искусства «ЛиК». Высокий уровень профессиональной подготовки, глубокое знание технологических особенностей златоустовской гравюры и постоянное желание пробовать себя в разных аспектах творческой деятельности позволили ей разработать необычную серию женских ювелирных украшений из латуни и серебра, образцы серебряных мужских портсигаров. Эти предметы, украшенные растительным декором в классической манере исторических ретростилей XIX века, являются данью уважения и памяти русским мастерам серебряных и золотых дел и ювелирным фирмам старой России.

Как известно, для Златоустовской оружейной фабрики с середины XIX века был характерен выпуск таких бытовых вещей, как шкатулки и ларцы, украшенные в технике гравюры. В наши дни широкую популярность снова приобрели многие утилитарные предметы кабинетного назначения. Эти, на первый взгляд, сугубо бытовые аксессуары часто играют важную роль художественной и эстетической доминанты в организации интерьеров современного городского жилища. Поэтому немалую долю в ассортименте Мастерских «ЛиК» имеет производство именно ларцов и шкатулок из латуни и серебра с использованием уральских самоцветов, жемчуга и полудрагоценных камней.

Это направление по созданию дорогих заказных предметов камерного характера в деятельности фирмы курирует один из ее основателей Григорий Мануш. Руководитель и главный художник мастерской художественной обработки камня и изготовления каминов, он является автором многих эскизных проектов различных предметов декоративно-прикладного и ювелирного искусства, в том числе ларцов и шкатулок, кабинетных письменных наборов. Оригинальной конструкцией и нестандартным внешним видом отличаются не только вышеназванные вещи, но и настольные часы для мужских кабинетов, рамки для фото, настольные зеркала. В дизайне форм и декоре этих необходимых в повседневной жизни человека функциональных вещей чувствуется сознательная многодельность и мужская логика архитектурного мышления их автора и создателя. Используя различные элементы архитектурного характера в конструкции предмета, Г. И. Мануш выстраивает в четкую композиционную схему всю декоративную отделку каждого конкретного изделия. Результатом подобного художественного решения, например в изготовлении шкатулок и ларцов, несмотря на кажущуюся сложность их дизайна, становится особая, присущая только изделиям Мастерских «ЛиК» выразительность формы предмета. Именно это подчеркивает его необычность и выделяет из среды подобных вещей.

Для усиления эстетической функции и положительного зрительного восприятия в производстве камерных предметов кабинетного назначения Г. И. Мануш широко применяет яшму и малахит, накладные металлические детали (клейма с изобразительной символикой, ажурные накладки со вставками из прозрачных ограненных или кабошонами камней, различные гербы и монограммы). Сложный позолоченный растительный декор, выполненный с восточной пышностью по эскизам Н. В. Лохтачевой, служит необходимой дорогой отделкой металлической поверхности и окончательно делает настольные часы или

92. Эскиз настольных часов. 1996

93. Ювелирная композиция «Манхэттен». 2002

ларец драгоценным предметом обихода. Напротив, письменные приборы в исполнении Г. И. Мануша отличаются изысканной простотой и лаконичностью художественного замысла. В них максимально выявляется красота и благородная текстура уральского камня. Все металлические детали предельно функциональны и выполняют исключительно формообразующую роль. В работе с металлом этого художника привлекает в первую очередь возможность художественного осмысления его возможностей, пластичность и конструктивные особенности, позволяющие создать авторское произведение искусства. Постоянный творческий поиск и желание соответствовать требованиям времени, высокий уровень технического исполнения в каждом изделии — таково жизненное и профессиональное кредо этого замечательного мастера авторского искусства.

В начале XXI века на фоне постоянно появляющихся новых синтетических материалов и хай-тековских технологий изделия из металла не утратили своего важного значения художественных предметов, способных к эстетико-культурным преобразованиям предметного мира современной цивилизации. Более того, именно в вещах из металла наиболее отчетливо чувствуется тенденция современной материальной культуры, направленной на создание и существование в быту дорогих заказных произведений декоративно-прикладного искусства в авторском исполнении. Подобного рода ситуация хорошо известна в истории искусства первой половины XX века. Например, в период между двумя мировыми войнами всеобщее развитие в странах Европы и Америки получило производство бытовых и интерьерных предметов элитного характера, одновременно имевших высокий статус произведений декоративно-прикладного искусства. Все они создавались талантливыми профессиональными художниками в частных студиях или мастерских из самых дорогих и экзотических материалов с применением старинных дорогостоящих техник в модной эксклюзивной манере ар деко. На российском рынке антиквариата эти стильные вещи высоко ценятся, особенно знатоками и любителями искусства, за свою непредсказуемую оригинальность, конструктивистский дизайн, фантазийность и блестящую технику исполнения в дорогих природных материалах.

Художники и мастера «ЛиКа» напряженно ищут свой творческий и стилевой канон в контексте златоустовских традиций XIX–XX веков, вырабатывают общий для объединения авторский почерк, постоянно экспериментируют в области художественного конструирования предметов быта и проектирования нового эстетического облика самых разных изделий интерьера. На этом пути они добились самого высокого успеха и признания, и именно это стимулирует к дальнейшим творческим поискам и прорывам. Высокая требовательность к себе и большая ответственность за сохранение и дальнейшее развитие искусства родного города не позволяют творческому коллективу «ЛиКа» останавливаться на достигнутых результатах. Напротив, на его плечи возложена сложная и благородная задача глубоко духовного осмысления и переложения на современный язык декоративно-прикладного искусства всего комплекса сохранившихся художественных традиций в области обработки металла. Мастерские декоративно-прикладного искусства «ЛиК» выполняют сегодня важную миссию постепенного возрождения забытых в нашей стране за последние 85 лет традиций производства и существования в жизни респектабельных слоев общества откровенных предметов роскоши – дорогих заказных вещей самого широкого профиля, ювелирных изделий, предметов сервировки и украшения обеденного стола и сувениров авторского исполнения, способных удовлетворить самые высокие притязания и подарить радость соприкосновения с настоящим искусством.

З. А. Малаева

94. Ведерко для льда «Столичное». 1996
95. Поднос «Российский». 1995–1996

96. **Поднос «Россия». 1995–1996**

Мастерские «ЛиК» награждены дипломом за создание высокохудожественных произведений с изображением государственных символов РФ.

97 *Набор «Пиала». 1999*

Отмечен дипломом за изготовление уникальных произведений, посвященных 1000-летию города Казани (Казань, 2003).

98 *Кубок «Лето». 1998*

99 *Набор для чая. 1999*

100. Набор для вина «Праздничный». 2002

101. Набор для чая. 1996

102. Набор для вина «Величальный». 1999

103. Набор для вина «Очарование» (с чарками). 2001

104. Поднос «Северное сияние». 2000

105 Набор для вина «Северное сияние»: подсвечник, два кубка, блюдо (с фрагментом). 2001

106 Набор «Юбилейный». 1998

107 Поднос «Ехал Ваня...». 1991 ►

г. Златоуст. 1992

108. Кубок «Торжество». 2002

109. Набор «На посошок» (с фрагментом). 1998

110. Поднос «Свадебный» (слева), дарница, поднос «Букет» (с фрагментом). 1997–2000

111 Поднос «Птица Сирин». 1994

112, 113. Подносы декоративные с цветочным орнаментом. 1991–1992

114. Поднос декоративный. 2003

115. Эскиз набора для шампанского. 1997

СОВЕТ ДА ЛЮБОВЬ
ЗЛАТОУСТ 90

116 Эскиз подарочных кубков, свадебных блюд и канделябра. 1999–2002

117 Декоративный предмет «Артефакт XXI века». 1996

118. Поднос подарочный «Саратовская губерния» (с фрагментом). 2002

119. Колокольчик настольный. 2003

САРАТОВСКАЯ ГУБЕРНИЯ
КРАСНЫЙ ПАРТИЗАН · ЛЫСЫЕ ГОРЫ · МАРКС · НОВОУЗЕНСК · НОВЫЕ БУРАСЫ · ОЗИНКИ · ПЕРЕЛЮБ · ПЕТРОВСК · П.СВЕТЛЫЙ · ПУГАЧЕВ · РОВНОЕ · РОМАНОВКА · РТИЩЕВО · САМОЙЛОВСКИЙ · САРАТОВСКИЙ · СОВЕТСКИЙ · ТАТИЩЕВО · ТУРКИ · ФЕДОРОВСКИЙ · ХВАЛЫНСК · ШИХАНЫ · ЭНГЕЛЬС · АЛЕКСАНДРОВ-ГАЙ · АРКАДАК · АТКАРСК

124, 125. Кубки «Каменный пояс Урала». 2003
126. Эскизы подарочных кубков. 2001

ЛК Златоуст 2001г

127 Эскизы праздничных кубков. 2000

128. Кубок подарочный. 1999
129. Кубок «Театральный». 2001

130. Кубок «Балет». 2001
Гран-при для Международного конкурса артистов балета и хореографов.

131. Кубок «Москва – Санкт-Петербург» (с фрагментом). 2003

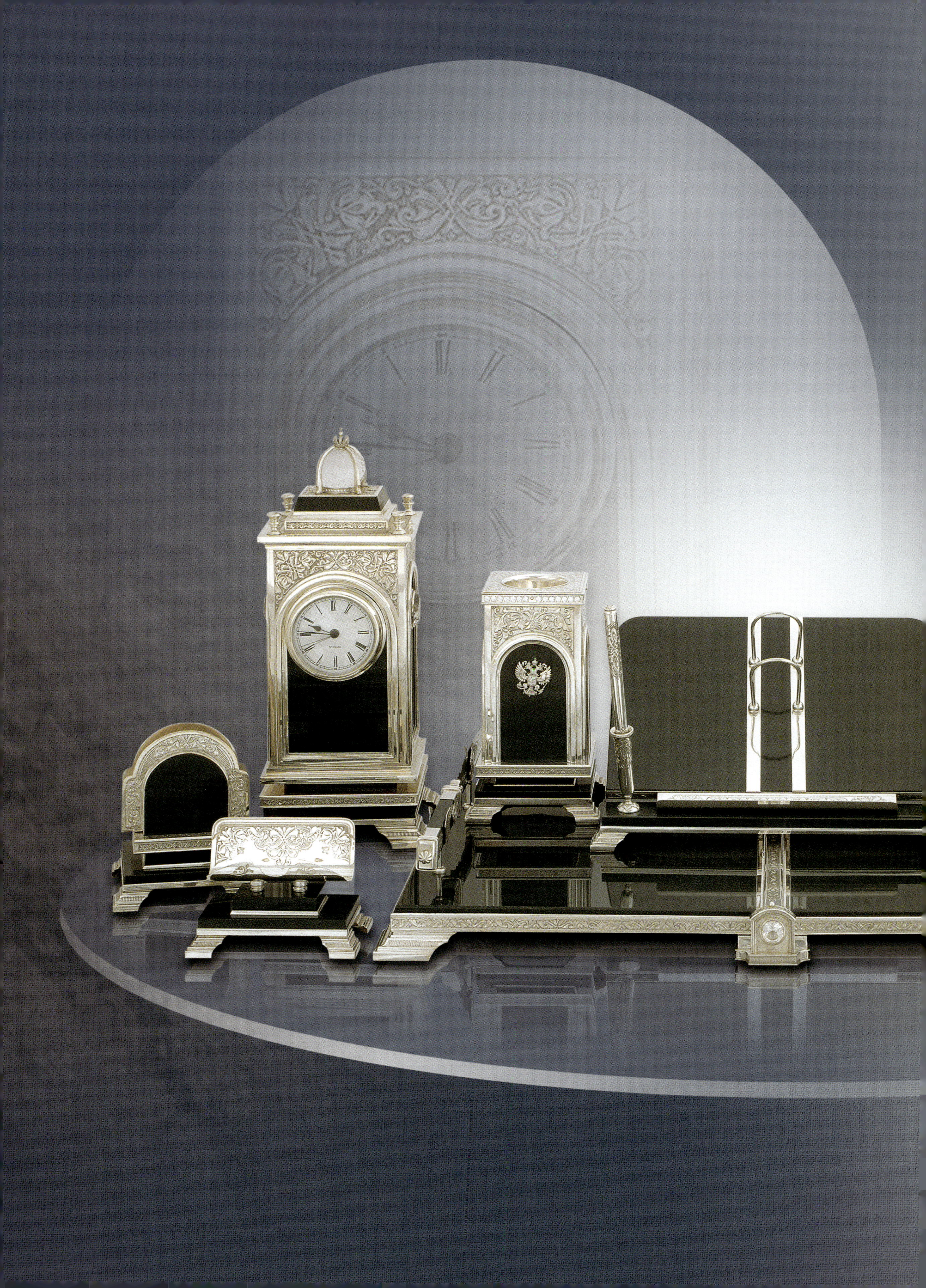

132. **Письменный прибор «Рифей». 2001**

Награжден дипломом в номинации «Ювелирная пластика» на Московской международной ювелирной выставке «Ювелир-2001».

133. Письменный прибор. 1999

134. Письменный прибор «Малахитовый цветок». 2001
Отмечен дипломом выставки, посвященной 1000-летию города Казани (Казань, 2003).

135. Эскиз предметов из письменного прибора. 1999 ►

МАЙ
26

Златоуст
99

136. Часы кабинетные. 2001
Отмечены дипломом выставки, посвященной 1000-летию города Казани (Казань, 2003).

137. Ларец «Жемчужная свадьба». 2002

138. Эскиз настольных часов. 2000

139. **Часы настольные. 2000**

140. **Ларец «Династия Романовых». 1998**

141. **Кубок подарочный «Торжественный». 2002**

Награжден дипломом в номинации «Лучшее внеконкурсное изделие» на выставке «УралЮвелир» (Екатеринбург, 2002).

112. Эскизы ларца «Династия Романовых». 1995

143. Эскиз настольных часов. 1998

144. Часы настольные. 1997

145. Минора «Кристалл». 2002
146. Эскиз настольных часов. 1998

147. Эскиз ларца. 2000

148. Ларец (с фрагментом). 2002

149. Поднос «Золотой Остап». 2003

150. Гран-при «Ангел». 2000

154 *Поднос «Поставщик двора Его Императорского Величества». 1999*

152. Дарница и поднос «Победа» (с фрагментом). 2003
Дар Государственному Историческому музею

1943
БЕЛГОРОД
ХАРЬКОВ
ОРЕЛ
КУРСК
НОВГОРОД
ЛЕНИНГРАД
КИЕВ
СМОЛЕНСК
СССР
ПОБЕДА

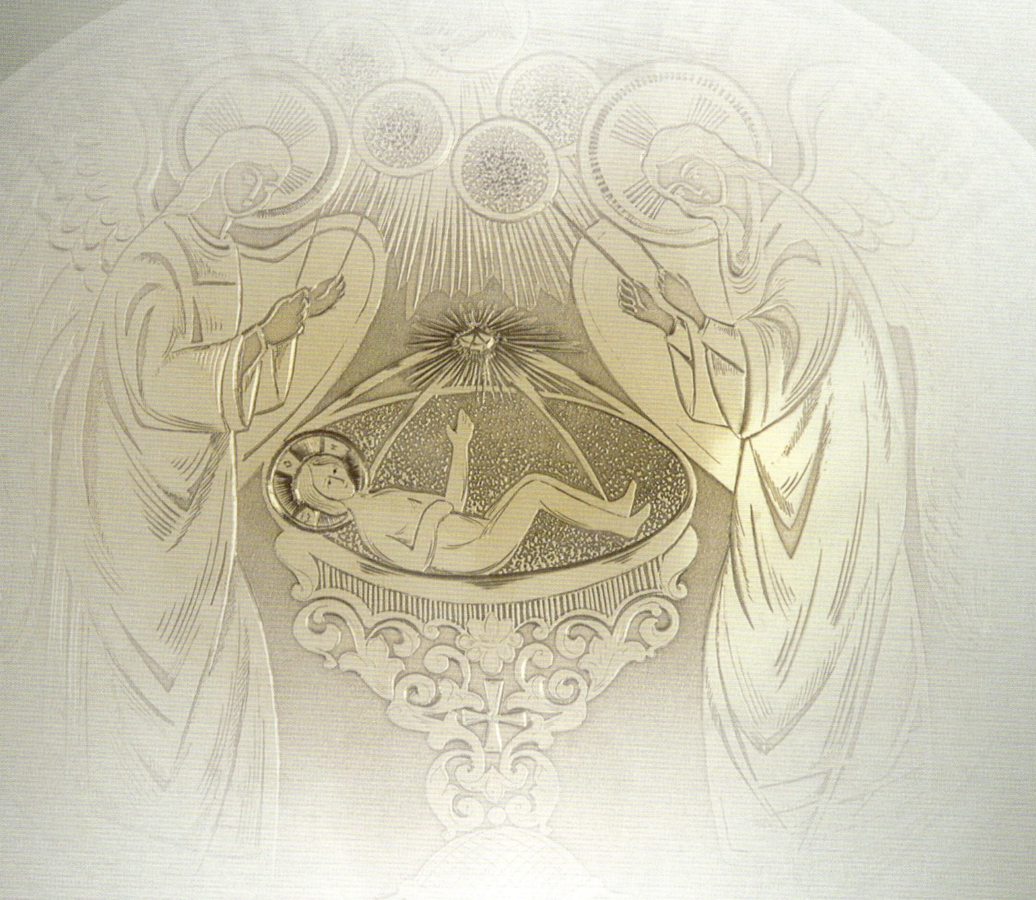

ЦЕРКОВНОЕ ИСКУССТВО

С древних времен на Руси так повелось, что лучшие мастера, талантливейшие умельцы отдавали все свое умение и жар сердца на благо Православной церкви, с усердием служа ее укреплению и прославлению. Лучшие творения человеческих рук во всех областях искусства, будь то архитектура, живопись или скульптура, призваны были возвеличить Имя Божие.

Уральские мастера всегда были востребованы церковным искусством. Известно, например, что на уральских гранильных фабриках — Колыванской и Екатеринбургской — в XIX столетии исполнялись заказы по убранству интерьеров главных санкт-петербургских соборов. Наиболее грандиозные работы были выполнены при оформлении храма Спаса-на-Крови. Для главного престола этого храма была изготовлена в русском стиле роскошная дарохранительница[1] из яшмы различных зеленоватых оттенков на постаменте из родонита.

На протяжении всего XIX века русские мастера декоративно-прикладного искусства, в том числе златоустовские умельцы, охотно исполняли вещи «по заказу, на манер старинных». Тем не менее понятие «старинное благолепие», к которому часто прибегал митрополит Московский Филарет (Дроздов), величайший духовный светоч прошлого столетия, не утратило своего смысла и значения по сей день.

Восхищение произведениями ушедшей эпохи не покидает современных «златокузнецов», и возрождение былых традиций мы наблюдаем в настоящее время — дарохранительница главного собора России вновь изготовлена на Урале, воссоздана руками мастеров златоустовских Мастерских декоративно-прикладного искусства «ЛиК».

Впервые свои произведения церковного назначения Мастерские «ЛиК» экспонировали в 1997 году на православной выставке «Многая лета, Москва», посвященной 850-летию основания Москвы.

Художники «ЛиКа» представили целую коллекцию произведений, выполненных в технике златоустовской гравюры на металле: комплект евхаристической утвари, серию плакет «Православие» с образами святых, первый авторский вариант дарохранительницы и другие.

Выставка проводилась по благословению Святейшего Патриарха Московского и Всея Руси Алексия II, который проникновенно отозвался об участниках этой экспозиции:

А. И. Лохтачев за работой над дарохранительницей

«Радует, что наши труженики стремятся всеми силами вернуть к жизни многие ремесла, мужественно преодолевая при этом экономические трудности нынешнего периода и даря людям через свое искусство гармонию, красоту и утешение».

Действительно, во все века мастера стремились прежде всего к образности и гармонии форм произведений, а также к их украшению, несущему тепло человеческих рук, свет и красоту.

В этом стремлении к совершенству связь времен, преемственность традиций и мастерства имели первостепенное значение. В православных храмах России идея соборности и единства мироздания воплощалась в особенно праздничной декоративности, которая «звучала» во всех предметах церковной литургии.

В таинстве причастия главными евхаристическими сосудами являются дискос[2] и потир[3], берущие свое начало от Тайной вечери. С глубокой древности эти сосуды старались делать сообразно величию таинства, на них совершаемого, — из драгоценных материалов, то есть из золота и серебра. В 1997 году Мастерскими декоративно-прикладного искусства «ЛиК» был впервые исполнен в технике златоустовской гравюры на металле комплект богослужебной утвари для храма Христа Спасителя. Он включал в себя потир, дискос со звездицей[4], лжицу[5] и копие[6].

В работе над этим евхаристическим набором мастера ориентировались на лучшие образцы русского ювелирного искусства, преображая их в своем творчестве в совершенно новую реальность. Пользуясь традиционными техническими приемами златоустовской гравюры и не отходя ни на шаг от церковного канона, Александр, Денис и Нина Лохтачевы создали такое произведение искусства, в котором орнаментация не перегружает форму, а чередование золоченых и никелированных, матовых и полированных до зеркального блеска поверхностей придает изделию особую нарядность, декоративность и одновременно праздничность, торжественность.

На чаше потира в овальных медальонах выгравированы поясные изображения Спасителя, Богоматери и Иоанна Предтечи. Вверху, по ободу чаши, расположена резная надпись, исполненная стилизованным полууставом, — текст причастного стиха: «Тело Христово приимите источника безсмертнаго вкусите».

На дискосе выгравирован текст из евхаристического канона литургии святителя Иоанна Златоуста: «Приимите, ядите: сие есть Тело Мое за вы ломимое во оставление грехов». В центре дискоса исполнена резцом композиция «Литургия ангелов», или «Се агнец»: два ангела с рипидами[7], склоненные над чашей с младенцем — бескровной жертвой. Ориентированная на древние образцы композиция тем не менее выдает руку современного мастера. Это проявляется в свободе фигур, стилизованной трактовке одеяний и крыльев ангелов, в ликах и иных чертах. Однако сцена дивно вписана в круг, не перегружена деталями и пронизана воздухом. Дискос украшен цитринами светло-желтого цвета, символизирующими тело Господне. В украшении потира использованы гранаты, символизирующие кровь Христову, средокрестие звездицы увенчано огромным ограненным топазом, означающим бездонное пространство Вселенной. Все камни тонко подобраны в соответствии с христианской символикой.

Евхаристические сосуды также украшены необыкновенной красоты полудрагоценными камнями. Над их фантазийной огранкой трудился златоустовский мастер-огранщик Владимир Блинов, в полной мере чувствующий красоту камня, умело выявляющий его «душу».

Творческий союз Лохтачевых с В. В. Блиновым привел к созданию поистине раритетного ансамбля богослужебной утвари, выставленного в настоящее время в музее храма Христа Спасителя как одно из лучших произведений русского

Эскиз дарохранительницы для храма Христа Спасителя в Москве, выполненный К. Тоном. 1879

декоративно-прикладного искусства последних лет. За евхаристический набор, серию плакет «Православие», а также за авторский вариант дарохранительницы Мастерские декоративно-прикладного искусства «ЛиК» получили в 1999 году статус «Патриарших» на выставке «Патриаршество в России: традиции и современность», посвященной 70-летию Алексия II.

В апреле 1997 года творческий коллектив художников и мастеров «ЛиКа» получил благословение Святейшего Патриарха Московского и Всея Руси Алексия II на изготовление дарохранительницы для возрождаемой святыни Русской Православной церкви и памятника Отечественной войны 1812 года — храма Христа Спасителя. В письме А. И. Лохтачеву, подписанном Святейшим Патриархом, говорилось: «Благодарю Вас и коллектив ТОО «ЛиК» за готовность выполнить ответственную и уникальную работу — изготовить дарохранительницу для главного Престола возрождаемой Святыни — храма Христа Спасителя. Да благословит Вас Всеблагий Господь на этот во всех отношениях своевременный и богоугодный труд! С уважением и пожеланием благословенных успехов, Патриарх Московский и Всея Руси Алексий II».

При закладке храма 10 ноября 1839 года митрополит Филарет (Дроздов) в речи, обращенной к императору Николаю I, отметил: «Есть для некоторых важных дел особенная судьба Провидения Божия, по которой одному избранному дается возвышенная мысль, а другому предоставляется величественное исполнение».

Так торжественно митрополит Филарет отозвался о мастерах, призванных осуществить грандиозную национальную идею — постройку в Москве одного из главных храмов России. Эти прочувствованные слова митрополита можно адресовать и людям, воссоздавшим вновь, в конце XX столетия, храм Христа Спасителя. В их числе были и златоустовские мастера из фирмы «ЛиК», которые отнеслись к трудной задаче восстановления облика главной дарохранительницы храма Христа Спасителя в полном смысле слова как к «величественному исполнению».

Поскольку характер работ был обусловлен общим замыслом воссоздания храма, Александр, Нина и Денис Лохтачевы, а также другие мастера прежде всего обратились к истории самого памятника.

Храм Христа Спасителя являлся крупнейшим монументальным ансамблем XIX столетия, в котором органично воплотились национальные идеи синтеза искусств.

Весь храм — от архитектурного замысла до утвари — исполнен в едином, неовизантийском, стиле. Особой оригинальностью архитектурного решения отличался главный иконостас храма, представлявший собой мраморную восьмигранную часовню, увенчанную высоким шатром. Часовня имела четыре яруса, соответствующие четырем ярусам иконостаса, и одновременно служила надпрестольной сенью.

Идея создания такой необыкновенной часовни-иконостаса — как бы «храма в храме» — принадлежала митрополиту Московскому Филарету (Дроздову). Его представления о христианском храме как о «святом хранилище Тела и Крови Христовых» нашли свое воплощение в архитектурной

А. И. Лохтачев с рабочей моделью дарохранительницы

композиции самого храма Христа Спасителя, а также в его внутреннем убранстве.

При составлении богословско-архитектурной программы храма святитель Филарет особое внимание сосредоточил на устройстве дарохранительного ковчега — ядра и сердца храма. «Если на нем должны быть изображения, то преимущественно требуются изображения Христа Спасителя... Апостолов и Святителей, особенно с передней стороны. Верх его или глава должна быть осенена крестом. Чтобы внутренность большого ковчега не представляла пустоты неблагообразной, прилично было бы внутри его сделать возвышенность на трех ступенях и на нем внутренний ковчег в виде гробницы... Прилично было бы, чтобы сию гробницу осеняли с двух сторон крылами два ангела, как было над Ковчегом Завета в ветхозаветном храме. Такой внутренний вид при отверстии пространных дверей внешнего большого ковчега соответствовал бы хранящейся в нем святыне», — таков был замысел святителя Филарета, воплощенный в XIX столетии в главной дарохранительнице храма Христа Спасителя мастерами-ювелирами московской фирмы И. П. Хлебникова.

Надо сказать, что происхождение богослужебного сосуда (дарохранительницы) обусловлено древним обычаем сохранять часть Святых Даров в храмах для тех, кто заболел или по каким-то другим причинам не смог приобщиться к Святым Дарам в храме. В первые века христианства встречались дарохранительницы в виде голубя, их подвешивали над престолом.

В XVIII—XX веках дарохранительницы выполнялись в виде храма или часовни с символическим Гробом Господним под сенью. В XIX веке некоторые из них представляли собой целые скульптурные композиции с литыми фигурами апостолов по углам, фигурками ангелов с рипидами и жен-мироносиц у Гроба Господня. Изготавливались дарохранительницы из золота, серебра, реже олова; декорировались гравировкой, чернью, сканым орнаментом. Часто на дарохранительницах помещали сцены из Евангелия, выполненные в технике чеканки или расписной эмали. Помимо металлических, в XIX веке в столичных храмах встречались дарохранительницы из поделочных камней.

Дарохранительница главного алтаря храма Христа Спасителя являлась незаурядным произведением декоративно-прикладного искусства, выполненным в неовизантийском стиле. Она была сделана в последний период сооружения храма, когда завершалась отделка его интерьера и изготовлялись предметы церковного обихода и утвари. Дарохранительница выполнена по рисунку архитектора Р. Шмеллинга, утвержденному комиссией по строительству храма 5 октября 1879 года. Выполненная дарохранительница немного отличалась от задуманной. Несколько по-другому были решены фигуры ангелов и евангелистов, изменена форма и отделка ковчега, имелись отличия в рисунке орнамента ряда деталей. Однако общая композиция, основные элементы и большая часть деталей отвечали утвержденному проекту. Первоначально предполагалось делать основание дарохранительницы из шокшинского порфира, однако в окончательном варианте предпочтение было отдано серебру.

По утверждении проекта 1879 года дарохранительница была изготовлена на фабрике купца И. П. Хлебникова в 1880 году. Однако комиссия по строительству храма ее не одобрила и в 1882 году сделала новый заказ сыну умершего И. П. Хлебникова — купцу М. И. Хлебникову. Фигуры ангелов, евангелистов и барельефы для окончательного варианта дарохранительницы были выполнены по моделям профессора Императорской Академии художеств, скульптора Н. А. Лаверецкого. Николай Акимович Лаверецкий, ученик П. К. Клодта, известен как автор скульптуры «Россия», исполненной им для Каслинского чугунного павильона, и ряда других памятников монументального искусства.

Судя по сохранившимся историческим документам, работа над созданием дарохранительницы для главного алтаря храма Христа Спасителя шла непросто. Вначале были сделаны две деревянные модели, которые затем отвергла комиссия. Умер, не закончив работу, И. П. Хлебников, и к мастерам золотого и серебряного дела присоединились профессиональные скульпторы. К несчастью, в 1931 году дарохранительница в числе других предметов утвари и убранства храма Христа Спасителя была безвозвратно утрачена при его уничтожении. Скорее всего, ее отправили в переплавку как произведение, «не имеющее художественной ценности».

Таким образом, творческий коллектив Мастерских «ЛиК» во главе с А. И. Лохтачевым оказался перед очень сложной и масштабной задачей воссоздания такого значительного памятника декоративно-прикладного искусства, какой представляла собой дарохранительница храма Христа Спасителя. Приступая к его реконструкции, златоустовские мастера были вынуждены ориентироваться на оставшиеся в небольшом количестве кино- и фотоматериалы, собранные ими по крупицам, а также на некоторые документы, сохранившиеся в архивах Москвы.

Основываясь на старых фотографиях, художники выстраивали вновь по светотени все пропорции, сечения и детали.

Прежде всего был изготовлен макет в натуральную величину. На нем отрабатывались все сложные конструктивные элементы. Этот макет был представлен в Москве, на заседании экспертной комиссии по воссозданию храма Христа Спасителя. С учетом всех замечаний в 1997 году был создан авторский вариант дарохранительницы из латуни, чтобы на этом этапе определиться с деталями орнаментации, гравировки и декорировки изделия.

Авторский вариант дарохранительницы в сентябре 1999 года экспонировался на ювелирной выставке «Сокровища России» (Москва), а также на Всероссийской художественной выставке «Имени Твоему» (2000), посвященной двухтысячелетию Рождества Христова. Произведение, выполненное в традициях златоустовской гравюры на металле, украшенное голубыми топазами ручной огранки и камнями горного хрусталя массой по 1570 карат каждый, поразило всех техническим совершенством, гармонией и чистотой исполнения.

Над ним трудились художники, ювелиры, граверы, токари, гальваники, камнерезы, то есть целый коллектив мастеров, создавший «всем миром», как говорили в старину, величественное произведение искусства.

Работа по воссозданию дарохранительницы заняла, по словам Дениса Лохтачева, руководителя мастерской церковной утвари, почти три года: три месяца шли подготовительные конструкторские работы, пять месяцев создавалась модель, полгода модель дорабатывалась, затем изготавливали первоначальный вариант в металле и только после этого в течение семи с половиной месяцев переводили изделие в драгоценный металл — серебро. Орнаментированная в технике златоустовской гравюры на металле, дарохранительница приобрела новое звучание.

Дарохранительница для алтаря храма Христа Спасителя представляет собой сооружение в виде часовни или небольшого храма с развитой ярусной композицией. Основание ее выполнено из калганской зеленой яшмы, верхняя часть — из позолоченного серебра. Двухъярусное основание в плане имеет квадратную форму, усложненную выступающими срезанными углами. В средней части цоколя, по архивным данным, с одной стороны ранее находилась накладка с надписью: «Повелением благочестивейшего государя нашего...». Теперь текст заменен на другой: «Дарохранительница воссоздана по

Александр и Денис Лохтачевы передают дарохранительницу Патриарху Московскому и Всея Руси Алексию II

Высочайшему благословению Святейшего Патриарха Московского и Всея Руси Алексия II и благодаря искусным художникам и мастерам фирмы «ЛиК» из Златоуста к 2000-летию Рождества Христова». Выступающие на диагональных осях углы решены как подиумы для скульптур, изображающих сидящих евангелистов с их символами. На торцах подиумов помещены овальные медальоны с рельефными поясными изображениями святителей Василия Великого, Григория Богослова, Иоанна Златоуста и Иакова, брата Господня.

Поверхности между подиумами выглядят как наклонные плоскости, заполненные текстом, в котором заключена законченная иконографическая программа в соответствии со сценами Страстного цикла.

Сцена «Тайная вечеря»: «И когда они ели, Иисус взял хлеб и, благословив, преломил и, раздавая ученикам, сказал: приимите, ядите, сие есть Тело Мое. И взяв чашу и благодарив, подал им и сказал: пейте из нее все, ибо сие есть Кровь Моя Нового Завета, за многих изливаемая во оставление грехов» (Мф. 26, 26—28). Сцена «Распятие»: «Ибо всякий раз, когда вы едите хлеб сей и пьете чашу сию, смерть Господню возвещаете, доколе Он придет» (1 Кор. 11, 26). Сцена «Снятие со креста»: «Я Хлеб Живый, сшедший с Небес; ядущий Хлеб сей будет жить вовек; Хлеб же, который Я дам, есть Плоть Моя, которую Я отдам за Жизнь мира» (Ин. 6, 51). Сцена «Положение во гроб»: «Но Он изъязвлен был за грехи наши и мучим за беззакония наши; наказание мира нашего было на Нем, и ранами Его мы исцелились» (Книга Пророка Исаии 53, 5).

Помимо глубокого сакрального смысла, эти надписи, сделанные изящным стилизованным уставом, выполняют немаловажную декоративную функцию, украшая постамент дарохранительницы.

Основание дарохранительницы (цоколь) служит базой для основного сооружения в виде девятиглавой часовни — кивория. В центре находится ковчег для Святых Даров, по сторонам которого поставлены две статуи ангелов, держащих рипиды.

Верхняя часть дарохранительницы напоминает низкий шатер, по углам которого помещены главки с крестами. Шатер расчленен на четыре крестообразно выступающих объема в форме усеченных конусов, также увенчанных главками с крестами. Самая крупная глава с богато украшенным крестом завершает композицию дарохранительницы. Все части сооружения декорированы разнообразным, сложным по рисунку орнаментом растительно-геометрического характера. Шатер выделяется сетчатым орнаментом, состоящим из ромбов с равноконечными крестами. Поверхности внутренних объемов позолочены.

Скульптурные образы ангелов с рипидами, созданные А. И. Лохтачевым, по пластике исполнения соответствуют традиционной трактовке, но решены в неовизантийском стиле, что отвечает историческому прототипу XIX века, созданному профессором Академии художеств Н. А. Лаверецким. На начальной стадии, то есть при разработке и корректировке будущего произведения, а также при исполнении его окончательной модели, скульптор использовал мягкий материал. Затем была осуществлена отливка из бронзы и впоследствии из серебра. Фигуры ангелов отлиты в традициях каслинских мастеров художественного литья прошлого столетия. В декоративном оформлении памятника использованы драгоценные металлы и ограненные драгоценные камни. Основание воссозданной дарохранительницы выполнено из калганской яшмы серо-зеленого цвета, однотонной, без разводов (она наиболее близко попадала под описание шокшинского порфира). На заседании художественной комиссии в Москве был утвержден самый твердый (технический)

Патриарх Московский и Всея Руси Алексий II рассматривает созданную мастерами «Лика» дарохранительницу

сорт яшмы. Камнерезу из уральского города Миасса Александру Шафикову, участвовавшему в работе над дарохранительницей, пришлось перепилить 150 килограммов яшмы, чтобы подготовить подходящие пластины.

В центральной части дарохранительницы находятся рельефные композиции, иллюстрирующие основные сюжеты Страстного цикла из Евангелия: Тайная вечеря, Распятие Христово, Снятие со креста, Положение во гроб. Эти гравированные изображения на дарохранительнице, сделанные в иконописной традиции, выполняют прежде всего литургическую функцию, тесно связанную с той, какую имеет икона, и раскрывают богослужебное предназначение предмета. Указанные сюжеты на исторической дарохранительнице XIX века в точности повторяли композиции картин, размещенных на стенах храма. Так, Тайная вечеря детально копировала в рельефе живописную работу Генриха Семирадского, остальные три сцены — живописные полотна В. В. Верещагина.

Сцены Страстного цикла, размещенные на воссозданной дарохранительнице, отличаются высочайшим мастерством гравировки в сочетании с тонкостью, изяществом силуэтных линий фигур. Перед автором эскизов этих композиций А. И. Лохтачевым стояла непростая задача: лаконичными средствами, такими как силуэт фигуры, поза, движение рук, передать настроение, переживание и раскрыть внутренний духовный смысл наиболее пронзительных сцен Страстного цикла Евангелия. Александр Иванович Лохтачев, не имея точно воспроизведенных оригиналов этих композиций и находясь в рамках церковного канона, тем не менее нашел удачное и единственно возможное решение, вписав эти сцены в арочную форму пластин. Композиции как бы вытянуты по горизонтали. В них сочетаются классическое спокойствие и бурная внутренняя динамика.

Удивительный факт, бесспорно убеждающий в «творческой» правоте А. И. Лохтачева и его соратников: уже после окончания работ над дарохранительницей была обнаружена ее уменьшенная копия начала XX века (в настоящее время находится на престоле Елоховского Богоявленского собора). Сопоставление подлинных рельефов Страстного цикла с гравированными композициями, исполненными по эскизам А. И. Лохтачева, не имевшего перед собой точного прототипа, показало, что они стилистически совпадают, несмотря на технологические и временны́е различия. Этот факт свидетельствует о том, что златоустовские мастера, посвятившие не один год воссозданию облика утраченной дарохранительницы главного престола храма Христа Спасителя, точно проникли в суть той эпохи, которой принадлежала вся церковная утварь главного храма России. В то же время в исполнении этого памятника нашли свое отражение и стилевые влияния современности, и высочайший уровень мастерства, и применение современных технических средств.

И сцены Страстного цикла, и гравированные надписи — цитаты из Евангелия, расположенные на четырех сторонах каменного подиума, — подготавливают восприятие центральной и главной части дарохранительницы, а именно ковчега для хранения «Божественных Таин больных ради». Ковчег, часто исполнявшийся в форме гробницы или саркофага, символизировал место распятия, погребения и воскресения Христова и одновременно Ковчег Завета ветхозаветной церкви, в котором находилась Святая Святых.

Изображения ковчега не сохранилось, и молодой художник Денис Александрович Лохтачев, нашел собственное оригинальное решение. Съемную крышку он декорировал самоцветами: красными гранатами. Сложный символический декор дополнил медальонами с хризмой [8], первой и последней буквами греческого алфавита — α и ω, употребление которых часто сопровождает хризму и означает: «Я есмь Альфа и Омега, начало и конец, говорит Господь, который есть и был и грядет, Вседержитель» (Откр. 1, 8).

В Рождество Христово 2000 года дарохранительница, воссозданная руками златоустовских мастеров «ЛиКа», была установлена на престоле главного алтаря храма Христа Спасителя. Она производит величественное впечатление, прекрасно вписываясь в общий храмовый ансамбль. Более того, главный храмовый иконостас в виде беломраморной восьмигранной часовни, увенчанной позолоченным бронзовым шатром, и сам походит на грандиозную дарохранительницу, которая всегда является живым подобием всего храма.

Без сомнения, воссозданная дарохранительница для главного алтаря храма Христа Спасителя может быть отнесена к произведениям монументально-декоративного искусства, в ней сочетаются архитектурные, скульптурные и декоративные элементы. Тончайшая линейная гравировка, сочетание матовой и глянцевой поверхности металла благодаря легкому травлению, проканфаренный фон и гладкие орнаментальные детали создают разнообразную фактуру произведения. Подобная гравировка по глянцу использовалась древнерусскими златокузнецами на протяжении многих столетий. Особенного ссвершенства она достигла в XVI—XVII веках в церковной утвари ярославских серебряников.

Техника резьбы по серебру особенно близка технике иконописи, вернее, одному из первых этапов работы над иконой, когда изображение вначале «знаменится», то есть начерчивается, а затем «графится», то есть гравируется иглой.

«Знаменить... рисунок — признается у иконописцев наиболее ответственной частью работы, — писал в книге «Иконостас» Павел Флоренский, — ведь назнаменовать перевод — значит передать множеству молящихся свидетельство Церкви об ином мире, и малейшее изменение не только линий, но и тончайшего их характера придает этой отвлеченной схеме иной стиль, иную духовную структуру».

Работа златоустовских мастеров над восстановлением дарохранительницы была по достоинству оценена. Авторы проекта были отмечены наградами Русской Православной церкви. Орденом Святого благоверного князя Даниила Московского III степени награжден Александр Лохтачев, художественный руководитель проекта, генеральный директор Мастерских «ЛиК»; орденом Святой равноапостольной великой княгини Ольги III степени — Нина Лохтачева, руководитель работ по декорировке дарохранительницы, главный художник Мастерских; орденов преподобного Серафима Саровского были удостоены Денис Лохтачев, руководитель ювелирных работ, автор технологических разработок изготовления дарохранительницы, а также Владимир Блинов, автор и исполнитель ювелирной огранки уральских самоцветов. Медали преподобного Серафима Саровского получили ювелир Андрей Фоминых, гальваник Валентина Егорова, художник-гравер Мария Терентьева.

После столь грандиозной работы над дарохранительницей храма Христа Спасителя мастерская церковной утвари «ЛиКа», возглавляемая Денисом Лохтачевым, успешно продолжила свою работу. Так, были изготовлены малые дарохранительницы в форме часовни для небольших храмов (две из них уже переданы в местные церкви), семисвечники, потиры, наборы для таинства елеопомазания, дарницы (сосуды для хранения святынь), сосуды для освященного масла.

При воплощении творческих замыслов художники «ЛиКа» широко применяют драгоценные ограненные камни, дополняя и подчеркивая глубинный смысл произведения.

Художественная обработка металла как один из разделов декоративно-прикладного искусства развивается в общем потоке искусства при постоянном совершенствовании и изменении форм, композиций и орнаментации.

Путь художников и мастеров фирмы «ЛиК» отмечен поисками новых художественных направлений, оригинальных идей и решений, виртуозностью и необыкновенно высоким техническим уровнем исполнения, блестящими перспективами в развитии такого прославленного, имеющего великие традиции вида прикладного искусства, как златоустовская гравюра на металле.

С. В. Гнутова

---

[1] **Дарохранительница** — один из главных священных предметов богослужения находящихся на престоле в алтаре православной церкви, специальный сосуд, в котором хранятся запасные Святые Дары, обычно для причащения на дому больных и умирающих. Иногда дарохранительницу называют «Сионом» или «Иерусалимом», что олицетворяет храм Воскресения Христова над Гробом Господним в Иерусалиме.

[2] **Дискос** (греч. — круглое блюдо) — образ того блюда, с которого Иисус Христос на Тайной вечери взял хлеб и претворил его в свого плоть, раздав ученикам.

[3] **Потир** (греч. — сосуд для питья) — образ чаши, которую Иисус Христос на Тайной вечери преподал своим ученикам со словами: «Пейте из нее все, ибо сие есть Кровь Моя...».

[4] **Звездица** — образ Вифлеемской звезды, напоминающей о Рождестве Иисуса Христа. Богослужебный предмет состоит из двух металлических дуг, соединенных в центре. По окончании проскомидии (обряд подготовки таинства причащения, совершаемый незримо для молящихся в алтаре, на особом столе, жертвеннике, где священник подготавливает жертвенный хлеб и вино) звездицу, раздвигая крестообразно, поставляют на дискос со словами из Евангелия: «И пришедши звезда, ста вверху, идеже бе Отроча».

[5] **Лжица** — небольшая ложка с крестом на конце рукояти, употребляется для преподания мирянам Причастия из потира.

[6] **Копие** — образ того копья, которым воин, желая удостовериться в смерти Христа на кресте, пронзил его в ребра. Копие предназначено для вырезывания частиц просфоры во время проскомидии. Из самой большой просфоры священник вырезает часть, называемую Агнцем. Из второй — вынимается часть в честь Богоматери. Из третьей просфоры — в честь Иоанна Предтечи, пророков, апостолов, Иоакима и Анны, родителей Марии, в честь святого, поминаемого в этот день, и всех чинов святости. Из четвертой просфоры вынимаются частицы за здравие живых, а из пятой — за упокой умерших.

[7] **Рипида** (греч. — опахало) — символизирует присутствие небесных сил во время литургии и является необходимой принадлежностью архиерейского богослужения.

[8] **Хризма** — монограмма, составленная из начальных букв имени Христа и в начертании образующая крест.

Храм Христа Спасителя: общий вид и интерьер верхней церкви Преображения Господня ►

153. *Дарохранительница для храма Христа Спасителя (с фрагментами). 1997–2000* ►

ТАЙНАѦ ВЕЧЕРѦ

СВ. ЄУ. МР.

СВ. ЕѴ. МР.

ЯДЫЙ ХЛѢБЪ СЕЙ ЖИВЪ БУДЕТ ВО ВѢКИ

ЯДЫЙ МОЮ ПЛОТЬ,
И ПІЯЙ МОЮ КРОВЬ,
ВО МНѢ ПРЕБЫВАЕТЪ

154. Первый (авторский) вариант дарохранительницы. 1997

155. *Дарохранительница малая. 2002*

КЪ ВЫШНИХЪ. БЛАГОСЛОВЕН

156. Евхаристический набор (потир, дискос со звездицей, копие, лжица) для храма Христа Спасителя. 1997–1999

157. Дискос со звездицей из евхаристического набора. 1997–1999

160. Потир «Евхаристия». 2000

161. *Набор для елеопомазания. 2003*

162. *Сосуд для елея с крышкой. 2003*

Каталог

ХУДОЖЕСТВЕННОЕ ХОЛОДНОЕ ОРУЖИЕ

1. Кортик «Урны Санкт-Петербурга» (фрагмент)
Из серии «Петербургские мотивы». 1997
См. кат. № 73

2. Набор «Охотничий»: нож и кинжал. 1999
Авторы: Мануш Г.И., Лохтачева Н.В.
Сталь, латунь, кап березовый
Рисовка кистью, гравировка иглой по лаку, травление, гравировка резцом, золочение, никелирование
Длина ножа 25*, длина кинжала 32

3. Набор «Морской»: кортик и компас. 1999
Авторы: Лохтачев А.И., Лохтачева Н.В.
Сталь, серебро, янтарь, топазы, цирконы
Рисовка кистью, гравировка иглой по лаку, травление, гравировка резцом, золочение, огранка камней
Длина кортика 38

4. Сабля (фрагмент). 2000
См. кат. № 34

5. Ножны охотничьего ножа. 1998
См. кат. № 49

6. Кинжал «Урал». 1999
Авторы: Мануш Г.И., Лохтачева Н.В.
Сталь, латунь, кап березовый
Рисовка кистью, гравировка иглой по лаку, травление, гравировка резцом, золочение, никелирование
Общая длина 38

7. Палаш «300 лет Санкт-Петербургу» (фрагмент). 2001
См. кат. № 10

8. Тесак и нож в ножнах «Былина». 2001
См. кат. № 25

9. Сабля «Восточная». 2003
Авторы: Лохтачева Н.В., Лохтачев Д.А.
Сталь, латунь, кап березовый, кожа
Рисовка кистью, гравировка иглой по лаку, травление, гравировка резцом, золочение, никелирование
Общая длина 110

10. Палаш «300 лет Санкт-Петербургу». 2001
Авторы: Лохтачев А.И., Лохтачева Н.В., Лохтачев Д.А.
Сталь, латунь, кап березовый, ювелирные камни
Рисовка кистью, гравировка иглой по лаку, травление, гравировка резцом, золочение, никелирование
Общая длина 111

11. Трости. 2000
Авторы: Мануш Г.И., Лохтачева Н.В.
Латунь, дерево
Рисовка кистью, гравировка иглой по лаку, травление, гравировка резцом, золочение
Длина 80

12. Палаш «Морской». 2000
Авторы: Лохтачев А.И., Лохтачева Н.В.
Сталь, латунь, кап березовый, бархат
Рисовка кистью, гравировка иглой по лаку, травление, гравировка резцом, никелирование, золочение
Общая длина 108

13. Сабля «Восточная» (первый вариант). 2000
Авторы: Лохтачев А.И., Лохтачева Н.В., Лохтачев Д.А.
Дамасская сталь, серебро, ореховое дерево, кожа, топазы, горный хрусталь, цирконы
Рисовка кистью, гравировка иглой по лаку, травление, гравировка резцом, золочение, огранка камней
Общая длина 110

14. Сабля «Восточная» (авторский вариант). 2001
Авторы: Лохтачев А.И., Лохтачева Н.В., Лохтачев Д.А.
Сталь, серебро, агат, топазы, лазурит, аметисты
Рисовка кистью, гравировка иглой по лаку, травление, гравировка резцом, огранка камней
Общая длина 110

15–17. Мечи «Памяти и Благодарности народам стран — участниц антигитлеровской коалиции». 1995. Созданы к 50-летию Победы в Великой Отечественной войне
См. кат. №№ 20, 21, 22

18. Щит Победы. 1995. Создан к 50-летию Победы в Великой Отечественной войне
Авторы: Лохтачев А.И., Лохтачева Н.В., Мануш Г.И., Блинов В.В.
Сталь, латунь, бархат, горный хрусталь, цирконы, танзаниты
Рисовка кистью, гравировка иглой по лаку, травление, гравировка резцом, никелирование, огранка камней
На щите нанесена надпись: «Россияне! Не уроним чести и плечом к плечу сомкнемся впредь. Выстоять дано нам только вместе, порознь — только умереть!..»
(автор К. Скворцов)
Диаметр щита 95
Установлен в Центральном музее Великой Отечественной войны в мемориальном комплексе на Поклонной горе. Москва

19. Меч Победы. 1995. Создан к 50-летию Победы в Великой Отечественной войне
Авторы: Лохтачев А.И., Лохтачева Н.В., Мануш Г.И., Блинов В.В.
Сталь, латунь, дерево, горный хрусталь
Рисовка кистью, гравировка иглой по лаку, травление, гравировка резцом, огранка камней
Длина 215

* Размеры изделий даны в сантиметрах.

20. Меч «Памяти и Благодарности народу Америки». 1995
Авторы: Лохтачев А.И., Лохтачева Н.В., Блинов В.В.
Сталь, латунь, бархат, дуб, горный хрусталь, цирконы
Рисовка кистью, гравировка иглой по лаку, травление, гравировка резцом, золочение, никелирование, огранка камней
На клинке нанесена надпись:
«Народу Америки благодарная Россия»
Общая длина меча 112, длина клинка 90

21. Меч «Памяти и Благодарности народу Франции». 1995
Авторы: Лохтачев А.И., Лохтачева Н.В., Блинов В.В.
Сталь, латунь, бархат, дуб, горный хрусталь, цирконы
Рисовка кистью, гравировка иглой по лаку, травление, гравировка резцом, золочение, никелирование, огранка камней
На клинке нанесена надпись:
«Народу Франции благодарная Россия»
Общая длина меча 112, длина клинка 90

22. Меч «Памяти и Благодарности народу Англии». 1995
Авторы: Лохтачев А.И., Лохтачева Н.В., Блинов В.В.
Сталь, латунь, бархат, дуб, горный хрусталь, цирконы
Рисовка кистью, гравировка иглой по лаку, травление, гравировка резцом, золочение, никелирование, огранка камней
На клинке нанесена надпись: «Народу Англии благодарная Россия»
Общая длина меча 112, длина клинка 90

23. Сабля «Офицерская». 1997
Авторы: Лохтачев А.И., Лохтачева Н.В.
Сталь, латунь, кап березовый, бархат
Рисовка кистью, гравировка иглой по лаку, травление, гравировка резцом, золочение, никелирование
Общая длина 104

24. Тесак и нож в ножнах «Диана». 2002
Авторы: Мануш Г.И., Лохтачева Н.В.
Сталь, латунь, кап березовый, кожа
Рисовка кистью, гравировка иглой по лаку, травление, гравировка резцом, золочение, никелирование
Общая длина 55

25. Тесак и нож в ножнах «Былина». 2001
Авторы: Мануш Г.И., Лохтачева Н.В.
Сталь, латунь, кап березовый, бархат
Рисовка кистью, гравировка иглой по лаку, травление, гравировка резцом, золочение, никелирование
Общая длина 60, длина ножа 24,5

26. Эскиз тесака с двумя ножами. 1998
Автор: Мануш Г.И.

27. Нож «Мотивы Востока». 2002
Авторы: Мануш Г.И., Лохтачева Н.В.
Сталь, латунь, кап березовый, кожа, бархат
Рисовка кистью, гравировка иглой по лаку, травление, гравировка резцом, золочение, никелирование
Общая длина 34

28. Кортик «Олений». 1999
Авторы: Мануш Г.И., Лохтачева Н.В.
Сталь, латунь, рог, кожа
Рисовка кистью, гравировка иглой по лаку, травление, гравировка резцом, золочение
Общая длина 87

29. Эскиз кортика «Олений». 1996
Автор: Мануш Г.И.

30. Шпага «Парус». 2003
Авторы: Лохтачев А.И., Лохтачева Н.В., Лохтачев Д.А.
Дамасская сталь, серебро, кожа, аметист
Рисовка кистью, гравировка иглой по лаку, травление, гравировка резцом, ручная огранка камня
Общая длина 117,5, ширина эфеса 23

31. Сабля «Офицерская». 1997
Авторы: Лохтачев Д.А., Лохтачева Н.В.
Сталь, латунь, кап березовый
Рисовка кистью, гравировка иглой по лаку, травление, гравировка резцом, золочение, никелирование
Общая длина 108

32. Сабля «Офицерская» (авторский вариант). 2001
Авторы: Лохтачев А.И., Лохтачева Н.В.
Сталь, латунь, кап березовый, бархат
Рисовка кистью, гравировка иглой по лаку, травление, гравировка резцом, золочение, никелирование
Общая длина 104

33. Сабля роты почетного караула. 1995
Авторы: Лохтачев А.И., Лохтачева Н.В.
Сталь, латунь, кап березовый, бархат
Рисовка кистью, гравировка иглой по лаку, травление, гравировка резцом, золочение, никелирование
Общая длина 104

34. Сабля. 2000
Авторы: Лохтачев А.И., Лохтачева Н.В.
Сталь, латунь, кап березовый
Рисовка кистью, гравировка иглой по лаку, травление, гравировка резцом, золочение, никелирование
Общая длина 104

35. Кинжал «Жар-птица». 2001
Авторы: Лохтачев А.И., Лохтачева Н.В.
Сталь, латунь, кап березовый
Рисовка кистью, гравировка иглой по лаку, травление, гравировка резцом, золочение, никелирование
Общая длина 45,5

36. Нож «Золотое руно». 2000
Авторы: Мануш Г.И., Павлючкова Н.
Сталь, латунь, кап березовый
Рисовка кистью, гравировка иглой по лаку, травление, гравировка резцом, золочение, никелирование
Общая длина 22

37. Кинжал «Крест». 1994
Авторы: Лохтачев А.И., Лохтачева Н.В.
Сталь, латунь, кап березовый
Рисовка кистью, гравировка иглой по лаку, травление, гравировка резцом, золочение, никелирование
Общая длина 49

38. Кортик «Адмиральский». 2002
Кинжал «Крест». 1998
Авторы: Лохтачев А.И., Лохтачева Н.В.
Сталь, латунь, кап березовый
Рисовка кистью, гравировка иглой по лаку, травление, гравировка резцом, золочение, никелирование
Общая длина кортика 43, общая длина кинжала 48
Тесак и нож в ножнах «Диана». 2002
См. кат. № 24

39. Кортик «Царская охота». 2001
Авторы: Мануш Г.И., Лохтачева Н.В.
Сталь, латунь, кап березовый, кожа
Рисовка кистью, гравировка иглой по лаку, травление, гравировка резцом, золочение, никелирование
Общая длина 65

40. Кортик «Морской». 1999
Авторы: Лохтачев А.И., Лохтачева Н.В.
Сталь, серебро, янтарь, топазы, цирконы
Рисовка кистью, гравировка иглой по лаку, травление, гравировка резцом, золочение, огранка камней
Общая длина 38

85. Кубок «Золотое кольцо России». 2002
Авторы: Лохтачев А.И., Лохтачева Н.В., Лохтачев Д.А.
Серебро 925°, горный хрусталь, цирконы
Рисовка кистью, гравировка иглой по лаку, травление, гравировка резцом, золочение, ручная огранка горного хрусталя
Высота 22

86. Ювелирные камни фантазийной огранки. 1998
Автор: Блинов В.В.

87. Поднос «Птица Сирин». 1994
Дарница. 2000
Подносы декоративные. 1999
Автор: Лохтачева Н.В.
Латунь
Полировка, рисовка кистью, гравировка иглой по лаку, травление, гравировка резцом, никелирование, золочение
Диаметр подноса «Птица Сирин» 32, высота дарницы 13, диаметр подносов 28 и 21

88. Поднос «Букет» (фрагмент). 2000
Автор: Лохтачева Н.В.
Латунь
Полировка, рисовка кистью, гравировка иглой по лаку, травление, гравировка резцом, никелирование, золочение
Диаметр 28

89. Ларец. 2002
Авторы: Мануш Г.И., Лохтачева Н.В.
Серебро 925°, калганская яшма, горный хрусталь, цирконы
Рисовка кистью, гравировка иглой по лаку, травление, гравировка резцом, камнеобработка, ручная фантазийная огранка горного хрусталя, огранка камней
23х26,2х14,6

90. Браслет «Снежная королева». 2002
Автор: Лохтачева Н.В.
Серебро 925°, цитрин
Рисовка кистью, гравировка иглой по лаку, травление, гравировка резцом, золочение, огранка ювелирных камней
Высота 7

91. Ключ символический. 1997
Авторы: Мануш Г.И., Лохтачев А.И., Лохтачева Н.В.
Латунь, горный хрусталь
Рисовка кистью, гравировка иглой по лаку, травление, гравировка резцом, золочение, ручная огранка горного хрусталя
Длина 39

92. Эскиз настольных часов. 1996
Автор: Мануш Г.И.

93. Ювелирная композиция «Манхэттен». 2002
Авторы: Лохтачев А.И., Лохтачев Д.А.
Платина, золото 750°, сапфиры иолиты, бриллианты, рубины, жемчуг черный и белый
Огранка ювелирных камней
Высота 9,5

94. Ведерко для льда «Столичное». 1996
Автор: Лохтачев А.И.
Латунь
Полировка, рисовка кистью, гравировка иглой по лаку, травление, гравировка резцом, никелирование, золочение
Высота 19

95. Поднос «Российский». 1995–1996
Автор: Лохтачев А.И.
Латунь
Полировка, рисовка кистью, гравировка иглой по лаку, травление, гравировка резцом, никелирование, золочение
Диаметр 28

96. Поднос «Россия». 1995–1996
Автор: Лохтачева Н.В.
Латунь
Полировка, рисовка кистью, гравировка иглой по лаку, травление, гравировка резцом, никелирование, золочение
Диаметр 28

97. Набор «Пиала». 1999
Автор: Лохтачева Н.В.
Латунь
Полировка, рисовка кистью, гравировка иглой по лаку, травление, гравировка резцом, никелирование, золочение
Диаметр подноса 32, высота пиал 9 и 10

98. Кубок «Лето». 1998
Авторы: Лохтачев А.И., Лохтачева Н.В.
Латунь
Полировка, рисовка кистью, гравировка иглой по лаку, травление, гравировка резцом, никелирование, золочение
Высота 17

99. Набор для чая. 1999
Автор: Лохтачев Д.А.
Серебро 925°, янтарь, цирконы
Рисовка кистью, гравировка иглой по лаку, травление, гравировка резцом, золочение, огранка камней
Диаметр подноса 32, высота подстаканников 7,3

100. Набор для вина «Праздничный». 2002
Автор: Лохтачева Н.В.
Латунь
Полировка, рисовка кистью, гравировка иглой по лаку, травление, гравировка резцом, никелирование, золочение
Диаметр подноса 32, высота стопок 6, высота подсвечника 31

101. Набор для чая. 1996
Авторы: Лохтачева Н.В., Лохтачев Д.А.
Латунь
Полировка, рисовка кистью, гравировка иглой по лаку, травление, гравировка резцом, никелирование, золочение
Поднос 46х26,3, высота сахарницы 13, высота чайника 17

102. Набор для вина «Величальный». 1999
Авторы: Лохтачев А.И., Лохтачева Н.В.
Серебро 925°, бриллианты
Рисовка кистью, гравировка иглой по лаку, травление, гравировка резцом, золочение, огранка ювелирных камней
Высота кубка 22, диаметр чаши 14, диаметр подноса 30,2

103. Набор для вина «Очарование». 2001
Авторы: Лохтачева Н.В., Лохтачев Д.А.
Латунь, чароит
Полировка, рисовка кистью, гравировка иглой по лаку, травление, гравировка резцом, никелирование, золочение
Диаметр подноса 32, высота чарок 8

104. Поднос «Северное сияние». 2000
Автор: Лохтачева Н.В.
Серебро 925°, топазы, цирконы
Рисовка кистью, гравировка иглой по лаку, травление, гравировка резцом, золочение, огранка ювелирных камней
Диаметр 32

105. Набор для вина «Северное сияние». 2001
Авторы: Лохтачев А.И., Лохтачева Н.В.
Серебро 925°, топазы, цирконы
Рисовка кистью, гравировка иглой по лаку, травление, гравировка резцом, золочение, огранка ювелирных камней
Высота малого кубка 17, высота большого кубка 18,5, диаметр подноса 32, высота подсвечника 31

106. Набор «Юбилейный». 1998
Авторы: Лохтачева Н.В., Лохтачев Д.А., Павлючкова Н.
Серебро 925°, аметисты, цирконы
Рисовка кистью, гравировка иглой по лаку, травление, гравировка резцом, золочение, огранка ювелирных камней
Высота 18,5, диаметр подноса 32

107. Поднос «Ехал Ваня...». 1991
Автор: Лохтачева Н.В.
Сталь
Никелирование, золочение, синение
40x30

108. Кубок «Торжество». 2002
Авторы: Лохтачев А.И., Лохтачева Н.В.
Серебро 925°, топазы
Рисовка кистью, гравировка иглой по лаку, травление, гравировка резцом, золочение, огранка ювелирных камней
Высота 20

109. Набор «На посошок». 1998
Автор: Лохтачева Н.В.
Латунь
Полировка, рисовка кистью, гравировка иглой по лаку, травление, гравировка резцом, никелирование, золочение
Диаметр подноса 32, высота чарок 8

110. Поднос «Свадебный». 1997
Дарница. 2000
Поднос «Букет». 1997
Автор: Лохтачева Н.В.
Латунь
Полировка, рисовка кистью, гравировка иглой по лаку, травление, гравировка резцом, никелирование, золочение
Диаметр подноса «Свадебный» 32, высота дарницы 13, диаметр подноса «Букет» 28

111. Поднос «Птица Сирин». 1994
См. кат. № 87

112. Поднос декоративный с цветочным орнаментом. 1991—1992
Автор: Лохтачева Н.В.
Латунь
Полировка, рисовка кистью, гравировка иглой по лаку, травление, гравировка резцом, никелирование, золочение
Диаметр 32

113. Поднос декоративный с цветочным орнаментом. 1991—1992
Автор: Лохтачева Н.В.
Латунь
Полировка, рисовка кистью, гравировка иглой по лаку, травление, гравировка резцом, никелирование, золочение
Диаметр 32

114. Поднос декоративный. 2003
Автор: Лохтачева Н.В.
Латунь
Полировка, рисовка кистью, гравировка иглой по лаку, травление, гравировка резцом, никелирование, золочение
Диаметр 32

115. Эскиз набора для шампанского. 1997
Автор: Мануш Г.И.

116. Эскиз подарочных кубков, свадебных блюд и канделябра. 1999—2002
Автор: Мануш Г.И.

117. Декоративный предмет «Артефакт XXI века». 1996
Автор: Лохтачев Д.А.
Латунь, кап березовый
Полировка, рисовка кистью, гравировка иглой по лаку, травление, гравировка резцом, никелирование, золочение, деревообработка
Высота 14

118. Поднос подарочный «Саратовская губерния». 2002
Автор: Лохтачева Н.В.
Латунь
Полировка, рисовка кистью, гравировка иглой по лаку, травление, гравировка резцом, никелирование, золочение
Диаметр 28

119. Колокольчик настольный. 2003
Авторы: Мануш Г.И., Лохтачева Н.В., Лохточев Д.А.
Латунь, горный хрусталь, калганская яшма
Рисовка кистью, гравировка иглой по лаку, травление, гравировка резцом, золочение, огранка горного хрусталя, художественная обработка камня
Высота 15,5

120. Эскиз кубка. 1994
Автор: Мануш Г.И.

121. Кубок подарочный с подносом. 2002
Авторы: Трошев В.И., Лохтачева Н.В.
Серебро, горный хрусталь
Полировка, рисовка кистью, гравировка иглой по лаку, травление, гравировка резцом, никелирование, золочение, огранка горного хрусталя
Высота кубка 20, диаметр подноса 21

122. Кубок «Золотое кольцо России». 2002
См. кат. № 85

123. Кубок подарочный «Санкт-Петербург». 2002
Авторы: Лохтачев А.И., Лохтачева Н.В.
Серебро 925°, горный хрусталь
Рисовка кистью, гравировка иглой по лаку, травление, гравировка резцом, золочение, ручная огранка горного хрусталя
Высота 22

124. Кубок «Каменный пояс Урала». 2003
Автор: Мануш Г.И.
Серебро 925°, нефрит
Рисовка кистью, гравировка иглой по лаку, травление, гравировка резцом, художественная обработка камня
Высота 22

125. Кубок «Каменный пояс Урала». 2003
См. кат. № 124

126. Эскизы подарочных кубков. 2001
Автор: Мануш Г.И.

127. Эскизы праздничных кубков. 2000
Авторы: Мануш Г.И., Лохтачева Н.В.

128. Кубок подарочный. 1999
Авторы: Мануш Г.И., Лохтачева Н.В.
Латунь
Полировка, рисовка кистью, гравировка иглой по лаку, травление, гравировка резцом, никелирование, золочение
Высота 20

129. Кубок «Театральный». 2001
Авторы: Мануш Г.И., Лохтачева Н.В.
Латунь
Полировка, рисовка кистью, гравировка иглой по лаку, травление, гравировка резцом, никелирование
Высота 22

130. Кубок «Балет». 2001
См. кат. № 84

131. Кубок «Москва — Санкт-Петербург». 2003
Авторы: Мануш Г.И., Лохтачева Н.В.
Серебро 925°, горный хрусталь, цирконы
Рисовка кистью, гравировка иглой по лаку, травление, гравировка резцом, золочение, фантазийная огранка горного хрусталя, огранка камней. Высота 22

132. Письменный прибор «Рифей». 2001
Авторы: Мануш Г.И., Лохтачева Н.В.
Серебро 925°, калганская яшма, горный хрусталь, цирконы
Рисовка кистью, гравировка иглой по лаку, травление, гравировка резцом, художественная обработка камня, огранка камней, ручная фантазийная огранка горного хрусталя
67,2x32x21

133. Письменный прибор. 1999
Авторы: Мануш Г.И., Лохтачева Н.В.
Латунь, яшма, горный хрусталь
Рисовка кистью, гравировка иглой по лаку, травление, гравировка резцом, художественная обработка камня, золочение, ручная фантазийная огранка горного хрусталя
67,2x32x21

134. Письменный прибор «Малахитовый цветок». 2001
Автор: Мануш Г.И.
Серебро, малахит, горный хрусталь, цирконы
Рисовка кистью, гравировка иглой по лаку, травление, гравировка резцом, никелирование, золочение, огранка камней
67x32x21

135. Эскиз предметов из письменного прибора. 1999
Автор: Мануш Г.И.

136. Часы кабинетные. 2001
Автор: Лохтачев Д.А.
Латунь, яшма
Лепка, литье, рисовка кистью, гравировка иглой по лаку, травление, гравировка резцом, художественная обработка камня
Высота 20

137. Ларец «Жемчужная свадьба». 2002
См. кат. № 83

138. Эскиз настольных часов. 2000
Автор: Мануш Г.И.

139. Часы настольные. 2000
Автор: Мануш Г.И.
Латунь, яшма, горный хрусталь
Рисовка кистью, гравировка иглой по лаку, травление, гравировка резцом, никелирование, золочение, художественная обработка камня
Высота 32

140. Ларец «Династия Романовых». 1998
Автор: Мануш Г.И.
Латунь, горный хрусталь, яшма
Рисовка кистью, гравировка иглой по лаку, травление, гравировка резцом, никелирование, золочение, огранка горного хрусталя, художественная обработка камня
30x25,7

141. Кубок подарочный «Торжественный». 2002
Авторы: Мануш Г.И., Лохтачева Н.В.
Серебро 925°, яшма, горный хрусталь
Рисовка кистью, гравировка иглой по лаку, травление, гравировка резцом, художественная обработка камня, ручная огранка горного хрусталя. Высота 23,5

142. Эскизы ларца «Династия Романовых». 1995
Автор: Мануш Г.И.

143. Эскиз настольных часов. 1998
Автор: Мануш Г.И.

144. Часы настольные. 1997
Автор: Мануш Г.И.
Латунь, малахит, горный хрусталь
Рисовка кистью, гравировка иглой по лаку, травление, гравировка резцом, никелирование, золочение, художественная обработка камня, огранка камней
Высота 34

145. Минора «Кристалл». 2002
Авторы: Лохтачев А.И., Лохтачева Н.В., Лохтачев Д.А.
Латунь, горный хрусталь
Полировка, рисовка кистью, гравировка иглой по лаку, травление, гравировка резцом, золочение, никелирование, ручная огранка горного хрусталя
Высота 43

146. Эскиз настольных часов. 1998
Автор: Мануш Г.И.

147. Эскиз ларца. 2000
Автор: Мануш Г.И.

148. Ларец. 2002
Авторы: Мануш Г.И., Лохтачева Н.В.
Латунь, калганская яшма, горный хрусталь, цирконы
Рисовка кистью, гравировка иглой по лаку, травление, гравировка резцом, художественная обработка камня, ручная фантазийная огранка горного хрусталя, огранка камней
32x23x12,5

149. Поднос «Золотой Остап». 2003
Автор: Лохтачева Н.В.
Латунь
Полировка, рисовка кистью, гравировка иглой по лаку, травление, гравировка резцом, никелирование, золочение
Диаметр 21

150. Гран-при «Ангел». 2000
Автор: Лохтачев А.И.
Серебро 925°
Лепка, литье
Высота 37

151. Поднос «Поставщик двора Его Императорского Величества». 1999
Автор: Лохтачева Н.В.
Латунь
Полировка, рисовка кистью, гравировка иглой по лаку, травление, гравировка резцом, никелирование, золочение
Диаметр 28

152. Дарница и поднос «Победа». 2003
Автор: Лохтачева Н.В.
Латунь, горный хрусталь, цирконы
Рисовка кистью, гравировка иглой по лаку, травление, гравировка резцом, золочение, ручная огранка горного хрусталя, огранка камней
Диаметр подноса 32, высота дарницы 13
Дар Государственному Историческому музею

ЦЕРКОВНОЕ ИСКУССТВО

153. Дарохранительница. 1997–2000
Авторы: Лохтачев А.И., Лохтачева Н.В., Лохтачев Д.А., Блинов В.В.
Серебро 925°, серебро 999,9°, золото 999,9°, калганская яшма, цитрины, гранаты
Рисовка кистью, гравировка иглой по лаку, травление, гравировка резцом, золочение, художественная обработка камня, огранка ювелирных камней
147,5x56x56
Храм Христа Спасителя. Москва

154. Первый (авторский) вариант дарохранительницы. 1997
Авторы: Лохтачев А.И., Лохтачева Н.В.,
Лохтачев Д.А., Блинов В.В.
Латунь, горный хрусталь
Рисовка кистью, гравировка иглой по лаку,
травление, гравировка резцом, золочение, никелирование
147,5x56x56

155. Дарохранительница малая. 2002
Авторы: Лохтачева Н.В., Лохтачев Д.А.
Серебро 925°, золото 999,9°, топазы, цирконы
Рисовка кистью, гравировка иглой по лаку, травление,
гравировка резцом, золочение, огранка камней
Высота 44

156. Евхаристический набор:
потир, дискос со звездицей, копие, лжица. 1997–1999
Авторы: Лохтачев А.И., Лохтачева Н.В.,
Лохтачев Д.А., Блинов В.В.
Латунь, серебро 925°, горный хрусталь, гранаты,
цитрины, цирконы, топазы
Рисовка кистью, гравировка иглой по лаку, травление,
гравировка резцом, золочение, фантазийная огранка
горного хрусталя, огранка камней
Потир – высота 43,6
Дискос – диаметр 38,5, высота 13,2
Звездица – высота 17,3
Лжица 31, копие 36
Храм Христа Спасителя. Москва

157. Дискос со звездицей. 1997–1999
См. кат. № 156

158. Потир из евхаристического набора. 1999
Авторы: Лохтачев А.И., Лохтачев Д.А.
Латунь, серебро, цирконы
Рисовка кистью, гравировка иглой по лаку,
травление, гравировка резцом, золочение,
закрепка камней
Высота 43

159. Эскиз потира. 1999
Автор: Мануш Г.И.

160. Потир «Евхаристия». 2000
Авторы: Лохтачев А.И., Лохтачев Д.А.
Серебро 925°, золото 999,9°, топазы, гранаты
Рисовка кистью, гравировка иглой по лаку, травление,
гравировка резцом, золочение, закрепка камней
Высота 43,6

161. Набор для елеопомазания. 2003
Авторы: Лохтачев Д.А., Лохтачева Н.В.
Серебро, горный хрусталь
Рисовка кистью, гравировка иглой по лаку, травление,
гравировка резцом, золочение, огранка камней
Высота сосуда 15, диаметр подноса 21

162. Сосуд для елея с крышкой. 2003
См. кат. № 161

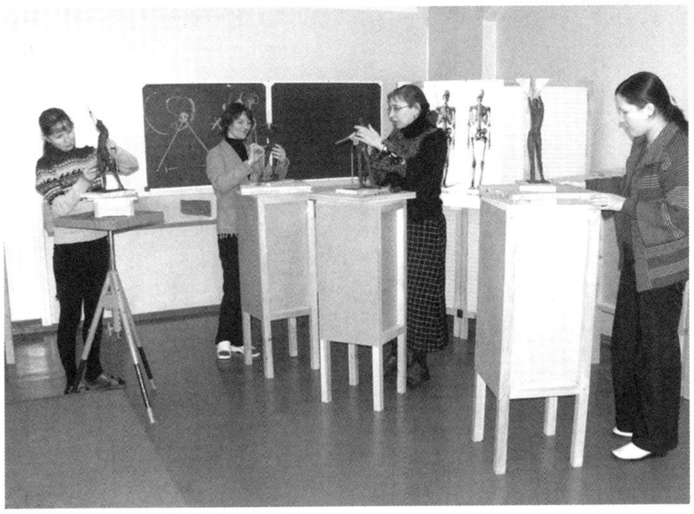

В 1996 году по инициативе Александра Ивановича Лохтачева на базе Мастерских декоративно-прикладного искусства «ЛиК» и при значительной финансовой поддержке этого предприятия в Златоусте был открыт филиал Южно-Уральского государственного университета (специальность «технология художественной обработки материалов»). Под руководством преподавателей, среди которых есть и ведущие художники «ЛиКа», студенты изучают не только классические дисциплины, такие как рисунок, композиция, живопись, история искусства и др., но и овладевают мастерством златоустовской гравюры на металле. А. И. Лохтачев и его соратники уверены: истинный художник должен видеть свое предназначение не только в создании произведений искусства, но и в сохранении и передаче накопленных знаний и опыта талантливой молодежи.

Ведущие художники и руководители Мастерских «ЛиК»

ЛОХТАЧЕВ Александр Иванович (род. 1948) — художник-педагог, инициатор возрождения искусства Златоустовской гравюры на металле. Создатель и организатор первой в городе мастерской декоративно-прикладного искусства «ЛиК» (Лохтачев и Компания) в 1990 году. Выпускник Златоустовского педагогического училища (1971), в течение нескольких лет возглавлял Златоустовские художественные мастерские. В настоящее время — художественный руководитель фирмы «ЛиК». Русской Православной церковью награжден орденом Святого благоверного князя Даниила Московского III степени. Участник всероссийских и международных специализированных выставок.

ЛОХТАЧЕВА Нина Владимировна (род. 1948) — член Союза художников России, Международной ассоциации изобразительных искусств (АИАП) ЮНЕСКО (с 1989), заслуженный художник России (с 1997). Руководитель и главный художник мастерской гравюры на металле. Выпускница Магнитогорского государственного университета. С 1992 года возглавляет коллектив художников-граверов Мастерских «ЛиК». Воспитала целую плеяду мастеров этого уникального искусства. Русской Православной церковью награждена орденом Святой равноапостольной великой княгини Ольги III степени. Автор декорировки произведений ювелирного и декоративно-прикладного искусства. На протяжении более чем 20 лет является участницей всесоюзных, всероссийских и международных выставок.

МАНУШ Григорий Иванович (род. 1949) — художник-график, член Союза художников России, Международной ассоциации изобразительных искусств (АИАП) ЮНЕСКО (с 1995). Руководитель и главный художник мастерской художественной обработки металла и природного уральского камня. Выпускник Нижнетагильского педагогического института (1981). Один из организаторов Мастерских «ЛиК». Автор эскизных проектов, дизайна, художественного решения изделий декоративно-прикладного и ювелирного искусства. Участник многих всероссийских и международных выставок.

ЛОХТАЧЕВ Денис Александрович (род. 1971) — художник, член Союза художников России, Международной ассоциации изобразительных искусств (АИАП) ЮНЕСКО (с 1998), лауреат конкурса «Будущее России» (1996), победитель конкурса ЮНЕСКО «Новые имена планеты» (1996), удостоен президентской стипендии. Руководитель мастерской церковной утвари. Выпускник первого набора (1996) факультета «Художественная обработка материалов» Златоустовского филиала Южно-Уральского государственного университета. Русской Православной церковью награжден орденом преподобного Серафима Саровского III степени. Участник областных, региональных, всероссийских и международных выставок, форумов, конкурсов.

ЛОХТАЧЕВ Андрей Александрович (род. 1975) — выпускник Челябинского государственного университета (1996, степень бакалавра менеджмента), слушатель Академии народного хозяйства при правительстве Российской Федерации. С 1996 по 2000 год работал менеджером отдела маркетинга Мастерских «ЛиК». С 2001 года является генеральным директором Мастерских декоративно-прикладного искусства «ЛиК». За успехи в сфере бизнеса фирма «ЛиК» в 2003 году награждена премией «Российский национальный Олимп» в номинации «Выдающиеся предприятия малого и среднего бизнеса».

Участие в выставках и основные награды

1993

Международная выставка «ЭКСПО-93» (Аделаида, Австралия)

Выставка компании «ЛиК» во Всероссийском музее декоративно-прикладного искусства (Москва)

1994

Международная выставка-ярмарка ножевых изделий «Blade Show» (Чаттануга, США)

1996

Выставка, посвященная 300-летию Российского флота (Москва)

Выставка «Народные художественные промыслы России», посвященная 100-летнему юбилею Нижегородской ярмарки (Нижний Новгород)

Персональная выставка художника Н. В. Лохтачевой (Эшборн, Берлин, Германия)

1997

Выставка «Народные художественные промыслы России» на Нижегородской ярмарке (Нижний Новгород)

Православная выставка «Многая лета, Москва», посвященная 850-летию основания города (Москва)

Дни российской культуры (Ипсвич, Великобритания)

1999

Выставка «Патриаршество в России: традиции и современность» (Москва)

Ювелирная выставка «Сокровища России» (Москва)

2000

Всероссийская художественная выставка к 2000-летию Рождества Христова «Имени Твоему» (Москва)

Московская международная ювелирная ярмарка. Диплом в номинации «Классика»

2001

Международная выставка-ярмарка ножевых изделий «Blade Show» (Атланта, США)

Московская международная выставка «Ювелир-2001» Диплом в номинации «Ювелирная пластика»

Всероссийский конкурс ювелиров «Признание Петербурга» (Санкт-Петербург). Лучшее украшение года в номинации «Художественное оружие»

5-я ежегодная выставка «Клинок — традиции и современность». Победитель конкурса в номинации «Среднеклинковые украшенные изделия»

«Дни Челябинской области в Москве» (Москва). Диплом

2002

Всероссийский конкурс ювелиров «Признание Петербурга» (Санкт-Петербург). Лучшее украшение года в номинации «Ювелирные изделия, посвященные 300-летию Санкт-Петербурга»

Выставка «Государственные символы России» (Москва). Диплом за создание высокохудожественных произведений с изображением государственных символов Российской Федерации

Конкурс ювелирных изделий «УралЮвелир» (Екатеринбург). Диплом в номинации «Лучшее внеконкурсное изделие»

Международный салон украшений, предметов искусства и подарков класса «люкс» «Luxury-2002» (Москва)

2003

Всероссийский конкурс ювелиров «Признание Петербурга» (Санкт-Петербург). Диплом I степени

Конкурс ювелирных изделий «УралЮвелир» (Екатеринбург). Диплом «За гармонию формы и исполнения»

«Дни Челябинской области в Республике Татарстан» (Казань). Диплом за изготовление уникальных произведений, посвященных 1000-летию города Казани

Премия «Российский национальный Олимп» в номинации «Выдающиеся предприятия среднего и малого бизнеса» за значительный вклад в социально-экономическое развитие России

1998—2003

Московская международная выставка «Ювелир»

Международная отраслевая ювелирная выставка «Junwex» (Санкт-Петербург)

Международная оружейная выставка «Клинок — традиции и современность» (Москва)

Содержание